BLOOD BOND #10
THE HANGING ROAD

William W. Johnstone
with J. A. Johnstone

PINNACLE BOOKS
Kensington Publishing Corp.
www.kensingtonbooks.com

PINNACLE BOOKS are published by

Kensington Publishing Corp.
850 Third Avenue
New York, NY 10022

PUBLISHER'S NOTE
Following the death of William W. Johnstone, the Johnstone family is working with a carefully selected writer to organize and complete Mr. Johnstone's outlines and many unfinished manuscripts to create additional novels in all of his series like The Last Gunfighter, Mountain Man, and Eagles, among others. This novel was inspired by Mr. Johnstone's superb storytelling.

All Kensington titles, imprints, and distributed lines are available at special quantity discounts for bulk purchases for sales promotions, premiums, fund-raising, educational, or institutional use. Special book excerpts or customized printings can also be created to fit specific needs. For details, write or phone the office of the Kensington special sales manager: Kensington Publishing Corp., 850 Third Avenue, New York, NY 10022, attn: Special Sales Department; phone 1-800-221-2647.

PINNACLE BOOKS and the Pinnacle logo are Reg. U.S. Pat. & TM Off.

ISBN-13: 978-0-7860-1871-0
ISBN-10: 0-7860-1871-2

First printing: June 2007

10 9 8 7 6 5 4 3 2 1

Printed in the United States of America

Man is born unto trouble,
as the sparks fly upward
—Job 5:7

A ruckus is the natural order of things
—Scratch Morton

Chapter 1

The crackle of gunfire drifted to the ears of the two young men riding across the prairie and made them sit up straighter in their saddles as they reined their mounts to a halt.

"Now that sounds interestin'," Matt Bodine drawled. He was somewhere between twenty-five and thirty years of age, a handsome, muscular young man with dark brown hair under his pushed-back Stetson. Even when he was mounted, it was easy to tell that he was tall and rangy, though the width of his shoulders indicated that there was plenty of power packed into his form.

The rider next to him was about the same age and almost could have been cut from the same cloth. His hair was darker, as black as a raven's wing, as were his eyes, black to Bodine's blue. His deeply tanned skin bore a faint coppery hue that Matt's did not. His cheekbones were slightly more prominent. And he carried only one walnut-butted Colt holstered on his hip, compared to the pair of six-guns sported by Matt Bodine. His name was Sam August Webster Two Wolves. His father had been

Medicine Horse, a Cheyenne chief; his mother a white woman Medicine Horse had met, fallen in love with, and married while being educated at an Eastern school.

Most importantly, Sam Two Wolves was blood brother to Matt Bodine. They were *Onihomahan*— Friends of the Wolf. Brothers of the Wolf, some said.

Brothers of the gun, definitely.

Sam grunted and jerked a thumb over his right shoulder. "We could turn around and ride the other way, you know," he pointed out.

A grin stretched across Matt's rugged face. "Yeah, we could," he agreed, "but you don't really want to, do you?"

"You'd never let me hear the end of it if we did, now would you?"

"Probably not," Matt said. He dug his boot heels into the flanks of his mean-eyed gray stallion and sent the animal leaping forward into a gallop. Sam was only an instant behind him on a big paint horse.

They raced toward a tree-dotted ridge. The shooting came from the other side of the rise. The flat reports of numerous handguns were interspersed with the sharper whip-cracks of at least a couple of rifles. From the sound of things, a small-scale war was going on up ahead.

Matt Bodine and Sam Two Wolves knew about war. Though they were too young to have participated in the great struggle between the Blue and the Gray, they had instead witnessed, and on occasion taken part in, the bloody clash between red men and white. They had been there, watching from a nearby hill overlooking the stream called the Greasy Grass by the Indians and the Little Big Horn by the whites, as a large detachment of the Seventh Cavalry under Colonel George Armstrong Custer had been wiped out by an army of warriors gathered from the various Plains tribes. Sam's father, Medicine Horse, had died in that battle, riding with an empty rifle up the slope toward the hilltop where Custer had rallied his troops for the final battle. He had counted coup on the notorious Yellowhair himself before falling with a fatal wound. The smells of blood and gun smoke and tragedy had been thick in the air that day.

Bodine and Two Wolves had smelled gun smoke again many times, in battles of their own. They were well-to-do; each owned a profitable ranch in Wyoming. But those ranches were run by others, because restlessness ruled the natures of these two young men. They were fiddle-footed, as folks said, always on the drift, not looking for trouble but not running from it, either. When the Good Lord made them, He had included not an ounce of backup.

So now they rushed toward the gunfire rather than away from it, as more prudent souls might have done.

Nobody had ever accused these two young hellions of being prudent.

They surged up the ridge and topped the crest. The slope fell away in front of them, down to a level plain crossed from right to left by a stagecoach road. A vehicle careened along that road, but it wasn't one of the red and yellow Concord coaches. It was a wagon with a squarish canvas cover over the back, rather than the rounded, arching Conestoga sort of wagon that had carried thousands of pioneers from the East to new homes in the West. Dust boiled up from the hooves of the six-horse team pulling the wagon, as well as from the rapidly turning wheels. Gray smoke spurted from under the canvas cover at the back of the vehicle—powder smoke.

Nearly a dozen men on horseback gave chase to the wagon, firing after it with revolvers as they galloped along the road. Matt and Sam had no idea who was inside the wagon or why the men were chasing it. But as they reined in for a second at the top of the ridge and their keen eyes took in the scene, they exchanged a glance and each knew that the other had seen the same thing.

The person driving the wagon, hunched over on the seat and sawing at the reins, was a woman. Long, curly red hair streamed out behind her head.

Any gents who would sling lead at a woman were bad hombres in the blood brothers' book. Matt yanked his Winchester from its saddle sheath and sent his stallion plunging down the slope. Sam followed suit.

Matt guided his horse with his knees as he worked the rifle's lever, jacking a round into the chamber. Smoothly, he brought the Winchester to his shoulder. The hurricane deck of a galloping horse wasn't the best platform for accurate shooting, but Matt Bodine wasn't an average marksman. The rifle kicked hard against his shoulder as he fired.

A hat leaped off the head of one of the men giving chase to the wagon. Startled, the rider hauled back on the reins so hard that his mount's hooves skidded on the dirt of the road. The horse reared up violently. With a yell, the rider went out of the saddle and crashed to the ground.

While that was going on, Sam opened fire, too, and his first shot creased the arm of another man, who howled in pain as his gun flew out of suddenly nerveless fingers. Gripping the reins tightly with his other hand, he wheeled his horse and shouted, "Look out! Up on the ridge!"

Several of the gunmen slowed their pursuit of the wagon and turned to pepper the slope with bullets as Matt and Sam descended. As a slug whistled past his ear, Matt knew the men were shooting to kill, so he returned the favor. His Winchester cracked again, and one of the men was driven backward off his horse by the .44-40 round that smashed into his chest. Dust puffed up around him as he landed in a limp sprawl signifying death.

Sam growled as he felt the fiery kiss of a bullet that tore his shirt and scraped along his ribs. He levered his Winchester and fired again. One of the gunmen hunched over and sagged in his saddle, but he managed to drop his gun, grab the saddle horn, and stay mounted. His horse bolted, probably spooked by the sudden smell of blood.

Halfway down the slope, Matt veered his stallion to the left. Several of the horsebackers were still giving chase to the wagon and shooting at it, so Matt went after them while Sam continued dealing with the ones who had given up the pursuit and stopped to meet the new threat. In both cases, the odds were four to one against the blood brothers.

They had faced worse in their time. Much worse.

Matt slid the Winchester back in its sheath and leaned forward over his horse's neck to urge the stallion on to greater speed. Cutting down the slope at an angle, he was able to intercept the riders. The pair of six-guns fairly leaped into his hands as he opened fire on the pursuers, raking their flank with deadly accurate shots. One man flew out of the saddle and another slewed sideways but was able to hang on.

Bullets plucked at the sleeves and the sides of Matt's buckskin shirt, but with the cool fatalism of a born gunfighter he ignored them. His time was up when it was up, and until then he was going to do everything he could to help that woman on the wagon and whoever was with her.

Another gunman threw up his arms and toppled off his horse as one of Matt's bullets punched through his body. That left only one man, and he whirled his horse around to flee. Matt snapped a shot at him but missed. The rider leaped his horse over a gully, rode through some trees, and disappeared from sight. Matt let him go.

He had another problem to deal with now. The team pulling that wagon was out of control. The horses leaned against their harness and raced madly along the road, never slowing even when the trail curved. As Matt rode after the vehicle, he saw the wagon lean perilously to the side, almost to the point of tipping over before the wheels on the high side came back to earth with a crash. At this point, it was a toss-up what would happen first. Either the wagon would roll over or an axle would crack, causing a wreck that way. Matt urged, "Come on, big fella!" as the stallion stretched out in a blinding run.

Concern for his blood brother flickered across Bodine's mind, but he shoved that out of his thoughts. Sam would have to take care of himself.

There weren't very many hombres better at that than Sam August Webster Two Wolves.

The wagon was moving fast, but the big gray stallion was a magnificent animal with speed and sand to spare, much like the man who rode him. Matt drew closer and closer to the wagon. The dust billowing up from its wheels made it difficult for him to see into the vehicle, but he spotted some movement there and then a second later, the spurt of flame from a rifle muzzle. As the bullet whined high over his head, he shouted, "Damn it, hold your fire! I'm trying to help you!"

It was no use. Whoever was in the wagon couldn't hear him over the thunder of hooves and the rattle of wheels. He leaned forward as more shots were fired. Luckily for him, the riflemen inside the wagon weren't very accurate in their aim.

He was only a few yards behind the careening vehicle now. He guided the stallion to the left side of the trail so they could pass the wagon. As they drew even with the back of it, he glanced over and saw a woman crouched just inside the tailgate with a rifle in her hands. Matt ducked as she fired. He didn't know where the bullet went, but neither he nor the stallion were hit, so that was all that mattered at the moment.

Then he was galloping alongside the wagon, the stallion running flat out. As they came up beside the driver's seat, Matt saw why the team was even more out of control than it had been earlier. The redheaded woman was slumped to one side on the seat, either unconscious or dead. The reins had slipped out of her hands and fallen so that they now trailed loosely underneath the wagon. Matt knew he wouldn't be able to reach them.

That left him without many options. He kept the stallion moving at a gallop until they were next to the left-hand leader. Then Matt kicked his feet out of the stirrups, hauled in a deep breath, and launched himself into the air.

That diving, daring leap carried him over the leader. As he landed on the horse's back he grabbed for the harness. He felt himself starting to slip to the right. His momentum had taken him a little too far. His right boot hit the singletree, stopping him for the instant he needed to wrap his fingers around the horse's harness. He held on for dear life, knowing that if he fell underneath the team, their hooves would pound and slash his body until it didn't resemble anything human.

As Matt got his balance and steadied himself, he pulled back as hard as he could on the harness. The horse responded, slowing down. The other members of the team did likewise, following the example of the leader. Gradually, Matt brought the horses to a halt. A breeze swirled the cloud of dust that rose around the wagon.

"Charity!" a woman's voice screamed. "Oh, my God, Charity!"

Still sitting on the leader, Matt turned to look toward the wagon. He found himself staring down the twin bores of a double-barreled shotgun. A woman's face glared at him over the weapon.

"Careful with that Greener, ma'am," he warned her. "I mean you no harm, and it might go off."

Another woman leaned from the back of the wagon over the unconscious driver. Matt could see now that the redhead's chest was rising and falling. As the woman ministering to her lifted her into a sitting position, Matt saw a slightly bloody lump on the side of her forehead. She had taken a hard lick from something and probably been knocked out by it. Matt figured one of the violent bounces taken by the wagon had thrown her to the side and cracked her head against one of the supports holding up the canvas cover over the back of the vehicle.

Meanwhile, the woman with the shotgun was still pointing it at him. With the wagon team now under control, standing there with their heads down and their sides heaving, he let go of the harness and raised his hands to shoulder level where they were in plain sight.

"Who are you?" the woman demanded.

"Name's Matt Bodine. My brother and I saw those hombres chasing you and figured you could use a hand." He leaned a little to the side, trying to look past the wagon in hopes of seeing what had happened to Sam and the men he had been trading lead with. No more shots rang out, and Matt felt a surge of relief go through him as he spotted Sam jogging the paint up the road toward them.

Another female voice called from the back of the wagon, "Here comes another one! Lydia, what should we do?"

Lydia, who appeared to be the gal with the Greener, said, "Hold your fire." She asked Matt, "Is that your brother?"

Matt nodded. "Yep. Blood brother, actually. We don't have the same ma and pa, although some folks say you can't tell it to look at us."

"What about the men who were chasing us?"

Matt saw at least half-a-dozen bodies littering the trail. A similar number of riderless horses had drifted off the road and were now cropping at the grass alongside it.

"I don't think the ones who are still alive will be bothering you anymore," he said. "Looks like they all took off for the tall and uncut."

The redhead let out a moan and shook her head, then winced as the movement obviously hurt. She was coming back to her senses. Her eyelids fluttered as she leaned against the woman who was bracing her up. When her eyes opened and looked around in confusion, Matt saw that they were a vivid shade of green.

"What . . . what happened?" she said. "Did they get us?"

"No," Lydia told her. She nodded toward Bodine. "This fella and a friend of his ran them off and evidently killed some of them."

"Oh." Gingerly, the redhead lifted a hand to the lump on her head. She winced again as she touched it. "What happened to me?"

Matt said, "If I had to guess, I'd say you bumped your head on one of those bad bounces hard enough to knock yourself out. Are you wounded anywhere else?"

She looked down at herself for a moment and then shook her head. "I don't think so."

Sam reached the wagon and grinned at the sight of Matt sitting on the draft horse. "Changed mounts, did you?" he asked. Without waiting for Matt to respond, he turned toward the seat and politely took his hat off, holding it over his chest. "Ladies."

Lydia relaxed a little and said, "Ain't you the cultured one?"

"I try, but it's difficult sometimes when my trail partner is such an unlettered lout." Sam settled his hat back on his head.

"Wait a minute," Matt protested. "This lout, as you put it, is the one who saved these ladies' bacon. And I'm not all that unlettered. I've been to school, too, you know."

"Ignore him," Sam said to the women. "Are any of you wounded? Do you need medical attention? I think there's a town not too far from here."

"There is," the redhead said. Bodine recalled that one of the other women had called her Charity. "It's called Buffalo Flat. That's where we're headed." She turned her head and went on. "Anybody hurt back there?"

A chorus of female voices answered her, all assuring her that their owners were all right. Matt frowned. Were these women traveling alone? he wondered. It was unusual to find a group of ladies out here on the frontier without at least one man accompanying them.

That appeared to be the case, though. One of the women asked, "Can we get out and stretch our legs, Charity? I mean, our limbs?"

The redhead nodded. "I guess so. But we can't stop for long. I want to make it to Buffalo Flat by nightfall."

Matt and Sam could only sit and watch in amazement as half a dozen of the prettiest gals they had seen in a long time climbed out of the wagon and stood there looking around, blinking against the sunlight and the dust and the thin haze of gun smoke that still hung in the air.

Chapter 2

"All I'm sayin'," Scratch Morton declared, "is that I didn't know she was married."

"How old are you, Scratch?" Bo Creel asked.

"Huh? What do you mean, how old am I? You know how old I am. We been friends since we met durin' the Runaway Scrape!"

Bo nodded solemnly. "That's right. So I know good and well that you're old enough to know better. What did you think that ring on her finger meant, anyway?"

Scratch grinned and said, "Well, I didn't rightly see no ring. It was dark in the room!"

Bo just sighed and shook his head. "You're lucky you didn't get yourself tarred and feathered. Or worse yet, both of us!"

Scratch threw back his head and laughed. "I swear, it might've been worth it. That gal surely was enthusiastic."

"Worth it to you, maybe. Not to me. I'm too old for such foolishness."

Scratch leaned over in the saddle and slapped his friend on the back as they rode along a trail that twisted between brush- and cactus-covered hills. "A man's never too old for a little foolishness until he's dead! And my blood's still pumpin' just fine, thank you."

Bo didn't say anything. He had learned a long time ago that it was a waste of breath trying to talk sense into Scratch Morton's head.

But then, he reminded himself, if Scratch had been blessed with an overabundance of sense, he probably never would have jumped in front of that Mexican soldier at San Jacinto and Bo never would have lived through that sunny April day in 1836. He would have gotten a Mexican bayonet in the back instead.

That was the first time Scratch saved Bo's life. It wouldn't be the last. Of course, Bo had repaid the favor more than a few times over the years. The long, violent years . . .

The Morton family and the Creel family had come to Texas in the days before the revolution, when it was still part of Mexico and Stephen F. Austin had been continuing his father Moses's dream of founding a colony of Americans there. The families had settled in different places, the Mortons not far from San Antonio and the Creels near Victoria. So the two strapping boys, barely in their teens, hadn't met until their folks had been fleeing across Texas, away from the invading army of the dictator Santa Anna. The Runaway Scrape, that flight was called, and it had been a time of terror and panic among many of the American settlers who had taken to calling themselves Texicans. If not for a small but gallant band of defenders who had stalled Santa Anna at a little mission just outside of San Antonio de Bexar, the dictator's army might have swept every American clean out of Texas.

As it was, though, the brave men holed up in the Alamo had occupied Santa Anna long enough for Sam Houston to gather an army of his own. Bo's father had gone off to join that army, as had Scratch's pa. And the two youngsters, who had become fast friends almost at first sight, had hatched a plan between them to follow their fathers off to war. That damned Santy Anny wasn't gonna run roughshod over no Texicans, no, sir!

But the Alamo had fallen after its defenders fought to the last man and were all put to the sword, and the prisoners at Goliad had been massacred in a bloody slaughter, and things looked bad for the folks who had really wanted nothing except to be left alone to live their lives. Houston's army kept retreating until they reached a wide, grassy plain between Buffalo Bayou and the San Jacinto River. It was there the battle was finally joined.

By that time Bo and Scratch, carrying old muzzle-loading muskets, had slipped away from their families and run off to join the army. Their fathers didn't like it, but there wasn't much they could do about it except promise to blister the boys' britches once the war was over . . . assuming, of course, that any of them lived through it.

So Bo and Scratch had been among that long line of men advancing on the Mexican camp, where the invaders dozed at their siestas. They had shouted "Remember the Alamo!" and "Remember Goliad!" like all the other Texicans as the guns began to roar and the men rushed forward to meet their destiny. And during that battle Scratch had saved Bo's life, cementing a friendship that had lasted more than forty years so far.

After the revolution, in the newly founded Republic of Texas, they had tried to settle down. Bo had even gotten married, and he and his wife had a couple of fine young'uns. But then the fever came through the area, taking the two little ones and then Bo's wife. Scratch had been there for him then, too, helping him dig each grave in turn, and somehow he got Bo through the awful days when grief and blind rage at God had threatened to consume him. When Bo finally came out of that dark, dark valley in his life and Scratch had suggested that they get out of Texas for a while, the idea sounded good to Bo.

They'd been on the drift pretty much ever since.

They didn't need much money, just enough for some supplies and ammunition, so they only worked when they had to. They had cowboyed, gambled, driven freight wagons, packed shotguns as stagecoach guards, scouted now and then for the army, and even worn lawmen's stars from time to time, although Scratch was a mite uncomfortable with being that respectable. It went against the grain. Any job was all right as long as it was honest . . . and Scratch had been known not to worry about that too much, under the right circumstances.

And despite their best intentions—Bo's best intentions, anyway—they seemed to run into trouble on a regular basis. As Scratch put it, "I get antsy when too much time goes by without anybody shootin' at us."

Here lately, though, they had hit a peaceful stretch as they made their ambling way through Colorado. The only recent bump in the trail had been Scratch's dalliance with a married woman in a town about twenty miles behind them. Bo had managed to get them out of there a couple of jumps ahead of the woman's angry husband. Scratch had always had an eye for the ladies, and even though he claimed he hadn't known the gal was married, Bo had his doubts about that.

"Maybe you should hunt up a game in the next town we come to," Scratch suggested. "Our poke's gettin' a mite empty."

"We could look for a real job."

Scratch made a face. "You'd turn your back on your God-given talents like that?"

"What about *your* God-given talents?"

Scratch sighed and said, "Bein' handsome and charmin' don't pay as well as it used to."

He was handsome, or at least most of the ladies they met seemed to think so. He had a shock of silver hair under his cream-colored Stetson, and his rugged face was usually creased in a friendly grin. He wore a buckskin jacket and whipcord trousers tucked into high-topped, moccasin-style boots. His clothes, his saddle, and his gun rig were all old and well used, but he took good care of them.

In contrast to his somewhat dandified trail partner, Bo looked as sober as a judge or a parson in a black hat and dusty black suit. He usually had a string tie knotted around his neck. Despite looking like a preacher, Bo was by far the better poker player, and if they needed to run up a stake in a hurry, he could be counted on to do it at some green-topped table in any cow-town saloon. Scratch's emotions ran too close to the surface for him to be much good at cards.

Bo took his hat off and ran his fingers through his brown hair, which despite his age was still thick and only lightly touched with gray. The midday sun was hot, and he was starting to think that they ought to find a nice shady spot on some creek bank to rest a while and maybe eat some lunch. He tugged his hat back down and was about to suggest that when the sound of a shot suddenly broke the still air.

The shot was followed right away by several more. Scratch reined his horse to a stop and said, "What's that?"

"You know what it is as well as I do," Bo replied. "Trouble."

"Yeah, for somebody." Scratch turned to look at him as the shooting continued. "Reckon we ought to go see what it's about?"

Bo hesitated only a second before nodding. "Somebody might need our help."

"Yeah, you just can't resist the smell of powder smoke!" Scratch said with a grin as he jabbed his heels into his horse's flanks.

The two men sent their mounts along the trail at a fast run. The shots were only a couple of hundred yards away, and it didn't take them long to reach the spot. As the Texans rounded a bend in the trail, they saw gray smoke drifting up from a cluster of boulders.

About a hundred yards away on the trail sat a buckboard with a couple of horses hitched to it. The horses moved around skittishly but didn't run. From behind a rock next to the trail, a handgun barked. Whoever had fired it ducked back down as a slug ricocheted off the top of the rock.

Bo and Scratch brought their horses to a stop. "Bushwhackers in those boulders," Bo said.

"Yeah, and the poor bastard who was drivin' that buckboard had to jump for cover when they opened up on him," Scratch concluded. "Problem is, that rock ain't hardly big enough. They'll drill him sooner or later."

With his face set in stern, angry lines, Bo reached for a Henry rifle in a sheath strapped to his saddle. "I don't like bushwhackers," he said.

"Neither do I," Scratch agreed as he pulled his own Henry.

From where they were, they couldn't see the men hidden among the boulders, but that didn't matter. Both Texans lifted their rifles and opened fire anyway, sending several fast shots into the rocks. The slugs ricocheted crazily. At this point, Bo and Scratch didn't care if they hit anybody or not. They just wanted to flush the bushwhackers out of hiding and make the varmints run.

The bushwhackers emerged from the boulders, all right, four men on horseback. But instead of fleeing, they charged toward the two old-timers, blazing away as they came.

"Uh-oh," Scratch muttered. "Looks like we put a burr under their saddles, good an' proper."

Bo ducked as a bullet sizzled through the air above his head. "They're not happy!" he called. "Split up!"

Bo went to the left, Scratch to the right. The rifle in Bo's hands spoke again. One of the bushwhackers was jolted as the slug smashed into his right shoulder. He peeled off from the others, clutching at his wounded arm.

The others came on, still firing, and Bo and Scratch responded in kind. They didn't know what was behind the drygulch attempt on the driver of the buckboard or who these gunmen were, but the conflict had been boiled down to an elemental level now.

Those bastards were trying to kill Bo and Scratch, and the Texans were going to do their damnedest to keep that from happening.

Two of the men galloped at Scratch while the other remaining gunman came after Bo. Scratch stuck his rifle back in its sheath, and then his hands flashed to the pair of revolvers he wore belted around his hips. They were ivory-handled, long-barreled Remingtons, and even though Scratch liked them mostly because of the way they looked, they were fine guns and he was handy with them. He swung his horse around and charged right into the faces of the men who had been attacking him. The Remingtons spouted smoke and flame as he alternated shots from them.

The .36-caliber slugs tore into the two startled gunmen and drove them backward out of their saddles. One man flopped lifelessly to the ground. The other landed, rolled, and tried to get up. He had hung onto his gun somehow, and as he struggled to lift it for another shot, Scratch blasted a bullet through his head.

On the other side of the trail, Bo left his saddle and dropped to one knee, still holding the Henry. Coolly, he lifted the rifle to his shoulder even though he heard the wind-rip of bullets on both sides of his head. He settled the Henry's sights on the chest of the remaining gunman and pulled the trigger. The man flew out of the saddle, spun through the air, and slammed face-first into the ground. He didn't move again.

Bo got to his feet and looked around to see how Scratch was doing. He wasn't surprised to see his fellow Texan trotting toward him, still on horseback. Scratch had holstered one gun and was reloading the other weapon. Bo looked past him and saw the two horses with empty saddles and the pair of motionless forms on the ground.

"Looks like we got 'em all," Scratch said as he rode up.

"Except the one who lit a shuck after I drilled him in the shoulder," Bo said. "He's liable to go back where he came from and tell whoever hired them about what happened to the others."

"How do you know somebody hired them?"

Bo grimaced. "Four against one, and they had to hide to do that. That tells me they were in it for the money. A man fighting for himself or something he believes in does it out in the open."

"Yeah, I reckon." Scratch finished loading the gun and slid it back into leather. "Want to go see if the hombre with the buckboard is all right?"

"I thought we would." Bo's horse hadn't gone far. He walked over to it and caught the reins, then swung up into the saddle and joined Scratch. Together they rode toward the buckboard.

When they were about fifty feet away, Bo saw the barrel of a six-gun thrust over the top of the rock where the driver had taken cover. "Hold your fire," he called. "We're friends."

"Yeah," Scratch added. "You can tell by the way we ventilated those sons o' bitches who were tryin' to ventilate *you*."

As Bo reined in, he looked at the buckboard and saw that several crates and bags had been piled onto the back of it and then partially covered with canvas. If he had to guess, he would say that was a load of supplies bound for a ranch or a mine or someplace like that.

The gun sticking over the rock hadn't moved. Bo

began to worry that the driver had been wounded and might even be lying back there dead. He gripped his saddle horn and got ready to dismount. "I'd better go have a look," he told Scratch.

"Stay right where you are!" a high, clear voice called out, and Bo and Scratch both stared as the gun finally moved. The person holding it stood up and regarded them with blue eyes that were narrowed in suspicion. A vagrant breeze stirred the beautiful woman's long blond hair as she watched them warily over the barrel of the revolver.

Chapter 3

Matt Bodine did a quick head count just to make sure. Yep, there were six of the women: redheaded Charity, Lydia, who had light brown hair that fell around her shoulders, another brunette, and three blondes. Lydia seemed to be the oldest, maybe thirty, and none of the others had seen twenty-five winters yet. One of the blondes, in fact, probably wasn't even twenty. Some were short, some were tall, some were in between. And all six of them were shapely. That much was evident even though they wore plain dresses with long sleeves and buttoned-up necks.

The young blonde eyed Matt and Sam with obvious interest until the redhead glared at her and dug an elbow into her ribs. The girl muttered, "Sorry," and looked down at the ground demurely.

Charity looked at the two men. "Thank you for helping us. I don't know what would have happened if you gentlemen hadn't come along when you did."

Matt slid from the horse's back to the ground

and said, "The way that team was stampeding, likely the wagon would have crashed."

"I know. You saved our lives."

Sam put in, "I wouldn't go so far as to say that. It *is* a good thing we were riding along here, though. Do you have any idea why those hombres jumped you like that?"

Charity glanced at the other women, then said, "I have no idea."

Matt saw the look and thought that maybe the redhead was lying. Charity did have an idea why they had been attacked. With his curiosity aroused, he said, "So you're heading for Buffalo Flat?" He couldn't recall ever visiting the cow town before, but he knew it was ten or fifteen miles west of their current location.

"That's right."

"You ladies have business there?" Sam asked. Knowing his blood brother as well as he did, Matt could tell that Sam was curious, too.

"You could say that." Charity hesitated, then went on. "We're going there to be married. We made . . . arrangements . . . with the gentlemen who are going to meet us there and become our husbands."

"You're mail-order brides!" Matt exclaimed, his eyes widening in surprise.

"We don't care for that term," Charity snapped. "It sounds so crass."

"Well, I'm sure the fellas meeting you in Buffalo Flat will be very happy to see you." Matt turned his head and whistled for his stallion. The mean-eyed gray had drifted off after Matt jumped on the wagon team, but he hadn't gone far. He came trotting over, and Matt caught hold of the reins.

Sam suggested, "Why don't Matt and I ride on

into town with you, just in case you run into more trouble?"

Matt swung up into the saddle and nodded. "I was just thinking the same thing. My name is Matt Bodine, by the way, and this is Sam Two Wolves."

"We're pleased to meet you," Charity said with a polite nod, but then her chin rose with a touch of defiance and stubbornness. "But we're perfectly capable of taking care of ourselves. We're armed, and we know how to use the weapons."

In fact, Lydia was still holding onto that Greener, and a couple of the other women had Winchesters.

"I can see that," Matt said, "but the hombres who survived that little fracas might double back and try to attack you again. Better let us go along just in case."

"We couldn't put you to the trouble—"

"No trouble," Sam said. "We don't have to be any particular place at any particular time, so we might as well go to Buffalo Flat."

Lydia said, "Saddle tramps, eh?"

Matt grinned. He saw no point in telling the women that his ranch was one of the largest and most valuable in Wyoming Territory, and so was Sam's. "Shiftless but harmless, that's us."

Charity's gaze flicked toward the bodies sprawled in the trail behind the wagon. "Not so harmless to those men."

"Speaking of which," Sam said, "we'd better check them out. Some of them might still be alive, and even if they're not, we might be able to find out who they were and why they came after you ladies."

"Wait right here while we take a look," Matt said. He thought Charity looked like she wanted to argue, but one of the other women said, "We're all tired, Charity, and so are the horses. We could use a little rest."

"All right," she said, giving in, obviously reluctant to do so. "Just don't take too long about it."

"Be right back," Matt said, and he and Sam each raised a hand in farewell as they rode back along the trail toward the fallen gunmen.

It didn't take long to check the bodies. All six of the men were dead as mackerels. Sam dismounted to make sure of that, and when he rolled one of the corpses onto his back, Matt let out a low whistle and said, "Deuce Ballinger."

"You know him?" Sam asked.

"We were just nodding acquaintances. Never liked him. He hired out his gun. Last I heard of him, he was mixed up in some range war in Montana."

They moved on to the next carcass, and Sam said, "This one is Wilbur Hatch. Bank robber and rustler from Idaho."

Matt pointed. "The Laredo Kid, lying over there. Sam, that bunch was nothing but backshooters and hired killers. Scum of the earth."

Sam had a look at the other bodies, and even though neither he nor Matt recognized any of them, they were all the same sort: coarse-featured, beard-stubbled hard cases. He went through their pockets, finding a considerable amount of money along with the makin's and a couple of flasks of whiskey. There were no letters or anything like that, though, to explain why they had attacked the wagon.

As Sam swung back up onto his paint, he said, "I reckon the ones who got away were all the same no-good sort. You reckon they jumped the wagon just because they saw that a woman was driving it?"

"Men like that would be snake-blooded enough to do such a thing," Matt said. "Or it could be that they heard a group of mail-order brides was traveling through the area and decided they wanted the women for themselves. They might've been able to collect ransom from the men who made arrangements to marry them."

"Who might not have wanted them anymore after those varmints got through abusing them," Sam said with a bleak expression on his face. "It really *is* a good thing we came along when we did, Matt."

"Yeah. Let's get back to the wagon before that redheaded little spitfire gets impatient and takes off without us."

Sam waved a hand toward the dead men and asked, "What about them?"

"I guess when we get to Buffalo Flat we can tell the local law what happened," Matt said with a shrug. "If there's an undertaker in town he might want to come out and get them, so he can plant 'em for what's in their pockets."

As they rode slowly back toward the wagon, Sam said quietly, "Does something strike you as funny about this whole situation?"

"Funny as in strange?"

"Yeah."

Matt frowned in thought and said, "Those women are just about the best-looking mail-order brides I've ever seen."

Sam nodded. "That's what I was thinking. Young, good-looking women usually don't have any trouble finding husbands. It's the older, plainer ones who decide to become mail-order brides. Why would gals like these need to come all the way out here to the frontier and marry up with gents they've never even met?"

"You reckon they're lying?"

"I don't know. But I'm going to be mighty interested to see what happens when we get to Buffalo Flat."

So would Matt. It had occurred to him that maybe someone had hired those gunmen to see to it that the wagonload of women never made it to town, but he couldn't see why anyone would want to do that. Females were still scarce out here, especially young, pretty ones. It seemed more likely somebody would have hired men to make sure the women reached their destination safely.

Maybe Matt and Sam would find out the truth later. One thing Matt knew was that he and Sam weren't going to let those ladies out of their sight until they got to Buffalo Flat.

"Ready to go?" he asked as they came up to the wagon. All the women had gotten back inside the vehicle except for Charity, who stood next to the team, and Lydia, who was perched on the seat with the Greener in her hands. She obviously intended to ride shotgun the rest of the way.

"If you are," Charity replied. She nodded toward the corpses. "Did you find out anything from the . . . bodies?"

"Not really. Sam and I recognized a few of them. They were badmen, the sort who wouldn't have treated you ladies kindly if they had caught up to you."

From the wagon seat, Lydia said, "They might've gotten a warmer welcome than they expected." She patted the barrels of the shotgun cradled across her lap.

Charity started to pull herself up onto the seat, and Matt moved to dismount, saying quickly, "Let me give you a hand."

"Stay in your saddle," she told him. "I'm perfectly capable of climbing onto a wagon." To prove it, she hauled herself to the seat and turned around to settle down on it and give Matt a defiant look. But then she blinked, swayed a little on the seat, and put a hand to her head. "Guess I'm still a little woozy from that rap on the head," she muttered.

"One of us can drive," Sam offered.

"No, thanks," Charity said stubbornly. She lifted the reins, slapped them against the backs of the team, and called out stridently to the horses as she got them moving again.

Matt and Sam just exchanged a glance, then turned their horses and fell in alongside the wagon.

As they rode toward Buffalo Flat, Matt tried to engage Charity in conversation, but mostly he just got curt, short answers from her. When he asked where they were from, Charity admitted that they hailed from Kansas City but didn't volunteer any further information.

"You've got a last name, don't you?" Matt prodded.

"It's MacKenzie," she admitted after a moment.

"I'm Lydia Shannon," the shotgun-wielding brunette put in. "Back there in the wagon we've got Becky Hanson, Kathy North, Wilma Larrabee, and Janie Cantrell."

Hearing their names, each of the women looked out past Lydia's shoulder and said hello to Bodine and Two Wolves. The men nodded and touched fingers to the brims of their hats in acknowledgment of the introductions.

"So you came all the way out here by yourselves from Kansas City?" Sam asked.

"Why not?" Lydia demanded. "We can take care of ourselves. Today was the first time we ran into any real trouble, when we were almost where we're going."

"That's the thing about the frontier," Matt said. "You can't ever tell where danger is going to come from, or when it might strike. That's why you've got to always be ready to defend yourself. Most of the time out here, nobody's going to do it for you."

"We're used to it," Charity said. "Don't worry about us."

Matt shrugged. "I'm just sayin', that's all."

"Well, don't bother."

Matt was about to make some comment about red hair and the temper that went with it, but then he decided that probably wouldn't be a very good idea. Once in a great while, discretion really was the better part of valor.

He kept an eye on the sun as they continued westward, knowing that Charity wanted to reach Buffalo Flat before nightfall. Matt figured that would be a pretty good idea, too. The thought of having to camp overnight with six pretty young women wasn't that unappealing, but the prospect that those other gunnies might come after them again was. The ladies ought to be safe once they got to town, though.

The sun was down and twilight was starting to settle over the landscape when lights appeared up ahead in the distance. Sam pointed out the scattering of warm yellow glows and said, "That would be Buffalo Flat."

"Thank goodness," Charity said with relief

evident in her voice. "I was afraid we were going to have to spend another night on the trail." She flapped the reins and got the tired horses moving at a slightly faster pace.

As the group approached the town, Matt saw that Buffalo Flat was a good-sized settlement. A wide main street lined with businesses ran for six or eight blocks. There were an equal number of cross streets, and quite a few houses and cabins were scattered around the outer edges of the business district. A steeple rose from the whitewashed walls of a church at the far end of town. At the near end was a large windmill and public watering trough, along with a corral. There was no railroad line running through Buffalo Flat, but a stagecoach probably came through a couple of times a week. For the most part, this was ranching country, although Matt knew there were several mines in the low range of peaks to the west known as the Prophet Mountains.

"You say the fellas you're betrothed to are supposed to meet you here?" Matt said.

Charity didn't reply. She just stared straight ahead grimly as she kept the team moving.

Once again Matt was struck by the strong feeling that not all was as it seemed. In fact, he thought that Charity had out-and-out lied to him and Sam. Why she would have done that was her own business, but he couldn't help but wonder just what the truth was about these women.

As they reached the edge of town, Charity hauled back on the reins and brought the wagon to a halt. "We'll be safe enough now," she said. "Thank you, Mr. Bodine, and you, too, Mr. Two Wolves. You gentlemen won't have to bother with us anymore."

"It was no bother, ma'am," Sam assured her. "If

you like, we can stay with you until you find the
gents you're looking for."

"That won't be necessary," Charity said quickly.
"You can go on—"

"There they are!" a harsh male voice said loudly.
"There are the two gun-happy bastards who bushwhacked us!"

Chapter 4

Bo couldn't help but stare at the woman who stood behind the rock pointing a gun at them. Beside him, Scratch did more than stare. He ogled the woman in outright admiration and maybe a little lust that was unbecoming in a man of his age. After a moment he let out a low whistle.

"Settle down," Bo told him sternly. He raised his voice and called, "Ma'am, you don't have to be afraid of us. Like my partner said, we ran off the men who ambushed you."

"Who said I was afraid of you?" she asked, her voice cool and level. "And how do I know I can trust you any more than those no-good bushwhackers of Cole's?"

"Why, we're Texans," Scratch said, as if that explained everything. "We'd never hurt a gal. Where we come from, a fella who don't treat womenfolk proper finds himself on the wrong end of a whippin'."

"There are as many bastards from Texas as there are from anywhere else," the woman said. The barrel of the gun still didn't droop. She held the weapon rock steady as she asked, "Who are you?"

"My name is Bo Creel," Bo said. "This rapscallion with me is Scratch Morton."

"I'd probably be offended," Scratch said, "if I knew what the hell you were talkin' about." He snatched off his Stetson and held it over his heart as he bowed in the saddle. "It's a plumb honor to meet you, ma'am."

Bo saw that a smile was trying to tug at the corners of her mouth. "I'd say that the two of you are old enough to be harmless," she commented, "if I hadn't just seen you shooting it out with those gunmen." Finally she lowered the Colt in her hand. "I guess I can trust you. You *did* come along and pull my bacon out of the fire."

"We don't like bushwhackers," Bo said. He nodded toward the wagon. "Got a load of supplies there?"

"That's right," the woman replied. "I was taking it back to my ranch."

"*Your* ranch?" Scratch said.

"Damn right it's mine," the woman answered without hesitation. "And no skunk like Junius Cole is going to take it away from me."

Bo crossed his hands on the saddle horn and leaned forward. "That's the second time you've mentioned this fella Cole. Who is he?"

"The man who hired those bushwhackers to kill me. I knew I was taking a chance by leaving the ranch and going into Buffalo Flat, but we needed the supplies. I thought maybe I could slip into town, load up, and get back out before Cole or any of his gunnies spotted me." She grimaced. "Obviously, that wasn't the case."

"Buffalo Flat," Scratch mused. "I've heard of the place. Don't reckon I've ever been there, though."

"You haven't missed much," the woman said. "It's a little east of here." She nodded toward the west. "My spread is that way, in the foothills at the base of the Prophets. Rugged country, and not as good as some of the other ranches around here, but it's mine and I'm going to hang onto it."

Bo said, "Got to admire somebody who's determined to keep what's theirs. Why don't Scratch and I ride along with you and see to it that you get back to your ranch safely?"

The woman's eyes narrowed in suspicion again. "You wouldn't be up to any tricks, would you?"

"No, ma'am. But one of those hombres got away, and he's liable to go right back to that fella Cole you mentioned and tell him what happened. You know Cole better than I do. What's he going to do when he hears about it?"

"Send more gunmen after me if he thinks they've got a chance to catch me before I get home," she replied. "I guess you've got a point. We'd better get moving." She came out from behind the rock and slipped the Colt into a holster she wore around her waist.

She was a fine-looking woman; Bo wasn't so old that he failed to realize that. In her late twenties, maybe thirty, with honey-blond hair that fell in thick wings around her shoulders. She was slender but not skinny, with intriguing curves in the right places. She wore a long brown skirt and a white shirt that was open at the throat so that her tanned skin contrasted nicely with the fabric. Moving with a smooth efficiency, she stepped up to the driver's seat of the buckboard. As she picked up the reins, she said, "I'm Theresa Kincaid."

"We're mighty pleased to meet you, ma'am," Scratch said with a broad grin on his face.

"Give us a minute to take a look at those hombres who were shooting at you," Bo said, "and then we'll join you."

He and Scratch turned their horses around and rode back to the fallen gunmen. They didn't have to dismount to be certain that the men were dead. The glassy eyes and the way their limbs were sprawled on the ground were evidence enough of that.

"Recognize any of 'em?" Bo asked.

Scratch shook his head. "Nope. Ugly-lookin' polecats, though. Hired guns, like you said, Bo."

"I hate to just leave them here. It doesn't seem fitting."

Scratch snorted and said, "It don't bother me a bit. They were tryin' to kill us, and you can damn well bet that if they'd succeeded, they'd have ridden off and left us a-layin' here for the buzzards and coyotes."

"Maybe when we get to town we can tell the sheriff about it. He'll probably want to come out and collect the bodies."

Scratch looked like he thought that would be a waste of time and effort, but he didn't say anything. He had ridden with Bo plenty long enough to know how his pard felt about doing things right and proper.

They went back to the buckboard. As Theresa Kincaid got the vehicle moving and the two old-timers moved their horses up alongside it, Scratch said, "That little fracas was more fun than we've had in a month of Sundays."

"Trading shots with bushwhackers is fun for you?"

Theresa asked with a look of bafflement on her face.

"We've sort of gotten used to trouble," Bo said.

"That's puttin' it mildly," Scratch added.

Theresa frowned in thought as she regarded them. "You two wouldn't happen to be looking for jobs, would you?" she asked after a moment.

"Fellas like us who are ridin' the grub line are always lookin' for work," Scratch replied before Bo could shake his head. Only a short time earlier, Scratch had been talking about needing to increase their stake and get some supplies in the next town they came to, but he sure hadn't meant to go about it by means of manual labor. It made a difference, though, when a pretty woman came into the picture.

"So you're ranch hands?" Theresa asked. She looked at Bo. "You're not really dressed like a cowboy."

"Don't let that getup fool you," Scratch said. "Ol' Bo here may look like a parson, but he's a top hand. As good a man with a rope as you'll ever see."

"Is that true?" Theresa asked.

Bo shrugged. "I've done my share of cowboying."

"And I know you can shoot. I've seen that with my own eyes."

"Is that part of the job requirement?" Bo asked coolly. "Shooting?"

"You saw for yourself what happened when I tried to make a peaceful trip to town for supplies. I won't lie to you, Mr. Creel. If you sign on to ride for the Half Moon, you're liable to get even more trouble than you're accustomed to. Junius Cole wants that ranch, and he's not going to stop at anything to get it."

"Why is he that anxious to his hands on it?" Bo asked, interested in Theresa's dilemma despite himself.

"He has a spread just east of mine, and the creek that runs through it and provides most of the water for his stock has its source on my land. The creek is spring-fed, and the spring comes up on Half Moon range."

"What did you do, threaten to dam it up?"

Theresa shook her head. "Not at all. Cole is just afraid that someday I might interfere with the spring's flow. *I* don't rely on it for water, you understand. Another creek runs through my spread, and the spring that feeds Cole's creek is just barely over the boundary line. But legally I could dynamite it and close it off any time I wanted to, and Cole worries that I'll do just that."

Scratch looked horrified by the thought as he asked, "Why would any Westerner do such a thing?"

"There was . . . bad blood . . . between Cole and my husband."

Scratch's eyebrows rose. "You're married?" He glanced at Bo as if to say, *See? I'm checking beforehand.*

"I was," Theresa answered solemnly. "My husband was killed about a year ago."

"An accident?" Bo asked.

"Only if the low-down bastard who shot him in the back meant to shoot him in the front."

Bo and Scratch looked at each other. Scratch's eyebrows rose quizzically. Bo said, "Your husband was already having trouble with Cole when that happened?"

"That's right. But things got worse after William was ambushed. I'm sure Cole thought that I would just sell out and leave. He was furious when I told him I intended to hang onto the ranch and keep it going." She paused and then added dryly, "Junius Cole is a man who's used to getting his own way. He doesn't like it when anybody stands up to him. That's how he managed to get his hands on the biggest ranch in the county and half of Buffalo Flat."

"He's not just a cattleman, then?" Bo asked.

"No, he's a businessman and lives in Buffalo Flat rather than on his ranch. He's got a crew of hard-cases to run it for him. He owns the Colorado Palace Saloon, the largest in town, as well as the hotel and one of the livery stables and Lord knows what else."

"Sounds like a bad hombre to have for an enemy," Scratch commented.

"He is," Theresa agreed with a nod. "And if you go to work for me, he'll consider the two of you his enemies, as well."

"How many hands do you already have working for you?" Bo asked.

"Just four. Cole's gunmen scared off the rest. I've written to some friends of mine asking for help, so I'm hoping that some more men will show up sometime. But I don't know when that will be. I may be dead before anyone else can get here."

"Well, we can't let that happen," Scratch said without hesitation. "We'll coil our twine here and give you a hand, won't we, Bo?"

Bo was already thinking the same thing. The odds were against Theresa Kincaid. She was playing against a stacked deck full of ruthless men and hired killers. Bo never liked seeing anybody being dealt a hand like that.

He nodded and said, "If you'll have us, we'll ride for your brand, ma'am."

"You understand that it could be dangerous?"

"Shoot, we're hopin' it will be," Scratch said with a grin. "More entertainin' that way. How much farther is it to this ranch o' yours?"

"Not much farther," she replied. "About a mile."

The terrain had become more rugged as they traveled west toward the mountains. The hills were larger and more numerous, and rocky ridges ran between some of them. The slopes were dotted with pine and cedar trees.

But even though the valleys were smaller here, they were still carpeted with lush grass, and Bo knew that cows wouldn't have much trouble finding plenty of graze in these parts. Maybe the range wasn't quite as good as it was farther east, but it was good enough to make a cattle ranch profitable.

"Are we on your spread now?" he asked Theresa.

"That's right."

"Where does Cole's range start?"

"Back behind us a couple of miles. The road marks the southern boundary of his ranch. It runs to the north for a long way, parallel to the mountains. The Half Moon is narrower and extends farther south, but the two ranches share a good ten miles of boundary line."

"Any fences between the spreads?"

"Of course not."

Bo wasn't surprised. Farther east in Kansas, people were starting to fence in their land with barbed wire—the Devil's wire, some folks called it—but there was still a great deal of resistance to that idea out here, in places like Colorado, Wyoming, and Montana. As far as Bo could see, efforts to bring in fences were doomed in most parts of the West. Farmers might like barbed wire, but cattlemen had no use for it.

Theresa went on. "Cole's foreman, a man named Barlowe, keeps line riders out all the time, turning back strays that get too close to the line from either side. That's one reason so many of my hands drew their time and rode off. Cole's riders have a habit of taking potshots at anyone they see moving around on the Half Moon side of the line."

"Why doesn't the law do something about that?" Bo wanted to know.

Theresa gave a bitter little laugh. "The sheriff is in Cole's pocket, that's why. Cole claims that his men are protecting his spread from rustlers, and Sheriff Branch just accepts whatever Cole says."

"That's a lawman for you," Scratch said. "Always suckin' up to whoever's got the most money."

Bo frowned and thought about reminding Scratch that both of them had worn tin stars on occasion, but he knew his partner was just telling Theresa what he thought she wanted to hear. He figured Scratch was wasting his time. They were almost twice as old as Theresa, and the odds that she would take any romantic interest in either of them ranged from slim to none. But Scratch wasn't going to give up without a fight, bless his lecherous old heart.

Theresa turned the buckboard off the road onto a smaller trail that led north. The route wound around a couple of hills and then turned west again into a valley watered by a small stream. Just beyond a rocky stretch of streambed that served as a ford sat a large log house. The way the structure sprawled out at odd angles told Bo that it had been added onto several times in the past and had started out as a small cabin. Beyond the house were some outbuildings and corrals.

"That's it," Theresa said as she drew back on the reins and brought the buckboard to a halt. The sun was about to dip behind the peaks to the west, but its reddish-gold glow still washed over the landscape, painting a pretty picture. "That's the Half Moon."

Chapter 5

Matt and Sam both stiffened in their saddles at the sound of that angry, accusatory voice. Matt turned his head and saw four men coming out of the barn next to the public corral. The one who was slightly in the lead as the group stalked toward them wore a flat-crowned black hat with a concho-studded silver band. He glared at them from a raw-boned face and when he spoke, Matt knew he was the one who had called out first.

"I'm surprised they had the guts to come on into town. It takes a coward to shoot a man in the back."

Rage burned hotly through Matt, but although it wasn't easy, he kept a tight rein on his temper. With that wagonload of women sitting right beside him, he didn't have much choice in the matter.

"What's the matter?" demanded the man Matt already thought of as Concho. "Too gutless to admit that you're a pair of backshooters?"

Sam's voice was taut, showing that he, too, was struggling to control his anger as he replied, "I remember seeing you and your friends out there on the trail. You're lying about what happened."

Concho glared and tapped his chest with his clenched left fist. "You callin' me a liar, breed?"

"You called us cowards. I'd say you have no room to complain." Sam drew a deep breath. "And as for my heritage, both sides of my family are proud, noble people . . . unlike, say, the skunk and the hog that mated to produce you."

A tight smile tugged at the corners of Matt's mouth. "A skunk and a hog," he said. "That's a good one."

"Thanks. I thought it was appropriate."

Concho's face had darkened even more with fury. Matt watched the man's eyes closely. Some people made the mistake of watching an enemy's gun hand, but Matt knew that the eyes were the more reliable giveaway. In this case, he could tell that while Concho was working himself up to hook and draw, he wasn't quite there yet.

The three men with Concho were similar, hard-faced Coltmen who could kill without blinking an eye. One had a bloodstained rag tied around his upper left arm where one of the blood brothers' bullets had winged him during the earlier fight. These were the survivors from the gang that had jumped the wagon. Matt had no doubt of that.

"Where are the other two who got away?" he asked.

"After you bushwhacked us, you mean?" Concho spat. "Dodgson is dead. Died on the way into town. Higgins is down at the doc's office. Sawbones says he probably won't make it. That's two more marks against you murderin' bastards."

Charity spoke up from behind Matt and Sam. "You're nothing but a liar! You and those others attacked our wagon. You tried to kill me and my friends!"

"Shut up, you whore!" Concho yelled.

"Charity, get the wagon out of here," Matt said in a low, urgent voice.

"But he's lying," Charity insisted. "We all know he's lying. The townspeople need to know it, too."

The confrontation in the twilight was drawing some attention, all right. Several people had paused nearby in the street to listen to the angry words being exchanged.

"Somebody fetch the sheriff!" Charity urged the bystanders.

"Blast it," Matt grated. "You ladies get out of here—"

"The odds are two to one, Bodine," Lydia broke in. "But if you'll move your horse aside a little, this Greener of mine will help even them up."

The gunmen on the ground tensed, but not because of the threat from Lydia's shotgun, although any man would be a fool not to be a mite scared of such a fearsome weapon. One of the gunnies said, "Bodine? Matt Bodine?"

Matt nodded slightly. "That's right."

"Then the breed would be Sam Two Wolves." The gunman spat on the ground and shook his head as he started backing off. The others stayed where they were, tense but still ready to draw. "Forget it, Tully," the one who was retreating said to the man Matt thought of as Concho. "I didn't sign on to fight no damn Bodine and Two Wolves."

"Damn it!" Tully burst out. "They're just men! They bleed like anybody else, and I'll prove it!"

His hand stabbed toward the gun on his hip.

The wagon was still where it had come to a stop.

Matt knew that he and Sam couldn't afford to fool around with these hired killers. They had to finish this fast and accurately to cut down on the chances of any of the women being hit by a wild slug.

Both of Bodine's guns flashed up, faster than the eye could follow. The right-hand Colt spoke just a fraction of a second sooner than the one in Matt's left hand. He used it to blast two rounds into Tully's chest. The gunman was thrown backward by the impact of the bullets striking his body. He'd had his gun out of the holster, but it was still pointing toward the ground when his death spasms caused him to jerk the trigger. The revolver roared as the bullet smacked harmlessly into the ground at his feet. The fancy hat came off Tully's head and seemed to hang in the air for a heartbeat before it fell to the street.

Before either Tully or his hat hit the ground, the gun in Matt's left hand had roared twice. The bullets went a shade lower than he had intended, ripping through the belly of a second hired killer. That hombre had hold of his gun, but didn't get it out of leather before his guts were blasted apart by the pair of .45-caliber slugs. He doubled over with a groan and collapsed as he crossed his arms over his stomach and tried unsuccessfully to hold his insides in.

Meanwhile, Sam's gun had also leaped into his hand with amazing speed. He was a hair slower than Bodine, which made him faster on the draw than nine out of ten men he would ever meet. His first shot caught the third gunman in the left shoulder as the man suddenly shifted to his right. The slug punching into him rocked him and turned him half around, but he stayed on his feet and finished clawing his revolver from its holster. Sam fired again as the gun started up. This shot went where it was supposed to, into the man's chest, but somehow the man still didn't fall. Not only that, but the stubborn bastard kept on trying to lift his gun and get a shot off.

The third time, Sam shot him in the head. That did the trick. The slug left a small, black-rimmed hole in the man's forehead and a huge, gaping one as it blew out the back of his skull, taking a shower of blood, brains, and bone fragments with it. The man went down hard and didn't move again.

The fourth gunman had his hands shoved high in the air and was shaking his head emphatically as he continued to back away. "Don't shoot!" he yelled. "I'm out of it, I'm out of it!"

Sam swung his Colt to cover the man and ordered, "Unbuckle your gunbelt, just so you don't get tempted."

The man did as he was told, unbuckling his gunbelt and letting the holstered revolver hit the ground.

A quick glance at the three men lying in the street told Matt he didn't have to worry about them anymore. As the echoes of gun thunder were still dying away like the sound of distant drums, he turned to look at the wagon. Charity and Lydia sat there motionless on the seat, pale and wide-eyed, and the other four women peered out from behind them in the back of the wagon, looking equally shaken by the sudden outbreak of violence.

"Everybody all right?" Matt asked. He was pretty sure none of the gunmen had been able to fire a shot before dying.

Charity swallowed and then nodded. "Yes, I . . . I

think we're all fine." She looked around at her companions. "Aren't we?"

Lydia nodded, and so did the other women.

"What in blue blazes is going on here?" a man shouted. "Drop those guns!"

Matt turned his head and saw a sturdy-looking man with gray hair under a black Stetson and a bristly mustache hurrying toward them. Even in the fading light, Matt could see the badge on the man's vest—and the shotgun clutched in his hands.

"Take it easy, Sheriff," Matt said, keeping his voice calm and steady in an attempt to keep the lawman from getting antsy. "We're not gonna drop our guns, but we'll be glad to holster 'em." To demonstrate that, he lowered both Colts and slipped them into leather. Sam did likewise with his gun.

The sheriff didn't look happy about it, but he didn't force the issue. Instead, he gestured with the twin barrels of the scattergun and said, "Get off those horses."

"All right," Sam said. "Just be careful with that weapon. I hope it doesn't have a hair trigger."

"You let me worry about that," the sheriff snorted as Bodine and Two Wolves dismounted. "What the hell happened here?"

Matt nodded toward the bodies, noticing as he did so that the fourth gunman had taken advantage of the sheriff's arrival to pick up his gunbelt and run off. He was no longer anywhere in sight.

"Earlier this afternoon those hombres and several others bushwhacked the ladies in this wagon," Matt explained. "My brother and I came along and took a hand in the game. We ventilated some of them, and the others lit a shuck. Obviously, they got to town ahead of us and saw us when we rode in. They mouthed off a little, then that one"—Matt gestured toward Tully's body— "picked up the fight where it left off. The other two went for their guns, too."

The sheriff frowned at Matt, then said, "By God, I know that man! That's Ed Tully. He's no bushwhacker. He works for Mr. Cole."

"I wouldn't know about that," Matt drawled, "but he's a bushwhacker, all right. You've got eight people here who can testify to that."

"And probably half a dozen or more of your citizens can tell you that those gunslingers drew first," Sam put in. "We had no choice but to defend ourselves, and the ladies."

The lawman switched his gaze to the wagon and its occupants. "Who're these ladies you keep talking about?"

"They came here to meet their future husbands," Sam said.

"I haven't heard anything about any mail-order brides coming to town," the sheriff insisted. He stared at Charity and Lydia for a second, then exclaimed, "My God! You're the new whores!"

Matt and Sam glanced at each other again, each thinking of the conversation they had had earlier. While they had been inclined to give Charity and the other women the benefit of the doubt, it was true that except for their conservative clothing, they looked more like soiled doves than they did husband-hunting old maids. Matt recalled as well that Tully had called Charity a whore just before the shooting starting. At the time Matt had thought the man was just being insulting. Now he wasn't so sure about that.

Intensely curious, Matt and Sam both waited to

see how Charity was going to respond to the sheriff's crude accusation.

Finally Charity said, "My name is Charity MacKenzie. I've come here to assume ownership of the Silver Belle Saloon. I have the documents that were sent to me by an attorney named Ashmore—"

"Judge Ashmore practices law here, all right," the sheriff interrupted. "He told me that a while back that somebody in Kansas City named C.A. MacKenzie had inherited the Silver Belle."

"That's me," Charity said stiffly. "Charity Anne MacKenzie."

"But . . . but he said this fella MacKenzie was coming to open up the saloon again, and bringing a new bunch of girls with him!"

"Judge Ashmore misunderstood," Charity insisted. "I'm C.A. MacKenzie, and my friends and I are going to run that saloon. But we're not whores."

"Not anymore, maybe," the sheriff said. He laughed again, and it sounded just as ugly this time as it had the first time. "But what'd you do for a living back in Kansas City?"

Charity's lips clamped together and she didn't reply. Beside her, Lydia sat just as stone-faced. Matt knew from their reaction that the sheriff was right. Back where the women had come from, they had been prostitutes.

But to Matt's way of thinking, that didn't make any real difference now. If Charity had inherited that saloon, then it was rightfully hers to run as she saw fit.

The sheriff turned away from the wagon and gestured with the shotgun again. "You boys come on down to the office with me," he said. "I'll have to lock you up until I get to the bottom of these killings."

"I never cared for being on the wrong side of iron bars, Sheriff," Matt said. "Just ask some of the folks who saw it. They'll tell you those gunmen drew first. And you've already heard how they ambushed these ladies earlier."

"I heard it, but these aren't ladies and I'm not sure I believe the rest of it, either." The lawman's mustache bristled with anger. "Ed Tully worked for one of this town's leading businessmen. I don't think he'd bushwhack even a bunch of whores."

Lydia burst out, "Stop callin' us that!"

The sheriff sneered at her. "I call a spade a spade and a whore a whore. If you don't like it, you can get the hell out of Buffalo Flat."

"Forget it," Charity said wearily to Lydia. "Just forget it. You know how people are."

"Yeah," Lydia said flatly. "Unfortunately, I do."

"Well, what about it?" the sheriff asked Matt and Sam. "Are you coming along peaceful-like, or is the undertaker gonna have even more business tonight?" He hefted the shotgun meaningfully.

"Answer one question first, Sheriff," Matt said.

"I don't have to answer a damned thing! You answer to me, boy." The sheriff chewed his mustache. "But what is it you want to know?"

"This fella you said that hired killer worked for—"

"Mr. Junius Cole. A fine man."

"He wouldn't happen to own a saloon, would he?"

"The Colorado Palace," the sheriff said. "Finest establishment in town. Hell, in this whole part of the state!"

Sam took up Matt's line of thought. "So I suppose Mr. Junius Cole wouldn't particularly want a rival saloon that had been closed down to open up again, would he?"

The lawman glowered at him. "What are you getting at? You saying Mr. Cole was behind this? I really ought to blast you two rannihans—"

"Is that how you enforce the law in Buffalo Flat?" Matt cut in. "Shotgun law?"

The sheriff controlled his temper with a visible effort. "Get moving, you two," he ordered. "Or I might just forget that I've got this badge pinned on."

Matt and Sam looked at each other. They had ridden together for long enough that each knew what the other was thinking. If they jumped in opposite directions, the sheriff wouldn't be able to get both of them, even with a shotgun. One of them would be able to hook and draw and cut down the lawman.

But the blood brothers hadn't been raised to go around shooting sheriffs, even when the star-packer in question might well be corrupt and was almost certainly close-minded and quick to jump to conclusions.

Matt sighed and said, "Don't you think you ought to take our guns, Sheriff?"

"Yeah." The sheriff looked around and called to one of the townies. "Dugan, come get the guns off these fellas."

"No offense, Sheriff, but you didn't see 'em shoot," the man replied as he hung back. "I did."

"Damn it, do what I told you!"

Matt looked at the townie and nodded. "It's all right." He held his hands out at his side, well clear of the gun butts, as the citizen approached warily and plucked the weapons from their holsters. When he had Matt's Colts, he took Sam's gun as well, and then scurried clear of the line of fire from the sheriff's Greener.

"I suppose I should be proud of you," Sam said under his breath. "Was a time you'd have told that badge-toter to stick his shotgun and his tin star up his ass—and then made it stick."

"Yeah, I guess I'm gettin' downright civilized in my old age," Matt muttered. "But I don't have to like it."

The sheriff jerked the barrels of the shotgun. "Get moving!"

As Matt and Sam started walking down the street toward the sheriff's office and jail, Charity suddenly called after them, "Don't worry! I'll go see Judge Ashmore. We'll get you out of there!"

The sheriff chuckled unpleasantly as he walked after them, the scattergun trained on their backs. "Hear that, boys?" he asked. "You don't have a thing in the world to worry about. You got a red-headed whore on your side!"

Chapter 6

Junius Cole had been in his office at the Colorado Palace when he heard the gunfire break out down the street at the edge of town. He wasn't working at the moment, though. He was watching a woman named Anna Malone take off her clothes.

Cole's square white teeth clamped down hard on the cigar in his mouth at the sound of the shots. He'd been looking forward to spending some time with Anna—she was both limber and enthusiastic, a good combination—but he supposed he should go see what the commotion was all about.

Buffalo Flat was *his* town, after all.

But he was already in a bad mood because of what Ed Tully had told him earlier, and he'd thought that Anna might cheer him up a little. As he stood up from behind the desk he said, "Wait here. I'll be right back."

"Would you like me to get dressed again?" she asked. She had a faint accent, because she was originally from England. That was another thing Cole liked about her. Some of the things she said to him while they were in the throes of passion sounded even dirtier in an English accent.

"No, damn it," he snapped at her as he headed for the door. "Stay just like you are."

She shrugged, which made her bare bosom do interesting things. Cole just shook his head and jerked open the door. Whoever had just gotten themselves killed out in the street could have had the decency to die at a better time.

He pulled the door shut behind him as he stepped into the main room of the saloon, knowing that if he didn't, his bartenders would be trying to sneak a peek into the office at Anna instead of paying attention to their business.

Even though he had softened some in recent years, Cole was still a big, powerful man. His bulky shoulders testified to the strength he had developed as a young man working in the boiler room of a Mississippi riverboat. He had been glad to get out of that stinking, hellish job and had vowed never to go back to anything that bad. The time he had spent working in a Natchez tavern had taught him to be even more ruthless about getting what he wanted, no matter who stood in his way.

Now he was the richest man in these parts, wore fine suits, smoked expensive cigars, and drank only the best whiskey. His thick dark hair was carefully barbered and slicked down with pomade. A perfectly trimmed mustache hung over his wide mouth. The crowd in the saloon parted to make room for him as he stalked toward the entrance, not only because he owned the place, but also because Junius Cole possessed an indefinable quality that made men step aside from him.

The shots had fallen silent, but not before quiet-

ing down the noise in the big room. "Anybody
know what the hell's going on out there?" Cole
asked the room at large.

"Some sort of shootin' down by the public corral
and the livery stable," a townsman said.

"I know that, damn it." Cole slapped the batwings
aside and stepped out onto the boardwalk in front
of the Colorado Palace. He was aware that in the
dusk he was silhouetted by the light behind him,
but he wasn't particularly worried about that. He
had this town treed. Nobody in it would dare to
take a shot at him.

He chewed on his cigar as he looked toward the
eastern end of town. A wagon was parked down
there, and several bodies lay in the street near it.
Sheriff Sherman Branch stood near the wagon,
too, shotgun in hand as he talked to a couple of
tall strangers. As Cole watched, the sheriff had
one of the bystanders disarm the men. Then he
started marching them up the street toward the
jail, which brought them straight toward the Colorado Palace, too.

Cole looked past the sheriff and the two prisoners and saw the hat with the concho-studded band
lying in the dirt next to one of the dead men. "Son
of a bitch," Cole said softly. That was Ed Tully's hat.
Which meant that Tully was one of the dead men
sprawled in the street.

The wagon, the two strangers, Tully dead . . . It
didn't take Cole but a second to put it all together.
Those were the two men who had saved those
whores, Cole realized. Not only saved the whores,
but wiped out half of the men Cole had sent to stop
them. Tully and some of the other survivors must

have spotted them coming into town and braced them again.

The damned fools. It would have been better to wait until later, after nightfall, and cut them down with a shotgun from some alley mouth. Tully would have been too proud to do that, though. Failing at the job Cole had given him had hurt his feelings. He would have been determined to make amends and face those two sharpshooting bastards out in the open, to prove he was faster and a better shot. It was a common failing among hired guns.

And in this case, it had gotten Tully killed.

Cole stepped back, letting the batwings flap closed. He could still see over them, and he got a good look at the two men as Branch marched them past on the way to the jail. Cole was pretty sure he had never seen either of them before, but he didn't like their looks. Although fairly clean-cut, they were obviously tough hombres. Bad enemies to have.

But the sheriff appeared to be locking them up, Cole reminded himself. That was good. Once the meddling troublemakers were behind bars, Cole could see about arranging for an "accident" to befall them.

Then, with their protectors gone, it would be easy enough to deal with those women.

Women, Cole thought disgustedly as he turned away from the saloon entrance. He had more than his share of woman trouble on his plate right now.

But he also had Anna waiting in his office, and the night wasn't getting any younger.

"What was the shootin' about, Boss?" one of the bartenders asked as Cole walked toward the office again.

"Looked like Tully and some of the other boys got in a ruckus with a couple of strangers," Cole replied.

The bartender smirked. "Reckon the undertaker'll be plantin' those strangers, then."

Cole shook his head, surprising the man. "I'm afraid it's going to be the other way around," he said.

He went into the office and closed the door, leaving the startled bartender staring after him.

Even though Cole hadn't told Anna to finish disrobing, that was what she'd done while he was gone. She was lying on the divan across the office from the desk, a pillow under her head and a smile on her face. Cole let his eyes play over her body and felt some of the aggravation ease inside him. She knew how to get to him, he had to give her credit for that.

He took the cigar out of his mouth and was about to tell her how pretty she looked, when a soft knock sounded on the door that led from the office out into the alley behind the Colorado Palace.

"Son of a *bitch*!" Cole said.

Anna sat up and said quietly, "Perhaps I should just go on up to my room."

Cole motioned for her to stay where she was as he went over to the door. "Just wait a damn minute," he told her. Then he called through the door, "Who the hell is it?"

The reply came in a strained voice. "Donohue, Boss."

Cole could tell something was wrong. Even though he didn't like it, he turned to Anna and said, "Put your clothes on." He added to Donohue, "Hang on."

"Sure thing . . . Boss."

Donohue didn't sound good. Cole put the cigar back in his mouth and clamped his teeth on it impatiently as Anna got dressed. Watching a woman put her clothes on had some appeal, but it wasn't near as enjoyable as watching her take them off, Cole reflected. When she was dressed he gave her a curt nod, and she went to the main door and slipped out into the saloon. Only when she was gone did Cole unlock the alley door and swing it open.

He stepped back quickly as Donohue tumbled into the office. The right sleeve of the man's shirt was soaked with blood. Donohue had either passed out leaning against the door—or he was dead.

Cole leaned over, checked for a pulse, and found one. Donohue wasn't dead, then. Cole dragged him all the way into the office and closed the alley door. He picked up the bottle of whiskey that was sitting on the desk and knelt next to the wounded man. He hated to waste liquor this good on a hired gun, but he needed to know what the hell had happened. He put one hand under Donohue's head and lifted it, used the other to bring the bottle to the man's lips and tilt it. Whiskey splashed into Donohue's mouth and dribbled over his chin.

Donohue gasped and coughed and opened his eyes. "Wha . . . what happened?"

"You tell me," Cole snapped. "And you'd damned well better not die before you do."

"I . . . got shot."

"I can see that." From the way Donohue's right arm hung limp, Cole figured the shoulder had been smashed by a bullet. "Where are the others?"

"Dead," Donohue said. "All . . . dead."

An icy rage filled Cole. "You let a *woman* shoot all

four of you? I paid you good money to take care of her, blast it!"

"Wasn't . . . the Kincaid woman," Donohue got out. "Two men . . . strangers . . . jumped us after we . . . bushwhacked her."

Cole frowned as he repeated, "Two men? Strangers?" He couldn't help but think of the men Sheriff Branch had taken to jail after the shooting at the other end of town. Could it have been the same two hombres who had shot up Donohue and his companions?

No, that was impossible, Cole decided. The fracases had occurred in opposite directions, one east of Buffalo Flat and the other west. Earlier in the day, Cole had sent Ed Tully and most of the gunmen who worked for him to intercept those whores from Kansas City who were on their way to Buffalo Flat to take over the Silver Belle. He had gone to the trouble to have old Archibald MacKenzie, the previous owner of the Silver Belle, disposed of, and he didn't want to see anybody else coming in and opening the place up again.

But then later, he had gotten word that Theresa Kincaid was in town, buying supplies, and knowing that fate had presented him with an opportunity to get rid of her so that he could go ahead and take over the Half Moon, he had sent Donohue and three other men to ambush her. Donohue and the others weren't as ruthlessly efficient as Tully's crew, but Cole had figured they were good enough to take care of one woman, for Christ's sake!

Obviously, that hadn't been the case, since Theresa Kincaid had gotten some unexpected help. Cole couldn't help but wonder who those two men were. Two pairs of strangers approaching Buffalo

Flat on the same day, from opposite directions, and both pairs interfering in his business. What were the odds of *that* happening!

Cole leaned over the wounded man and asked, "What about the woman? What happened to her? Did you at least kill her before you got shot up?"

Donohue opened his mouth, but couldn't get any words out. Cole had to dribble more of the whiskey into him before he could speak again.

"I don't think . . . she was hit," Donohue said. "She jumped off the wagon . . . hid behind a rock . . . Briggs and St. John were gonna . . . work around behind her . . . but before they could . . . those strangers showed up . . . opened fire on us. . . . We figured we'd . . . get rid of them first . . . then take care of the woman."

"But it didn't work out that way," Cole guessed. His face was set in grim lines.

"Got this bullet in my shoulder . . . right off," Donohue said. "I knew I was out of the fight . . . figured I'd better get back here . . . to let you know what happened."

"You ran out on your partners, in other words." Cole's angry words were scathing.

"No, I . . . I stayed long enough . . . to see what happened. Those bastards . . . gunned 'em down . . . all three of 'em . . . Briggs, Anderson, and St. John . . . I could tell . . . they was dead."

"The two men who interfered, what did they look like?"

Donohue swallowed and licked his lips, but Cole ignored the hint and didn't give him any more liquor. After a moment the gunman said, "They was . . . old. Old-timers. One wore buckskin . . . the other was dressed more like . . . a preacher. Could've been just . . . a pair of saddle tramps . . . but they were . . . damned good shots."

The descriptions didn't fit anyone that Cole knew. "Did you see the Kincaid woman after that?" he wanted to know.

Donohue shook his head. "No, I . . . lit a shuck . . . outta there. But I'm pretty sure . . . she wasn't hit." He took a deep, ragged breath. "Boss, I need . . . a sawbones. I'm hit hard . . . hurt like hell . . . lost a lot of blood . . . but I knew I had to get back . . . and tell you—"

He stopped short and sucked his breath in as his eyes suddenly widened. They began to glaze over, and as he released that last breath, it rattled in his throat. That sound and the glassy look in Donohue's eyes told Cole that the gunman was dead. Cole was a little surprised. The wound was messy, but hadn't appeared to be life-threatening. Obviously, Donohue had lost too much blood, and it had killed him. None too gently, Cole lowered the dead man's head to the floor and then stood up. He set the whiskey bottle on the desk and replaced the cork in its neck. He was glad that Donohue had lived long enough to at least warn him that Theresa Kincaid was still alive and might have two new allies in those old-timers who had pitched in to rescue her from the ambush.

Cole wondered who they were. They had to be pretty gun-handy to have dealt so efficiently with four hired killers. The question now was, had they moved on after helping the Kincaid woman, or had she recruited them to work on her ranch? As far as Cole knew, she had only a few hands left on the Half Moon, and she was probably desperate for help, especially help that could handle a gun.

He wished the woman had had enough sense to accept his offer to buy the ranch after her husband was killed. Cole had never dreamed she would be foolish enough to refuse. True, Cole had offered the widow only a fraction of what the spread was worth, but he had thought she would jump at it anyway.

Anger welled up inside him. He had the Kincaid woman being stubborn and hanging onto something he wanted, and he was faced with the threat of those whores coming into town, taking over the Silver Belle, and turning it into a real rival for the Colorado Palace. Thorns in both of his sides, damn it. And now to make things worse, four strangers who stuck their noses—and their guns—into his plans. The rage Cole felt was so overpowering he had to lash out at somebody or something.

So he kicked Donohue's corpse in the ribs twice, hard. That made Cole feel a little better, and Donohue, of course, didn't feel a damned thing.

Chapter 7

"What are we going to do, Charity?" Janie Cantrell asked as she leaned over the back of the wagon seat and anxiously watched the sheriff lead Matt Bodine and Sam Two Wolves away. "They helped us. We can't just let them be locked up!"

Janie was nineteen and hadn't been a soiled dove for very long, just a couple of years. Even though Charity was only twenty-four, she often felt like the gulf between their ages was huge. She could only imagine what it must feel like to be Lydia, who had been a whore for more than half her life.

Until Charity had offered her a chance to escape from all that, the same chance she had offered the other girls.

She knew Janie was upset not only because Matt and Sam had been taken into custody unjustly, but also because the younger girl had already fallen hard for Bodine. Charity had seen it in Janie's eyes. Men were usually the ones who were romantic fools—otherwise they wouldn't believe it when red-light ladies told them they loved them, or that they were the best they'd ever had—but the same crazy notions sometimes afflicted gals, too, especially ones like Janie. Just because Matt Bodine was tall and handsome, she had already convinced herself that she was in love with him.

"We can't stop the sheriff from locking them up," Charity told her, "but maybe we can help get them out of jail. We'll go see Judge Ashmore. I'm sure he can round up some witnesses who'll testify that those other men drew first and that Bodine and Two Wolves were just defending themselves. The sheriff won't have any choice but to release them."

"You're sure?"

"Of course. Haven't I been right about everything so far? We're here, aren't we?"

"We're here, all right," Lydia put in, "but from the sound of it, somebody doesn't want us here. Do you know anything about this fella Cole, Charity?"

"Not a thing," Charity said as she shook her head. "I never heard of him until the sheriff mentioned him." She lifted the reins and flapped them against the backs of the team. "Let's go find that lawyer's office."

Several times as she drove along the street, she called to men on the boardwalks, asking them where Judge Ashmore's office was. They either ignored her or just shrugged their shoulders and kept moving.

"Looks like they don't want to talk to you," Lydia commented.

"Maybe they don't know."

From the back of the wagon, petite Becky Hanson said, "Or maybe they just don't want anybody to see them talking to a bunch of floozies."

"That's all behind us now," Charity said stubbornly. "As far as anybody here in Buffalo Flat is concerned, we're just as respectable as anybody else."

"Oh, honey," Lydia said. "You know that's not

true. Hell, you heard what the sheriff said. The whole town must know who we are."

Charity caught her bottom lip between her teeth. She knew Lydia was right. She had tried her best to keep the truth from arriving before them. She had signed all the letters she'd sent to Judge Ashmore as "C.A. MacKenzie." Somehow, though, the word had gotten around.

"It doesn't matter," Charity said, and she knew she was trying as hard to convince herself as she was to make the others believe that. "It just doesn't matter."

The light was fading fast, but enough of it remained for her to spot a sign hanging from the awning over the boardwalk. It read JUDGE A.A. ASHMORE—ONE FLIGHT UP. An arrow pointed up a flight of stairs attached to the side of the building, the ground floor of which housed an apothecary shop. Charity brought the wagon to a halt and peered up the stairs. The second floor windows were lit. Somebody was up there.

"Stay here," she said as she looped the reins around the brake lever. "I'll go see about this."

Lydia patted the stock of the shotgun in her lap. "We'll be right here," she promised.

Charity jumped from the wagon to the boardwalk and started up the stairs, clutching the railing as she climbed. Her throat was tight. Despite the confidence she tried to exhibit, especially around the other women, she had known going into this thing that it wouldn't be easy. She had expected to encounter obstacles in getting the townspeople to accept them.

She hadn't figured on getting shot at, though.

When she reached the landing at the top of the

stairs, she rapped smartly on the door. A deep, gruff voice called, "Come in!"

An aromatic blend of pipe tobacco and old leather filled the air as Charity opened the door and stepped into the lawyer's office. The tobacco smell came from the briar clenched between the teeth of the man seated behind a paper-cluttered desk. Shelves full of thick leather-bound volumes contributed the other smell. They were sets of law books, Charity guessed.

The man was fat, with a round, ruddy face and a short, neatly trimmed gray-shot beard. He took the pipe out of his mouth as he looked up at her. "Judge Ashmore?" she asked.

"That's right. Ambrose Aloysious Ashmore, at your service, my dear. And you are?"

"Charity Anne MacKenzie," she told him.

The friendly, somewhat lecherous twinkle that had been in Ashmore's eyes an instant earlier vanished. "Miss MacKenzie," he said coolly. "You might have told me what the initials stood for instead of keeping me in the dark. I'm afraid you've made me look foolish."

"I'm sorry, but I don't see how that could be."

"Come in and close the door," Ashmore said. "When I executed old Archibald MacKenzie's will, I assumed he was leaving the Silver Belle to a *male* relative."

"And what difference does that make? Archibald was my great-uncle, and he wanted me to have the saloon. That's all that should matter."

Ashmore scowled. "We shall see, we shall see. In the meantime, I take it you've come to Buffalo Flat to take possession of the property?"

"That's right."

The lawyer sighed and reached for his hat. "Very well. I suppose I can take you over there—"

"Actually, there's another matter that needs to be dealt with first," Charity broke in. "I want to engage your services on behalf of two men who were just taken to jail by the sheriff."

Ashmore sat back in his chair and raised his rather bushy eyebrows. "Indeed?" His expression became shrewd. "This doesn't have anything to do with that shooting I heard a short time ago, does it?"

"As a matter of fact, it does. Two men who were defending me and my friends, as well as themselves, were forced to shoot some ruffians. It was a clear-cut case of self-defense in front of numerous witnesses. The sheriff had no right to arrest them."

Ashmore grunted. "Sherman Branch knows the boundaries of the law pretty well. If he locked up these friends of yours, I'm sure he thought he had good reason to do so."

Charity felt anger and exasperation go through her, and at the same time she wondered about Ashmore referring to Bodine and Two Wolves as her friends. Were they? She had known the two men only a matter of hours, but she recalled how both of them had risked their own lives without hesitation to help her and the other women. Yes, she decided, they were her friends, at least until they gave her reason to believe otherwise.

"Judge, my companions and I will all testify that there was no crime committed. I'm sure if you ask around you can find other witnesses who'll tell the sheriff the same thing. I think if we move fast we can get Mr. Bodine and Mr. Two Wolves out of jail tonight—"

Ashmore sat up sharply and held out a hand to stop her. "What did you say their names are?"

"Matt Bodine and Sam Two Wolves." Charity frowned. "Why do people keep reacting that way? One of the men who challenged them backed off when he found out who they were."

"I should think so. These two friends of yours, my dear, are notorious gunfighters. Why, I can't think of anyone who's killed more men than Matt Bodine except maybe Smoke Jensen."

Charity was shaken, but tried not to show it. She had seen for herself how proficient with their guns Matt and Sam were, but it hadn't occurred to her that they might be famous—or infamous, as the case might be.

"Regardless of their reputations, they're innocent of any wrongdoing in these shootings," she insisted. "You have to help them, Judge."

"I don't *have* to do anything, young lady," Ashmore said sternly. "But I suppose I can go down and have a talk with Sheriff Branch. By the way, who did they kill?"

"The sheriff said one of the men was named Ed Tully. That's all I know."

Ashmore caught his breath again. "Tully? The one who works for Junius Cole?"

"I think that's what the sheriff said. This man Cole should be investigated and probably locked up. I believe he must be the person who sent those men to ambush me and my friends."

"Oh, I doubt that," Ashmore said hastily. "Junius Cole is a respected businessman in this town."

"I've known a lot of respected businessmen, Judge. Some of them were real scoundrels."

Ashmore reached for his hat again. "Yes, I imagine

you *have* known plenty of businessmen," he said. He
heaved himself to his feet as Charity trembled a little
with anger at the insinuation. "I'll take you and your
friends to the Silver Belle," he went on. "Then I'll
look into this other matter."

She forced herself to nod. "I'm counting on your
legal integrity, Judge."

"Yes, yes," he muttered as he started toward the
door. "Sometimes integrity, legal and otherwise, is
a damned inconvenient thing to have."

The front doors of the Silver Belle were closed
and locked. Puffing slightly from the exertion of
walking two blocks, Judge Ashmore dug a key out
of his coat pocket to unlock them. "Nobody's been
in here since old Archibald died," he told Charity,
"and that was several months ago. So it may be a bit
dusty and musty inside."

"We can clean it up," Charity said confidently.

"We'll spruce it up just fine," Lydia added. She
still had the shotgun in her hands as she and Charity stood on the boardwalk with Ashmore. The
other four women remained in the wagon, but they
leaned out from under the canvas cover at the front
to watch as the lawyer opened up the saloon.

Ashmore stepped back to let Charity and Lydia go
first. It was dark inside, of course, but Charity had
brought one of the lanterns from the wagon, and as
she raised it in her hand, the glow from it spread
out around the big room. The long hardwood bar
was to the right, with a staircase to the second floor
at the end of it. To the left were round tables where
customers could sit and drink, plus faro layouts, a
roulette wheel, and several baize-topped tables for

poker games. A small stage was at the far end of the room with a real piano next to it. A player piano sat against the wall in the front left corner.

Charity lifted her eyes to the balcony that ran around the room. There were rooms up there on the second floor that could be rented out or used as sleeping quarters for her and the other girls. As to whether or not there would be anything else going on in those rooms . . . well, Charity hadn't made up her mind about that yet. The idea of coming here had been for her and her friends to give up their lives as soiled doves, but what was a frontier saloon without whores?

They would wait and see what happened with that part of the business, she told herself. For now it was enough to know that they would have to clean the place up, make sure it was well stocked with liquor, maybe hire a bartender or two.

"Looks like the place is in pretty good shape," Lydia commented. "A little dusty, like you said, Judge, and some cobwebs here and there, but it won't take us long to have everything shining."

Charity set the lantern on the bar and looked up at the chandeliers hanging from the ceiling. "Including those," she said. "They're already pretty shiny, even with a layer of dust on them."

Ashmore grunted. "They're silver," he informed the two women. "Archibald paid a pretty penny to have them hauled out here from St. Louis, along with that big mirror behind the bar. He didn't mind putting money into the place, that's for sure. He was well on the way to making a big success of it when he got sick."

Charity frowned and asked, "What did he die of? I never was really sure about that."

"No way you could be sure when the doctor didn't even know."

That surprised Charity. "The doctor didn't know what was wrong with my great-uncle?"

Ashmore shook his head. "It was a mystery, Dr. Bradford said. He'd never seen anything like it before. Some sort of stomach grippe. Archibald couldn't keep any food down. It kept getting worse, and after a couple of weeks he just couldn't fight it anymore. He was getting along in years, you know."

Charity nodded as she said, "I know. Still, it's sort of strange that he would have gotten sick and died so quickly like that, isn't it?"

"You'd have to ask a physician, my dear. The law is my specialty, not medicine." Ashmore held out the key. "I suppose you'll be wanting this?"

"Yes, thank you." Charity took the key and tucked it into one of the pockets of her dress. "Thank you for everything."

Ashmore scowled and looked uncomfortable. "No need for thanks. Just doing my job. I don't have to like it."

Lydia said, "You don't like *us* very much, either, do you, Judge?"

"Buffalo Flat is a peaceful town," he replied. "I don't like to see people come in and stir everything up and cause trouble."

"Maybe it's peaceful only because nobody wants to stand up to Junius Cole," Charity pointed out. "Did you ever think of that?"

The lawyer's scowl darkened even more and he was about to say something else, but before he could get the words out, a scream sounded from outside, the sound carrying urgently through the open doors of the saloon.

Chapter 8

Earlier that afternoon, when Bo and Scratch arrived at the Half Moon Ranch with Theresa Kincaid, Bo was impressed with the layout. This was no greasy-sack outfit. It had been built up with care over the years. The main house especially looked sturdy and comfortable.

If you knew what to look for, though, there were signs that the place was going slightly downhill. The corral fences could have used some tightening up, and one of the hinges on a barn door was loose, causing the door to hang a little askew. The roof of the same barn needed some patching. Those were the sort of chores that went undone when a spread was short-handed, as Theresa had said that the Half Moon was.

"Mighty nice-lookin' place, ma'am," Scratch said, still playing up to the young woman. "We'll be tolerable proud to work here, won't we, Bo?"

"Looks like there's work to be done, all right," Bo said bluntly.

"Don't mind that old grump, Miss Theresa. Looks to me like the place has been kept up just fine. Bo could find somethin' to complain about if he was bein' served cake and cream."

Theresa laughed. "I know there are chores that need to be taken care of, Mr. Creel. We've had all we can do just tending to the stock and trying to stay alive."

"Yes, ma'am, I expect so," Bo agreed. "Maybe it'll all be a mite easier for you now that Scratch and I are here."

"I hope so." Theresa flapped the reins. "Let's go. I'll introduce you to the other hands."

As they splashed across the ford, several men emerged from a long, low, log building that Bo figured was the bunkhouse. They carried rifles and stood tensely alert. They had to have recognized the buckboard and its driver, but they didn't know who Bo and Scratch were. Given the dangerous situation in these parts, Bo couldn't blame them for being wary.

Theresa drove up in front of the ranch house and brought the buckboard to a halt. Bo and Scratch reined in beside her. The oldest of the hands, a middle-aged gent with a bristly gray mustache, stepped forward and said, "It's mighty good to see that you got back all right, Miss Theresa. You never should have gone off to Buffalo Flat like that by yourself."

Theresa laughed. "Don't scold me, Hardy. You're not my father."

"No, ma'am, I ain't." The man called Hardy regarded Bo and Scratch with narrowed eyes and asked, "Who're these two old pelicans?"

"Watch who you're callin' old, friend," Scratch said. "I'd say we don't have too many years on you."

Theresa said, "This is Mr. Morton and Mr. Creel.

They gave me a hand when some of Cole's gunmen ambushed me on the way home."

That made Hardy and the other ranch hands stiffen even more. "Are you all right?" Hardy asked.

"I'm fine, not a scratch. And I didn't lose any of the supplies, either, so the trip was a success all the way around." Theresa paused. "Plus I got two more hands out of it."

"You two figure to work here, do you?"

Bo said, "Miss Kincaid asked us to sign on and ride for the Half Moon. We said we would." His tone implied that once he and Scratch had given their word on something, that was the end of the matter.

Hardy grunted. His frown didn't go away, but he seemed to relax slightly. "In that case, light down. There are empty stalls in the barn for your horses."

The two drifters from Texas swung down from their saddles. Scratch stuck out a hand and introduced himself. "Scratch Morton."

Hardy howdied and shook hands with him. "Hardy Thomas is my name," he said. "These other rannies are Johnny Del Rio, Mort Skaggs, and Hector Ibañez."

"Bo Creel," Bo said as he shook hands in turn with the four punchers. Skaggs and Ibañez were well-seasoned cowboys in their thirties, while Johnny Del Rio was the youngest of the bunch, a strapping blond hombre around twenty years old.

None of the men seemed to have heard of Bo or Scratch before, which was just fine with the two drifters. They had been mixed up in enough fracases over the years that sometimes they ran into folks who recognized their names, but Bo preferred to soft-pedal their reputation, such as it was.

"Let's get these supplies unloaded while Mr. Morton and Mr. Creel are tending to their horses," Theresa said.

"I want to hear more about that ambush," Hardy said. "What happened to the bushwhackers? They get away?"

Theresa nodded toward Bo and Scratch. "Our two new friends happened to the bushwhackers. Only one of them got away, and I'm pretty sure he had a bullet in his shoulder as he galloped off."

"Dollars to doughnuts he ran straight back to Buffalo Flat and told Cole what happened," Hardy commented as he placed his rifle in the back of the buckboard and lifted one of the boxes of supplies. The other men moved to help him. Johnny hefted a couple of bags of flour and balanced one on each shoulder as he started toward the house.

As Bo and Scratch led their horses into the barn, Bo asked, "What do you think of the crew Miss Kincaid has left?"

"They seem like a decent bunch," Scratch replied. "Hardy strikes me as a salty old jigger. Can't really tell about the others, except the boy. He's got calf eyes for Miss Theresa." Scratch chuckled. "Can't say as I blame him, either. She's a mighty fine-looking woman."

"And young enough to be your daughter, to boot."

"I don't have a daughter," Scratch protested. "Leastways, not any that I know of."

They unsaddled their mounts, rubbed them down, and settled the animals in stalls. Scratch got a bucket of grain from a bin and split it between the two feed troughs. Bo took another bucket, went to the creek, and filled it for the horses. By the time they were through tending to those chores, all the supplies had been carried from the buckboard into the house.

"Something about that fella Hardy strikes me as familiar," Bo said quietly as they walked toward the house with their war bags slung over their shoulders. "I think I've seen him somewhere before."

"I wouldn't be surprised. We've been a whole heap of places since leavin' Texas."

Bo nodded and didn't say anything else about it. He didn't think he had ever met Hardy Thomas before, though. The more he thought about it, the more he believed he had seen the man's likeness on a wanted poster during one of his and Scratch's stints as lawmen.

Even if that was true, it didn't necessarily mean that Hardy was a real badman, Bo reminded himself. Drawings of him and Scratch probably had adorned more than one reward dodger in the past. Misunderstandings had gotten them in trouble with the law on several occasions. Maybe the same thing had happened to Hardy.

They went inside and found Theresa putting away the things she had brought from town. The house was well furnished, with thick hide rugs on the floors and heavy furniture and a massive fireplace on one wall. Bo didn't see any of the ranch hands, and assumed that the men had returned to the bunkhouse while he and Scratch were tending to their horses.

Theresa said, "Make yourselves at home. There are empty bedrooms here in the house if you'd like."

Before Scratch could say anything, Bo replied, "Thanks, but that wouldn't hardly be proper.

We'll bunk with the other hands if that's all right with you."

"Of course," Theresa said. "Whatever you like, Mr. Creel."

"That's another thing, ma'am. If we're going to be working for you, why don't you go ahead and call me Bo?"

"And I'm Scratch," his partner added. "No point in standin' on formality."

Theresa smiled. "All right. That's fine."

"What are your orders, ma'am?" Bo asked.

"You mean as far as the work goes? It's late enough in the day you don't need to worry about that. I'm sure Hardy will tell you what to do in the morning. He's my foreman, and he really runs things around here since William died."

Bo had taken off his hat when he came into the house. Now he turned it over in his hands and said, "I've been meaning to ask you about that, if you don't mind talking about it. You said he was shot in the back?"

She nodded, the smile disappearing from her face and being replaced by a look of anger more than sorrow. "That's right. He was out riding on our range when someone ambushed him. I'm convinced it was one of Cole's men, of course, but the sheriff said there was no proof of that since no one saw it happen. We'd been having some trouble with rustlers, losing some stock now and then—something else I'm convinced Cole is behind—and Sheriff Branch said it was more likely William was killed by a rustler. I'll never believe that, though."

The thing of it was, thought Bo, such an explanation might be true. He asked, "Who found your husband?"

Theresa's voice caught a little as she said, "I did. He was gone longer than I expected him to be, so I went out looking for him. Back then, I didn't realize it was quite so dangerous to be doing something like that."

"Was he a young fella?" Scratch asked.

Theresa shook her head. "No, William was considerably older than me. He started the Half Moon more than ten years ago."

"I thought it looked like the spread had been here for a while," Bo commented.

"Yes, William worked long and hard to make the ranch successful . . . and then it was all taken away from him in the time it takes to pull a trigger." Tears sparkled in her eyes as she spoke.

"Maybe we'd better mosey on out to the bunkhouse," Scratch suggested. "We didn't mean to upset you, Miss Theresa—"

"No, don't worry about it, please. Most of the time I'm fine. I just hate to think about Junius Cole getting away with all the terrible things he's done."

"Most folks get what's comin' to 'em sooner or later, one way or another," Scratch assured her. "But with me an' Bo here, maybe it'll be sooner instead of later for that hombre Cole."

"Just be careful, that's all I ask. I don't want to see anyone else get killed."

"I reckon that'll be up to Cole," Bo said with a curt nod.

Bo and Scratch said their good nights and left the house. The western sky was red with the swift approach of sunset. As Bo and Scratch approached the bunkhouse, they saw Hardy Thomas emerge hurriedly from the building.

"Either of you gents seen Johnny?" he asked.

"Not since y'all were takin' the supplies into the house," Scratch replied. "Somethin' wrong?"

Hardy cursed and said, "I think that damn hot-headed kid's gone and ridden into town to look for trouble. He was talkin' about how we couldn't let Cole get away with havin' his gunnies ambush Miss Theresa. Said somebody was gonna have to teach Cole a lesson. Now I can't find him."

"Check the barn for his horse," Bo suggested.

"That's just what I was on my way to do."

Hardy stalked into the barn with Bo and Scratch following him. The foreman let out another sulfurous curse when he saw an empty stall and said, "That's where Johnny always keeps his nag. The damn fool's gone after Cole!"

"I suppose Cole's got gunmen around him most of the time?" Bo said.

Hardy nodded. "Yeah. Kid'll get hisself shot to doll rags if he ain't careful. Somebody's got to go stop him from gettin' killed. It'd bust up Miss Theresa if he did." Hardy turned to another stall and reached for the saddle that was hung over one side of it.

"Better let us go," Bo said quickly. "We can find him and bring him back before he gets into trouble."

"Just point us toward town," Scratch added, obviously eager for a chance to visit Buffalo Flat.

Hardy frowned. "You fellas may not know what you'd be gettin' yourselves into—"

"We already tangled with Cole's men once today, remember?" Scratch said. "We came out on top, too."

Hardy rubbed his grizzled jaw for a second and then nodded. "Yeah, that's true. But your horses are about played out. You'd need to take fresh mounts."

"You know the stock better than we do," Bo said. "Pick out a couple of good horses and we'll get saddled up."

"If you're sure . . ."

Scratch nodded. "We're sure. Just don't say anything to Miss Theresa about it. No need in worryin' her. We'll find the boy and bring him right back here."

"All right. Don't waste any time. Johnny's already got a lead on you."

The three men moved quickly, especially considering that none of them were young anymore. In less than five minutes, Bo and Scratch were mounted on a couple of horses from the Half Moon's remuda, and Hardy had told them how to find Buffalo Flat. The trail would be easy to follow, even in the rapidly fading light.

"Cole spends most of his time in the Colorado Palace Saloon," Hardy told them. "He owns the place and lives there, too. You can't miss it. It's the biggest, fanciest saloon in town. Dollars to doughnuts that's where Johnny'll look for him."

"We'll find him," Bo said. He added silently, *In time, I hope.*

The Texans rode out, keeping their horses at a walk until they were across the creek and well away from the house, in hopes that Theresa wouldn't hear them leaving. If she did, she would want to know where they were going, and then Hardy would have to tell her about Johnny Del Rio. Bo and Scratch hoped to have the youngster safely back on the Half Moon before Theresa even knew that he was gone.

The sun had settled behind the Prophets as Bo and Scratch rode east toward Buffalo Flat. Twilight closed in quickly. The horses were well rested, so they pushed the animals to a fast pace, hoping to make up some ground on the young man they sought.

Even so, night had fallen by the time they reached the town. They spotted the glow of lights from windows and trotted into the settlement a few minutes later. Buffalo Flat was similar to a hundred other frontier towns they had visited over their years of drifting. Bo knew that the Colorado Palace would be somewhere near the center of town. His eyes were searching for it as he and Scratch rode past a wagon with a canvas cover parked on the left side of the street, in front of a building with a dim light burning inside it. Bo would have ridden right past the wagon, scarcely noticing it, if there hadn't been a sudden commotion at the rear of the vehicle.

"C'mon outta there, honey," a man's voice said harshly as he leaned into the wagon. Then he lurched away from it, dragging a shadowy shape with him. As he stepped into the faint glow coming from the window of the building, it became apparent that he was struggling with a woman. Blond hair flew around her head as she tried to free herself from his grip. The frightened scream she let out a second later made it even more obvious that she was female.

Bo and Scratch reined in sharply. They had hurried to Buffalo Flat from the Half Moon Ranch on a specific errand, but it just wasn't in their nature to ignore somebody in trouble, especially a woman.

"Ah, hell," Scratch said, and as Bo lunged out of the saddle, he couldn't help but agree.

Chapter 9

He was moving toward the struggling pair even as his boots hit the dusty street. Two fast steps brought him to them. His left hand closed over the man's shoulder and hauled him around.

"Let the woman go," Bo grated.

The man's breath was thick with whiskey fumes as he cursed. "Leggo o' me," he rasped. "Meddlin' ol' bastard!"

He released the woman and swung a punch at Bo's head, moving fairly fast despite being drunk. Not fast enough, though, because Bo was able to lean back and let the blow pass harmlessly in front of his face. He hooked a hard right into the man's belly, sinking his fist almost to the wrist. The drunk doubled over, more rotgut-laced breath exploding from his mouth. Bo hit him with a left that sent him stumbling against the boardwalk. The man fell over backward, sprawling on the planks.

As the man gasped for breath, he twisted onto his side and clawed at the butt of the revolver holstered at his waist. He stopped as he heard the metallic sound of a gun hammer being reared back.

"I wouldn't if I were you," Scratch said over the barrel of a leveled Colt. "We're in a hurry, and if you make me shoot, I don't have time to do anything but kill you."

The drunk lay there wide-eyed and moved his hand away from his gun.

Bo turned toward the woman and asked, "Are you all right, miss?" She swayed toward him, obviously shaken by the experience, and he put out a hand to steady her.

"Get away from her!" another woman's voice called angrily. "Let go of her or I'll blast you!"

Bo looked over and saw that two more women had just emerged from the building. One of them was pointing a shotgun at him. "Better be careful with that," he said. "You fire that scattergun and you'll kill your friend here, too."

The other woman on the boardwalk said sharply, "Janie, get away from him! Get back in the wagon!"

Bo heard a sound from the back of the wagon that he recognized as the lever of a Winchester being worked. "This ain't a shotgun, mister," yet another woman said. "And I'll drill you if I have to."

"Good Lord," Scratch said as he kept the drunk covered. "Is that blamed wagon full of females?"

"In case you ladies didn't notice," Bo said, "I was trying to help your friend."

The young blonde who had been dragged out of the wagon recovered her wits enough to nod and say, "He . . . he's right, Charity. It was that one who grabbed me!" She pointed at the man who still lay on the boardwalk.

The redheaded woman who had come out of the building said, "All right, it looks like we made a mistake. Put the shotgun down, Lydia."

"All right," the woman agreed as she lowered the Greener. "But I don't like the looks of those two old codgers. You can't blame me for jumping the gun."

Bo might have taken offense at that comment, but the next instant his attention was distracted by the sudden blast of a pistol shot somewhere up the street. He and Scratch looked at each other at the same time and said in unison, "Johnny."

As Bo stepped quickly toward his horse, he pointed at the man lying on the boardwalk and told him, "On your feet and rattle your hocks out of here, amigo. Otherwise we'll let that lady with the scattergun have you."

The man still seemed to be a little dazed from being knocked around, but he managed to scramble to his feet and lurch off down the boardwalk. Scratch said, "If he comes back, ma'am, don't hesitate to ventilate the son of a buck."

The woman with the Greener nodded and said, "Don't worry about that, old-timer."

Scratch frowned at being referred to that way but didn't say anything.

Bo put his foot in the stirrup and swung up into the saddle. Only one gunshot had sounded, and in a way, that was more worrisome than if there had been a whole flurry of them.

"Let's go see what happened," he said to Scratch. Side by side, they rode quickly up the street.

They didn't have to go very far, just a couple of blocks, before they spotted the Colorado Palace Saloon to their right. It was a large building, taking up one side of an entire block. The batwinged entrance was at the corner, providing easy access from both Main Street and the cross street. Yellow light spilled through big windows that flanked the doors.

The glass was decorated with fancy gilt curlicues. Impressive signs announcing the name of the place jutted out from the awnings overhanging the boardwalks on both sides of the saloon. A knot of men had gathered to peer over the batwings, and more were hurrying toward the place. It didn't take any great guesswork to know that the shot had come from inside.

"Son of a bitch," Scratch muttered as he and Bo drew rein in front of the Colorado Palace.

"Yeah," Bo agreed. He had been hoping that the shot they'd heard had come from somewhere else, and he knew Scratch felt the same way.

Hurriedly, they dismounted and wrapped their reins around a hitch rack already crowded with other horses. Then they stepped up onto the boardwalk and shouldered their way through the crowd, ignoring the curses and angry mutters that came from the displaced bystanders. The townies abruptly fell silent as they took good looks at Bo and Scratch. Long in the tooth the Texans might be, but they were still men to stand aside from whenever there was trouble.

They reached the batwings and pushed through, moving into the smoky atmosphere of the saloon. Not all the haze came from tobacco, though. Bo recognized the familiar tang of powder smoke.

A low buzz of conversation filled the room. Most of the customers had gone back to drinking or card playing or fondling the percentage gals in scanty, spangled outfits, whatever they had been doing before the brief outbreak of violence. People stepped around the body lying sprawled in front of the bar, leaking crimson into the sawdust that coated the floor. The sawdust was there to soak up spilled booze, but it did a decent job with blood, too.

Bo's face hardened as he recognized big, blond Johnny Del Rio. He glanced over at Scratch and saw that his partner's visage was equally grim. Johnny lay on his back. He had been shot once in the chest. His blue eyes stared sightlessly at the fancy crystal chandeliers suspended from the ceiling.

Feeling sick and angry at the same time, Bo caught the eye of a bartender and asked the balding man, "Are you in the habit in this town of leaving bodies lying in the floor, mister?"

The bartender didn't stop polishing the glass in his hand. "Undertaker's been sent for already. What the hell else do you expect us to do?"

With his left hand, Scratch pointed at Johnny's body and demanded, "Who shot this man?"

At one of the nearby tables, a man slowly rose to his feet. "I did," he announced in a gravelly voice. "What's it to you, cowboy?"

He was a tall, broad-shouldered hombre with coal-black hair under a tipped-back Stetson. His weathered face was angular, with a wedge of jaw that jutted out defiantly. An ivory-handled Colt rode easily in a black leather holster on his hip.

Bo said, "There was no call to kill him. He was just a kid."

The gunman shrugged. "He came in here demandin' to see Mr. Cole and blusterin' about how he was gonna kill him. Kid or not, he had to know better than to do something like that. I asked him to leave, and he went for his gun. Simple as that. Ask anybody in here if he didn't draw first."

Bo looked at the man's casual pose, thumbs hooked in his belt but with the right hand still dangerously close to the ivory butt of that gun, and knew that the killer was probably telling the truth. It was likely that Johnny had reached for iron first. But Bo would have been willing to bet there had been some goading before that. It wasn't hard for a gunslinger to prod a less experienced man into drawing first.

"Do we know each other?" Bo asked quietly. "You look a mite familiar."

"You don't," the gunman said bluntly. "You just look like an old man stickin' his nose in where it doesn't have any business bein'." He grinned. "But my name, if that's your way of askin', is Lucas Tate."

Bo nodded, and Scratch said, "Heard tell of you. You've killed, what, three men? Four?"

Tate's grin disappeared as he scowled. "Twelve," he corrected curtly.

Scratch chuckled, but there wasn't any real humor in the sound. "What I've seen here makes me wonder just how many of 'em were wet-behind-the-ears kids who didn't stand no chance against you."

Tate stiffened, and his right hand moved slightly so that it hovered over his gun, ready to hook and draw. The noise in the saloon had trailed away to nothing again, and folks started to move out of the way as unobtrusively as they could. Tate growled, "It's two against one, but I don't give a damn. I'm not afraid of you old buzzards."

A new voice said sharply, "Wait just a damned minute! There's not gonna be any more gunplay in here tonight!"

Bo glanced over his shoulder and saw a thick-bodied, middle-aged man coming through the batwings, followed by a tall, cadaverous-looking gent in a dark suit and hat who had to be the town undertaker. The older man had a lawman's star pinned on his vest and a shotgun in his hands. It had taken a while for him to get here, but the local law had arrived on the scene of the killing.

The badge-toter glanced at the bartender and went on. "Riley, fetch Mr. Cole."

"Sure thing, Sheriff." The man hurried out from behind the hardwood and disappeared through a door at the end of the bar.

While the bartender was gone, the sheriff came forward and glanced curiously at Bo and Scratch, then turned his attention to the killer and asked, "Is this one of yours, Tate?"

"The kid came in practically foamin' at the mouth," Tate said, "sayin' that he was gonna kill Mr. Cole. I told him to leave, and he went for his gun instead. I didn't have any choice but to ventilate him."

"I suppose you've got witnesses to back up that story."

"Ask anybody in here," Tate said. Then he gestured at Bo and Scratch with his left hand and added, "Except those two old-timers. They weren't even in here when it happened, but they seem to be takin' exception to it now."

The sheriff turned back to the Texans and frowned. "Who are you men? I haven't seen you around before."

"Name's Creel," Bo said. "This is Morton. We came into town looking for the kid. We all ride for the Half Moon spread."

The sheriff's bushy eyebrows went up. "The Half Moon! Then this killing is tied in with that crazy Kincaid woman?"

Scratch said, "Badge or no badge, Sheriff, you might want to be careful about calling a woman crazy."

"Several men ambushed Mrs. Kincaid this afternoon while she was on her way back to her ranch from buying supplies here in town," Bo explained. "She figured they worked for a fella named Cole. When Johnny Del Rio found out about what happened, it upset him. That's why he came to town, to have a showdown with Cole." He looked coldly at Tate. "That's when this fella stepped in."

"It's my job to protect Mr. Cole from troublemakers," Tate said. "And I do it the way I see fit."

"You do a fine job of it, too, Lucas," said a man who had emerged from the door at the end of the bar in time to hear Tate's statement. He was a big man with sleekly oiled dark hair and a mustache. He wore an expensive suit, and an equally expensive-looking woman with brown hair followed him out of what appeared to be a private office. The bartender came out last and went back behind the hardwood.

"I've already heard the details of this unfortunate incident, Sheriff," the man who had to be Junius Cole continued. "Lucas was just doing his duty by confronting that cowboy and trying to convince him to leave peacefully. You certainly can't blame him for defending himself when the kid started the ball."

"No, I reckon not," the sheriff agreed with a sage nod, and at that moment, Bo knew there was no point in turning to the local law for help. This star-packer was tucked away firmly in Cole's hip pocket.

The undertaker had been examining Johnny's body. He stood up now and said, "I'll get my wagon. I think I already have a coffin that'll fit him just fine."

As the man started past, Bo put out a hand to stop him. He took a twenty-dollar gold piece from his pocket and slapped it in the undertaker's palm. "Do it up right," he ordered.

The undertaker nodded. "Sure, mister. Is the deceased kin of yours?"

Bo shook his head. "Nope. Never even saw him until a couple of hours ago. But we rode for the same brand."

The undertaker nodded again and went out. The sheriff stepped over in front of Bo and Scratch, tucked the shotgun under his arm, and asked sternly, "Now, what's this about somebody trying to ambush Mrs. Kincaid?"

"Four men with rifles," Scratch drawled, "hidden in some rocks about halfway between here and her ranch."

"Was she hurt?"

"Nope. She was lucky. We came along about then and took cards in the game."

"What happened to the bushwhackers? They get away?"

"One of them did," Bo said. "I reckon the other three are still lying out there unless the wolves and the coyotes have dragged them off by now."

"What!" the sheriff burst out. "You just left them there?"

It was Bo's turn to shrug. "They tried to kill a woman," he said, "and then they did their damnedest to ventilate my partner and me. I don't figure to lose a whole lot of sleep worrying about what happens to skunks like that."

He had been watching Junius Cole very closely as he mentioned that three of the bushwhackers were dead, and he didn't see the least bit of surprise in the man's eyes. That meant Cole already knew about it, and that bit of knowledge confirmed the theory that the surviving bushwhacker had come back here to Buffalo Flat to report to Cole. Bo didn't know where the fourth man was now and didn't care. What was important was that he was convinced Theresa Kincaid was right about Cole being responsible for the attempt on her life.

The sheriff asked, "What's the connection between you two and Mrs. Kincaid?"

"They work for her," Lucas Tate said. "At least, that's what they claimed a few minutes ago."

"You might want to think twice about that, gents," the lawman said. "Mrs. Kincaid's got a lot of things mixed up in her head. She's been just about out of her mind with grief ever since rustlers killed her husband a while back."

Bo said, "She seemed plenty sane to me. Seemed like a woman who knows who her real enemies are."

"Anyway," Scratch put in, "I think we're gonna like it there. Figure on stickin' around for a while."

"Well, if you cause any trouble, you'll wind up in my jail," the sheriff blustered. "I already got some customers, but I can make room for more, you can count on that."

Bo ignored the man. He knew that the real threats in this room were Cole and Tate. And maybe that sleek brunette who had been back in the office with Cole. She was beautiful, but Bo could see a cold edge in her eyes. They reminded him a little of the eyes of a snake.

The undertaker and a couple of his helpers came into the saloon. As they picked up Johnny's body, Bo told them, "Remember what I said about taking care of him properly. We'll let you know whether he's to be buried here in town, or if Mrs. Kincaid would like for him to be interred out on her ranch."

"Whatever you say, mister," the undertaker agreed.

"It doesn't matter to me. I just plant 'em where I'm told."

The men left with their grim burden, carrying the body out to the wagon that was parked in front of the saloon. A swamper brought a bucket and a mop to clean up the blood from the floor. While that chore was being taken care of, the sheriff gave Bo and Scratch a hard look and asked, "Is there any other reason for you two men to stay in town tonight?"

"Not that I know of," Bo said.

"Since it looks like the official response to this killin' is just gonna be a yawn," Scratch added.

The lawman glowered at them and said, "Git. I don't want to see either of you again tonight."

"I reckon the feeling is mutual," Bo replied coolly. He and Scratch turned and walked slowly out of the Colorado Palace.

But as they went, they could practically feel the targets that had been painted on their backs. They had openly declared themselves in the struggle between Theresa Kincaid and Junius Cole. From here on out they would have to watch their backs at all times.

Which, of course, wasn't all that different from the way they usually lived. For a long time, trouble had had a habit of dogging their trail.

As they pushed through the batwings into the night, Bo heard the sheriff say disgustedly, "This used to be a peaceable town. Now there's killin's right and left."

Bo wondered what other violence had prompted that comment, but then he put the thought out of his mind. He already had plenty to think about, like how he and Scratch were going to tell Theresa, Hardy, and the others on the Half Moon that Johnny Del Rio was dead.

Chapter 10

"Take it easy," Sam Two Wolves said as he watched his blood brother pace from one side of the cell to the other. That didn't take long. The cell was only about ten feet by ten feet, with a bunk on each side and a high, barred window in the rear wall. Sam added, "We've been in worse places."

"I don't like bein' locked up," Matt grated.

"Hell, I'm the Indian," Sam said as he lay back on the bunk and laced his fingers together behind his head. "I'm the one who's supposed to hate being penned up so much."

"Yeah, well, I don't see how you can lay there takin' life easy," Matt said. "We never should have gone along with that damned lawman. It's obvious he's crooked. He's working for Cole, the same bastard who tried to have those gals killed just so they wouldn't come to Buffalo Flat and open up a saloon. He'll probably try to murder us in our sleep tonight."

"Then here's what you do," Sam suggested. "Don't sleep. I'll take care of that for both of us." He closed his eyes and heaved a deep sigh.

Inside that seemingly peaceful exterior, though, he was seething with anger just as much as Matt was. Sam's Cheyenne heritage meant that he *hated* being confined. He had been born to ride across the vast plains under a wide-open sky. Being stuck in a tiny cell behind gray iron bars was just about the worst thing he could endure.

In fact, the only way he had been able to tolerate it so far was to distract himself by adopting a care-free attitude that he knew would drive Matt crazy. But in reality, Sam feared that if he had to spend a whole night in here, he would go mad before morning.

"I thought that Charity gal said her lawyer would get us out of here," Matt groused as he continued to pace. "Hell, the whole thing was an open-and-shut case of self-defense. Tully and those other two hombres drew on us first. Everybody in the street saw it."

"Maybe nobody who saw it wants to get crossways with Junius Cole," Sam said. "I get the feeling that he's the big skookum he-wolf around here. People don't want to have him as an enemy."

"*Somebody's* got to speak up," Matt insisted. "If they don't, when that pompous jackass of a sheriff gets back, I'll . . . I'll . . ."

"You'll what?" Sam asked. "We're locked up, re-member?"

"You don't have to remind me!"

A short time earlier, Sheriff Branch had left the office after hearing a gunshot somewhere else in town. The door between the office and the cell block was open, so Matt and Sam had seen the lawman hustle out. It had been a while since that happened, and the sheriff hadn't come back.

What if he *didn't* return to the jail until morning? Sam felt his insides tighten up even more at the thought of that prospect.

A few minutes later, footsteps sounded on the boardwalk outside the sheriff's office. Sam sat up and swung his legs off the bunk, hoping that Branch was coming back. Matt went to the door of the cell and gripped the bars tightly.

The office door opened, but it wasn't Sheriff Branch who came in. It was Charity MacKenzie, accompanied by a fat, bearded man in a town suit. A lawyer if he'd ever seen one, Sam thought.

The man looked around and said, "Sheriff Branch doesn't appear to be here."

Sam stood up and joined his blood brother at the bars as Matt called, "Hey! Hey, we're back here! Don't leave!"

Charity hurried through the door between the office and the cell block, trailed by the lawyer. "There you are," she said. "Are you all right?"

"Why wouldn't they be?" the lawyer demanded before Matt or Sam could say anything. "Sherman Branch isn't the sort of man who would mistreat his prisoners."

"I feel a mite mistreated already, amigo," Matt said. "Being locked up unjustly will do that to a man."

"Well, we're here to see about that. I'm Judge A.A. Ashmore, Miss, uh, MacKenzie's attorney."

"I'm sorry it's taken us so long to get here," Charity said. "We went over to the saloon that I inherited, and then there was some trouble there—"

"We heard a gunshot a while ago," Sam put in. "Is that what you're talking about?"

Charity shook her head. "No, that was some-where else. We heard it, too."

"Then you're all all right?" Matt asked.

"Yes, we're fine. A drunk came along and pulled Janie out of the wagon, but a couple of old-timers stepped in and stopped him from doing anything worse. She was just scared, not hurt."

"It's good to hear that," Sam said.

"After that ruckus was over, Judge Ashmore and I went looking for witnesses to the earlier shooting, the one you were involved in," Charity went on. "Lydia and the other girls stayed at the saloon to start cleaning it up."

Matt frowned and said, "You reckon they'll be all right there?"

"As long as Lydia has her shotgun, I think they will be. Anyway, we found some people who were willing to give us statements—"

The outer door opened again, and this time it was the lawman who came in, stopping short as he saw Charity and Ashmore standing on the other side of the bars from Bodine and Two Wolves.

"What in blazes is goin' on here?" he demanded as he put his Greener back on the rack beside the door. "I didn't say those prisoners could have visitors!"

"You weren't here. Anyway, I think you should re-lease these two men, Sherman," Ashmore said. He reached inside his coat and pulled out several pieces of paper. "I have here statements from wit-nesses who are willing to testify that Ed Tully and the other two deceased hombres reached for their guns first. These gentlemen were just defending themselves and the ladies who accompanied them."

Branch gazed warily at the lawyer. "Are you sure you know what you're sayin', Judge?"

Ashmore sighed. "Indeed I do. Despite the fact that these men are strangers and the gents they killed worked for one of the town's leading citizens . . . legally you have no case against them, and as an attorney bound by the laws of this state, I would have no choice but to point that out to the presiding judge if the case ever came to trial."

"Who gave you those so-called statements?" Branch wanted to know.

"Casey McLennan, Drew Gilmore, and Phineas O'Toole, for starters."

"Men who aren't overly fond of Mr. Cole, in other words. They've had trouble with him in the past."

"Men who are respectable, honest citizens of Buffalo Flat," Ashmore corrected. "Their word is good, and folks know that, Sherman."

"Yeah," the sheriff agreed grudgingly. "I guess you're right." He walked over to the desk and picked up a ring of keys. "Step back away from the door and I'll let those two out."

Sam felt a wave of relief wash through him, but he tried not to show it. He wasn't going to have to stay locked up all night after all.

The sheriff unlocked the cell door and swung it open. He stepped back to let Matt and Sam come out. "I reckon you'll be giving us our guns back," Matt said.

Red in the face, Branch started to bluster. "I could impound them—"

"You don't have any cause to do that," Ashmore pointed out. "Unlike some towns, Buffalo Flat has no ordinance against carrying firearms. But perhaps that's something I should bring up at the next meeting of the town council."

"Yeah, you do that," the sheriff said in a surly

voice as he went to a cabinet and took out the gun-belts he had taken earlier from Matt and Sam. Their Colts had been replaced in the holsters. Sam felt even better once he had strapped on the belt and was packing iron again. He knew Matt felt the same way.

Matt twirled both Colts before settling them into leather. It was a bit of a show-off move, and Sam wondered if it was directed toward the sheriff—or Charity MacKenzie. He didn't know which of them Matt might be trying to impress.

"You're free to go," Branch said, "and if you're smart you'll get on your horses and get out of Buffalo Flat. There's nothing to keep you here."

"Oh, I don't know about that," Matt said. "We haven't had a chance to see much of your town yet except this jail. Could be we'll like it here and want to stay around for a while."

Branch's eyes narrowed. "I happen to know that the hotel is full up. No rooms to be had in town."

Sam doubted that, but before he could say as much, Charity spoke up. "Actually, that's not true," she said. "There are empty rooms upstairs in the Silver Belle." She ignored the warning look that Ashmore slanted in her direction. "I was thinking about renting them out, and I believe I've just decided to do so."

The sheriff looked at Ashmore. "Is that saloon really her property?"

"I'm afraid so," the lawyer replied with a grim nod. "Legally, she can do whatever she wants with it."

Branch shook his head. "Lord, the state things have come to!"

Charity ignored him and turned to Matt and

Sam. "How about it?" she asked them. "Would you like to stay at the Silver Belle?"

Matt grinned. "Why, we'd be honored, ma'am."

Actually, they hadn't even discussed what their next move would be, and Sam knew that Matt had accepted Charity's offer as much to annoy the sheriff as anything. But he agreed with the decision, because it was obvious that Charity and her friends had been dealt a tough hand to play, especially without any help. Six women alone wouldn't stand a chance against a man as ruthless as Junius Cole appeared to be. The fact that the local law didn't want to buck Cole made the situation even worse. Sam knew that he and Matt couldn't abandon them.

"Yes, we'll stay around for a while," he said quietly, backing Matt's decision.

"It's settled, then." Charity turned to Ashmore. "If you'll send me a bill for your services tonight, Judge, I'll see that it's paid."

An ugly laugh came from the sheriff. "The judge ain't married. Maybe he'd like to take out what you owe in trade, missy."

Sam put a hand on his blood brother's arm as he saw the look that ignited in Matt's eyes at Branch's coarse words. "Come on," he said. "Let's get out of here."

Bodine shrugged off the restraining hand. "In a minute." He looked hard at Branch and went on. "I've met a lot of fine lawmen in my time, Sheriff."

Branch started to grin smugly.

"You aren't one of 'em," Matt finished.

Branch's breath hissed between his teeth as the shit-eating grin disappeared. "Get the hell out of my office," he ordered.

Matt gave him a curt nod and said, "Be seein' you."
It sounded as much like a threat as anything else.

Judge Ashmore remained behind as Matt, Sam,
and Charity left the sheriff's office. Matt paused on
the boardwalk outside, drew a deep breath, and let
it out angrily.

"I know," Sam said. "That lawman's crooked as a
dog's hind leg, and an unpleasant cuss to boot. But
he's still a lawman. You gun him and we'll have
every star-packer in the state after us."

Matt nodded. "Yeah, I know. As long as he steers
clear of us, I'll steer clear of him. But if he was ten
years younger, I'd've put a fist right in his face and
taken my chances on givin' him a whippin'."

"If he was ten years younger, you'd have probably
had to stand in line behind me to do that," Sam
said with a smile.

Charity said, "If you two are through trying to impress me with how big and tough you are, those
rooms are waiting for you down at the Silver Belle."

"You really want us to stay there?" Matt asked.

With only the slightest hesitation, Charity
nodded. "I know that sometimes I'm too proud for
my own good, especially considering where I came
from and . . . what I used to do. But I'm not a fool,
Mr. Bodine. I know the deck is stacked against us
here in Buffalo Flat. The girls and I need someone
on our side, someone who can stand up to Cole
and his men."

"There's no guarantee we can do that," Sam
pointed out as the three of them started along the
boardwalk.

"On the contrary, you've already done it. I get
the feeling that nobody has traded shots with

Cole's men and come out on top for a long time, maybe ever."

"In other words," Matt said, "you want a war with him."

Charity shook her head. "No, that's not what I want. But Cole fired the opening shot, and I'm damned sure not ready to surrender. Cole's the one who wants the war."

"And you're going to give it to him," Sam said.

Charity nodded, her red curls bobbing. "I'm going to give it to him—in spades."

Chapter 11

When they got to the Silver Belle, they found the other women working industriously, despite the fact that the hour was getting late.

"We're used to workin' late," a grinning Lydia said by way of explanation.

Not like this, though, thought Matt. Becky was cleaning flyspecks off the big mirror behind the bar, while Wilma was polishing the hardwood itself. Around in front of the bar, Kathy worked on the brass foot rail, while behind it Lydia dusted the bottles arrayed below the mirror on the backbar. Janie had found a broom somewhere and was sweeping the floor. She already had a pile of dust swept up and was pushing it toward the open doors.

One of them had climbed up on a stepladder and filled and lit the oil lamps in one of the silver chandeliers, so plenty of light now illuminated their efforts. All the women had paused in their work as Charity came in with Matt and Sam. Janie leaned on her broom and smiled at Matt. "You're back!" she said excitedly. "I knew that ol' sheriff couldn't keep you locked up in jail, Mr. Bodine."

Matt nodded toward the redhead and said, "Actually, it was Charity here who was responsible for getting us out. And Mr. Bodine is my pa. I'm Matt, remember?" He looked around the room. "That goes for all of you."

"Are you going to be staying here?" Janie asked. It was obvious what she hoped the answer would be.

Charity answered the question. "We're going to rent a couple of the upstairs rooms to Mr. Bodine and Mr. Two Wolves . . . I mean, Matt and Sam."

Lydia looked surprised. "You're gonna charge 'em rent after what they've done for us so far?"

"Sam and I insist," Matt said before Charity could say anything. "In fact, we'd be plumb honored to be the Silver Belle's first paying customers under the new ownership, wouldn't we, Sam?"

"Sure," Sam agreed. In truth, the blood brothers had plenty of money and could easily afford to pay for their lodging, drinks, and food for as long as they wanted to stay here.

Matt took a coin from his pocket and dropped it on the bar. "Let's get started by having a drink," he suggested. "That is, if any of that who-hit-John left over from before is still fit to drink."

Lydia picked up one of the bottles she had just dusted and pulled the cork from its neck. She took a sniff, considered for a moment, and then nodded. "Smells like decent booze," she said. "Not too much strychnine, rattlesnake juice, and panther piss."

Matt laughed. "Fetch some glasses."

Sam put a hand on the bar and said, "Actually, if you could rustle up a pot of coffee, ma'am, I'd appreciate it. I'm not much of a drinker."

"That's right," Matt said as he jerked a thumb at

his companion. "He's half redskin. Can't handle his liquor because of it."

"And since I know that it means there's a smaller chance I'll wind up a drunken bum lying in some gutter . . . a fate that may well be waiting for *someone* I know." Two Wolves looked pointedly at Bodine as he spoke.

Lydia laughed. "I thought you two were friends. Blood brothers, right?"

"*Onihomahan,*" Sam said with a solemn nod. "Some say it means Brothers of the Wolf."

"That doesn't mean we can't see each other's faults," Matt added. "Right, you stiff-necked, over-educated half-breed?"

"Right, you drunken, irresponsible hillbilly."

"Come to think of it, though," Matt said, "a pot of coffee does sound pretty good right now."

"There's a kitchen in the back," Lydia said. She recorked the bottle of whiskey and returned it to the backbar. "I'll see what I can do."

She must have found a bag of coffee and a pot, because a few minutes later the familiar potent aroma of Arbuckle's drifted out of the kitchen into the main room of the saloon. While they were waiting for it, Charity motioned Matt and Sam over to one of the tables, and the three of them sat down.

"I just wanted you to know," she said quietly, "you don't really have to pay rent for those rooms. I appreciate your willingness to do that, but—"

Matt held up a hand to stop her. "Don't worry about that. We can afford it. What I'm more concerned about is how you intend to handle this problem with Cole."

"He's the one making it a problem, not me," Charity said. "I don't care about his saloon, I just want to run mine. If he leaves us alone, we'll leave him alone."

Sam said, "But we all know that's not the way it's going to be, more than likely. If he's worried enough—or arrogant enough—to want to wipe out the competition before it even gets to town, he's not going to just sit back and let you operate the Silver Belle unmolested."

She nodded. "I'm afraid you're right. He'll try something else. I just don't know what it is yet."

"Whatever it is, Sam and I will be here to help," Matt assured her.

Charity leaned back in her chair and smiled. "If this keeps up, I'm going to have to put you on the payroll." Suddenly she looked more serious as she said, "Wait a minute. I could give you each a share of this place in return for helping us."

"That's not necessary," Sam said. Matt shook his head.

Charity glanced over at her friends, who were still hard at work making the saloon more presentable, and said so that they couldn't hear, "The girls don't know it yet, but all of them are getting a share. It's only fair after they gave up their own lives to come with me and start over out here."

"I imagine that was a sacrifice they were more than willing to make," Sam said gently.

"Maybe so, but I still intend to do right by them. I'd like to do the same where you two are concerned."

"Well, you can forget about giving us shares," Matt said. "Shoot, the last thing in the world we want is to be tied down to some business. Isn't that right, Sam?"

"We *are* pretty undependable," Sam said. "Here today and gone tomorrow, as the old saying has it."

"Fiddle-footed, that's us."

"You won't catch us putting down roots."

"No, ma'am, we just naturally get ourselves an itch to mosey along—"

Charity held up a hand to stop them. "All right, that's enough," she said with a laugh. "I get the idea. But you'll stay until things are settled with Cole, won't you?"

Matt grinned. "We wouldn't miss it for the world."

Lydia emerged from the kitchen with the coffee-pot and a tray full of cups, and everyone gathered around as she began to pour. When they each had a cup of the strong black brew, Lydia lifted hers and said, "Maybe it's not an official toast without a little hooch involved, but here's to the Silver Belle . . . and to Charity McKenzie."

Charity swallowed hard and blinked back tears. "And here's to all of you, the best friends a girl could ever have."

"And to our new friends, Matt and Sam," Janie put in.

The eight cups clinked together over the bar.

Later that evening, when they were all ready to turn in, Janie offered to show Matt to his room. Charity overruled her and said she would take care of that herself. Matt was glad the redhead had stepped in. He had a feeling that if he'd found himself alone in a bedroom with Janie, she would have had her duds off in two shakes of a lamb's tail. Not that it wouldn't have been a mighty pleasant prospect, but it would have also been an added complication that none of them needed right now.

As was the case with the saloon downstairs, the upstairs rooms were still furnished, though rather frugally. Each of the rooms claimed by the blood brothers had a bed, a ladder-back chair, a small table with a washbasin on it, and a thunder mug under the bed. The single window was covered with a plain curtain. They had been in lots fancier places—but they had been in lots worse, too.

Even if there hadn't been a couple of gunfights involved, the day had been a long one, and with the natural ability of youth, Matt dozed off quickly and slept long and sound. He woke up the next morning feeling refreshed, and went downstairs to find Sam already sitting at one of the tables, a cup of coffee and a plate full of bacon and flapjacks in front of him.

"Sit down, Matt," Lydia called to him from behind the bar. "I'll bring you your breakfast."

"About time you rattled your hocks out of bed," Sam said with a grin as Matt took a seat. "Have you looked outside? That bright, shiny stuff is called sunlight."

"It's not that late," Matt said as he glanced through the windows at the brilliant morning and winced. "I'm a growing boy. I need my sleep." He grew more serious. "It was a quiet night, right? No trouble?"

"No trouble," Sam agreed. "Don't worry, you didn't sleep through another gunfight. I guess Cole felt like it would be pushing it to try anything else so soon."

"We need to go see this fella Cole," Matt growled. "Sort of introduce ourselves."

"I reckon we'll get around to that soon enough," Sam said.

Lydia came over to the table with another cup of coffee and a plate heaped high with food. "Here you go," she said to Matt as she set the meal in front of him.

"Where's everybody else?" he asked.

"Except for Charity, they're all upstairs asleep, I reckon. Like I said last night, we're more used to late hours, and I suppose it'll stay that way, runnin' a saloon. I sort of like to get up and rustle a good breakfast for folks, though."

"Where's Charity?" Sam asked. "You said she wasn't upstairs."

Lydia gestured toward the food. "We're runnin' low on supplies, just about used up all we brought with us. So Charity went over to the store to see about getting some delivered later today."

Matt frowned and sat up straighter, his morning languor disappearing. "She went by herself?"

"I'm not sure that's a good idea," Sam added. He wasn't as relaxed anymore, either.

Lydia sighed. "I told her that if she waited, one or both of you gents would probably be glad to go with her, but she wouldn't hear of it. She said she'd be perfectly fine in the middle of town in broad daylight, that Cole wouldn't dare try anything under those circumstances. That gal is nothin' if not headstrong," she added unnecessarily.

"And she's likely right," Matt said as he scraped his chair back to stand up. "But with no law except that tame sheriff to worry about, there's really no telling what Cole might do."

Sam got to his feet, too. "We'd better go make sure that she's all right."

"But your breakfast," Lydia protested.

"It'll have to wait," Matt said as he started toward the door.

It opened before he and Sam could get there, and Charity walked in. She frowned and said, "Where are you two going? Sit down and eat."

"You're all right?" Matt asked.

"I'm fine. I told Lydia it wouldn't be a problem for me to go to the store."

"And I told them," Lydia put in. "But they're about as stubborn as you are."

"You were coming to check on me," Charity said in a faintly accusatory tone.

Both men shrugged. "We've run into men like Cole before," Sam said. "They think they're a law unto themselves and can do whatever they want."

"Well, I'm touched by your concern. Right now, though, I want you to sit down and have your break-fast. I have a job for you later, if you want it."

"What's that?" Matt asked as he and Sam returned to the table.

Charity joined them there and explained. "After I went to the general store to buy some supplies—which will be delivered here later this morning, by the way—I stopped at the newspaper. I thought the editor might be interested in doing a story about the Silver Belle being open for business again."

"He take you up on it?"

"Well . . . no," Charity admitted ruefully. "I think he might have, but his wife was there. Evidently she keeps his books for him, and she didn't seem too keen on the idea that a place like this is news-worthy. But the editor also takes on outside print-ing jobs, so I made arrangements for him to print up some fliers advertising the business. Since they'd be making money on that, his wife agreed to it."

"Can we afford that?" Lydia asked.

"Barely. But they say you have to spend money to make money."

Matt and Sam exchanged a glance. If the gals ran short of funds, they would be glad to loan them some money. Charity might put up a fuss about taking it, though. Even though her name was Charity, she might insist she wasn't going to take any.

"Those fliers should be ready about eleven o'clock, he said," she went on. "I thought maybe you wouldn't mind getting them and tacking them up around town."

"Doesn't sound like too complicated a chore," Sam said.

"I reckon we can give it a try," Matt added.

"Good. I imagine word has already spread around town about the saloon opening again, but I want people to know that they can start coming here right away. While I was at the store I bought a sheet and a can of paint, too. I'm going to paint a big sign that says GRAND REOPENING and hang it up outside."

"That ought to get Cole's goat," Sam said.

"I don't care about Cole's goat or anything else about him. I just want to get the business off to a good start."

The blood brothers resumed their breakfast. For a retired whore, Lydia was a mighty good cook, Matt thought, but he kept that assessment to himself, just in case she might take it the wrong way.

Since they had some time before they would need to pick up the fliers at the newspaper office, they turned their hand to some chores around the saloon that the women might have trouble handling. A section of the railing around the balcony was a little loose, so Sam found a hammer and some nails in the storeroom off the kitchen and set about repairing it. Matt took a saw and a piece of lumber from a pile in the alley out back and began cutting a replacement board for one of the stair risers that had had a hole kicked in it sometime in the past. Those and a few other similar tasks kept them busy as the morning passed.

The other women were still upstairs asleep when Bodine and Two Wolves left the saloon and walked across the street and down a couple of blocks to the newspaper office. The editor and publisher, a man in his thirties with a neatly trimmed dark beard, had the fliers ready for them when they explained who they were.

"I've heard about you two," he said. "If you ask me, Junius Cole doesn't know what he's getting into if you're taking the side of those women."

"*Those women* have a right to be here," Matt said. "Miss MacKenzie is the legal owner of the Silver Belle."

"Oh, I'm not disputing that," the editor said quickly. He was alone in the office now, his wife obviously having gone home to prepare lunch. "And to tell you the truth, I wish Miss MacKenzie luck. There are a lot of people in Buffalo Flat who'd like to see Cole taken down a notch or two, and I'm one of 'em." He extended an ink-stained hand and introduced himself. "I'm Casey McLennan."

Sam recognized the name. "You're one of the men who gave statements to Judge Ashmore yesterday evening about that gunfight with Cole's gunnies."

McLennan nodded. "That's right. I saw the whole thing and was glad to speak up on your behalf. I would have put a story about it in next week's paper, but . . . my wife doesn't like stories that she says glorify violence."

"Standing up for what's right isn't the same thing as glorifying violence," Matt said.

"I agree with you, but some people don't."

"Well, then, I'm lucky I've never been one to give much of a hoot in hell about what some people think." Matt picked up the stack of fliers. "I believe Miss MacKenzie's already paid you for these?"

"That's right. And if I could offer one word of advice?"

"What's that?" Sam asked.

"Watch your backs. I know about your reputations, but Cole has some dangerous men working for him, especially one named Lucas Tate."

"Tate," Matt repeated. "I've heard of him. He's fast, and he's got ice water in his veins."

McLennan nodded. "That's him, all right."

"Despite what you may have heard about us," Sam said, "we don't go hunting for trouble. We'll keep an eye out for Cole's men, but we won't start any fights."

"Won't run from any, either," Matt added.

They left the newspaper office. Sam had brought along the hammer he had been using at the saloon and a pocketful of nails. He suggested, "Let's put some of these up by the corral and the public watering trough. Lots of folks pass by there in a day's time."

"I was thinkin' more about plastering the front wall of the Colorado Palace with them," Matt said.

"Remember what I said about not hunting for trouble? That's Cole's place."

Matt grinned. "I know." He walked toward the eastern end of town without complaining, though.

When they reached the corral, Matt handed one of the fliers to Sam, who tacked it onto a post with a couple of nails. The flier read, SILVER BELLE SALOON—NOW OPEN—NEW OWNER INVITES EVERYONE TO COME IN FOR THE BEST DRINKS AND BEST TIMES IN BUFFALO FLAT!

As Sam stepped back from the post and looked at the sign, then nodded in satisfaction, Matt said, "That'd get my attention, all right." They turned to walk away and look for another place to display one of the fliers.

They had gone only a few feet when shots roared out, shattering the midday calm.

Chapter 12

The night before, Hardy Thomas must have heard the hoofbeats as Bo and Scratch approached the ranch, because the Half Moon's foreman stepped out of the bunkhouse with a rifle in his hands and called anxiously, "Who's that yonder?"

"Bo and Scratch, Hardy," Bo replied.

Mort Skaggs and Hector Ibañez emerged from the bunkhouse, too, and joined Hardy as he hurried to meet the Texans. "Did you find Johnny?" Mort asked in a voice taut with worry.

"We found him," Scratch replied heavily, "but you ain't gonna like what we've got to tell you."

Mort began to curse while Hector crossed himself and muttered a prayer. Hardy sighed and said, "The kid's dead, ain't he?"

"I'm afraid so," Bo said. He and Scratch dismounted, and Bo went on. "We found him in the Colorado Palace. He'd been shot by a man named Lucas Tate."

"Tate!" Mort exclaimed. "That son of a bitch is nothin' but a murderin' gunslinger!"

Scratch said, "Yeah, I reckon he prodded young

Johnny into drawin' on him, knowin' full well that the kid didn't have a chance."

Hardy's hands tightened on the rifle he held as he said, "We ought to ride into town and—"

"And what?" Bo broke in. "Get yourself killed so that Mrs. Kincaid has even less help than she does now?" He shook his head. "I know Scratch and I are strangers here, and I don't mean to sound harsh, but it seems to me that the worst thing you could do right now is to give Tate and the rest of Cole's hired killers an opportunity to gun you down."

Hardy lowered the rifle to his side in his left hand and used the right to scrub wearily at his face as he sighed. "You're right, Creel," he said. "I know you're right. But it's mighty damned hard to sit back and do nothin' when that poor kid was as good as murdered."

"I know," Bo said with a nod. "But you've just got to tell yourself that in time Tate will get what's coming to him, and so will Cole."

"In time," Mort repeated. "How long a time? It passes damned slow when you're waitin' for justice."

"I know," Bo said, "but you've just got to have faith."

Hardy said, "Now here's the really hard part. Somebody's got to go in there and tell Miz Kincaid what happened."

"Did Johnny have any kinfolks around here?" Scratch asked.

Hardy shook his head. "Not that I know of. He claimed to be from down in the Texas border country somewhere. Could be that Del Rio wasn't even his real name. He might've left Texas two jumps ahead of the Rangers. Even good men get crosswise with the law sometimes."

"You don't have to tell us about that," Scratch said. "More than once, Bo and me have had star-packers tell us that we were ridin' down the hangin' road, bound for the gallows. And we're just as peaceable and innocent as any two jiggers could ever be!"

Bo didn't waste his breath pointing out all the evidence that put the lie to Scratch's last comment. He just said, "I'll talk to Mrs. Kincaid. She's going to have to decide whether she wants Johnny buried out here on the ranch or in town. His body is at the undertaking parlor tonight.

"There's a little burial ground up on top o' the hill back yonder," Hardy said as he inclined his head toward the slope rising behind the ranch house. "That's where the boss is laid to rest, along with his first wife and the baby they lost, and a few other hands who've bit the dust while they was workin' here."

"William Kincaid was married before, eh?"

"That's right, some years back. Wife died whilst givin' birth, and the young'un didn't make it, neither. Losin' 'em both like that hit Will mighty hard. Took him years to get over it. And then when he did get over it and married the current Miz Kincaid, it was only a few months before some murderin' bushwhacker shot him in the back. But at least he got to be happy again for a little while."

Bo turned to Scratch and said, "If you'll tend to the horses, I'll go talk to Mrs. Kincaid."

"Sure you don't want me to come along?" Scratch asked.

Solemnly, Bo shook his head. "No, I can handle this chore."

He left Scratch and the ranch hands standing in

front of the bunkhouse and strode toward the main house. All the windows were dark. Theresa Kincaid had turned in for the night not knowing that Johnny Del Rio had headed for Buffalo Flat to settle the score for the attempt on her life.

Bo climbed onto the porch, paused in front of the door, took a deep breath, and then knocked loudly. "Mrs. Kincaid!" he called. "Mrs. Kincaid, it's Bo Creel!"

He continued knocking and occasionally announcing who he was. After a couple of minutes passed, he saw a light through the window next to the door, and a moment later it swung open to reveal Theresa standing there holding a lamp. She wore a robe belted tightly around her waist, and her blond hair was tousled from sleep. Even though Scratch was the one who fancied himself a ladies' man, Bo appreciated a good-looking woman, too, and the intimate dishevelment Theresa displayed made her undeniably attractive.

"Bo," she said as she blinked in confusion. "What is it? Is something wrong?"

He took his hat off and nodded. "Yes, ma'am, I'm afraid so. I have some bad news for you."

"You and Scratch aren't leaving, are you?"

"No, ma'am. It's worse than that."

Theresa sighed. "Well, then, come on in. If it's that bad, I think I'd rather be sitting down to hear it."

They stepped into the parlor, where Theresa placed the lamp on a table and sat down on a divan, perching nervously on the edge of it. Bo remained on his feet.

"What is it?" she asked again.

"Earlier this evening, Johnny Del Rio left the ranch and rode to Buffalo Flat. He was angry about what happened this afternoon and wanted to have a showdown with Junius Cole. But he never got to see Cole. A man named Lucas Tate killed him in a gunfight in the Colorado Palace Saloon."

The words came out of Bo's mouth hard and flat, without any hesitation or inflection. He knew from painful experience that there was no good way to cushion the news of anybody's death. Better to just put it out there in the open and get the telling of it over with. But it was never pleasant, and that was true now, too.

"Johnny?" Theresa repeated in a hollow voice. "Johnny is . . . dead?"

Bo nodded. "I'm afraid so. Scratch and I went after him, in hopes that we could head him off before he got into trouble, but we were too late."

He didn't say anything about how the two of them had stopped to intervene when that drunk was manhandling the young blonde from the wagon. The shot that had killed Johnny had come *after* that incident, which meant that if they hadn't paused, they might have gotten to the youngster in time to keep him from drawing on Lucas Tate. The knowledge of that possibility had gnawed quite a bit on Bo's guts during the ride back out here from the settlement.

On the other hand, there was no telling what might have happened if he and Scratch hadn't stepped in to help the young woman. That might have ended tragically, too. A man couldn't dwell too much on what might have been, because it would drive him loco if he did.

Tears welled from Theresa's eyes and rolled down her cheeks as she looked up at him. "That . . . that foolish boy," she said. "He only did it because he was smitten with me."

Bo shook his head. "No, ma'am, I don't think so. I think it was more a matter of him riding for the brand. Hardy and Mort and Hector all wanted a shot at Cole, too. But they're old enough not to give in to the impulse."

"Johnny wasn't . . . and now he'll never get any older." Theresa wiped at her eyes.

Bo was glad he had come in here to break the news to her instead of Scratch. Scratch would have been sitting beside her on that divan by now with an arm around her shoulders as he tried to comfort her. He wouldn't have tried to really take advantage of a grieving, upset woman, of course—Scratch might be incorrigible, but he wasn't *that* incorrigible—but still, that wasn't what Theresa needed right now, at least not in Bo's view. He believed in a more practical, hardheaded approach to sorrow.

"Johnny's body is at the undertaker's in Buffalo Flat," he went on. "We'll need to ride into town first thing in the morning and let him know where the burial will be. Hardy and the boys said they didn't think Johnny had any family around here."

"If he did, I never heard about it," Theresa agreed. She nodded decisively. "He'll be buried here on the ranch. We have a small cemetery up on the hill."

"That's what Hardy told me. Sounds fine to me, ma'am. Scratch and I will take care of it in the morning."

"No," Theresa said sharply. "We'll take care of it. All of us. We'll all go to town to get him."

With a dubious look on his face, Bo said, "I don't know if that's a good idea. That would leave the spread undefended. It'd practically be an engraved invitation for Cole's men to come in and burn all the buildings to the ground."

Theresa frowned and bit at her lower lip for a second. "I didn't think about that. You're right, of course. We'll leave the other members of the crew here to keep an eye on the place. But I'm going along with you and Mr. Morton, and I won't listen to any arguments about that."

Bo shrugged. "We'll need to take the buckboard," he said. "I reckon you can drive it."

"That's what I was thinking."

"I guess it's settled, then. We'll start first thing in the morning. Ought to be back here by the middle of the day."

"That will be fine." Theresa stood up, came over to him, and laid a hand on his arm. "Thank you for trying to save him, Bo."

Bo allowed a touch of gentleness to come into his voice as he said, "I wish I'd been able to, ma'am." He put on his hat, nodded politely to her, and turned to leave.

Scratch was waiting for him on the porch, a quirly dangling from his lips. "How'd she take it?" he asked.

"About as well as can be expected," Bo replied. "She was upset, of course. She wants to take the buckboard into town in the morning to get Johnny and bring him back out here to be buried."

Scratch nodded. "That don't surprise me. We'll be goin' with her, I reckon?"

"Damn right. She first said everybody would go, but I pointed out that that would leave the place with nobody to watch it."

"Cole's men would get up to mischief for sure if that happened."

"Yeah," Bo said. "I pointed that out, and Mrs. Kincaid went along with me."

Scratch took a drag on the cigarette. "We'd better turn in, then, if we're gettin' an early start in the mornin'. It's been a long day."

Thinking of the violence that had marred it, Bo nodded and said, "Yeah. It sure has."

Thankfully, the rest of the night passed quietly. All the hands were up before dawn the next morning. Hardy handled the cooking chores in the shack next to the bunkhouse and had coffee and biscuits ready when the others rolled out of their soogans. After the rudimentary breakfast, Mort and Hector rode out to check on the stock. "Keep your eyes open," Hardy warned them as they started off. "You never know when some of Cole's gunslingers might be lurkin' hereabouts."

While Hardy began hitching the team to the buckboard, Bo and Scratch got their regular mounts ready to ride. Then they walked over to the house, where Scratch knocked on the front door. It opened almost immediately. Theresa Kincaid must have been waiting for them. She stood there in a stylish but sober traveling outfit, suitable garb for the grim errand on which she was going to be engaged today.

"Ready to go, ma'am?" Bo asked as he and Scratch took off their hats.

"Yes, just a minute." Theresa reached to one side of the door and picked up a rifle. It was a fairly new Winchester. As she tucked the weapon under her arm, she went on. "If anybody bothers us today, I'll be ready to make them wish that they hadn't."

"Yes, ma'am," Scratch said.

"If I'd had this rifle yesterday instead of just a pistol," Theresa said as the three of them walked out to the buckboard, "I'd have been able to put up a better fight against those bushwhackers."

"I'm hoping we won't run into any trouble today," Bo said. "Maybe Johnny's death will cause Cole to ease up a little on the pressure."

"Don't count on it." Theresa climbed onto the buckboard seat and took the reins from Hardy as he handed them to her. "Cole is the sort of man who's more likely to try to press his advantage."

"Well, if he does, we'll make him sorry," Scratch said. He and Bo swung up into their saddles and fell in on either side of the buckboard as Theresa flapped the reins and got the vehicle moving.

She kept the buckboard rolling along briskly as she headed for Buffalo Flat. With a night's rest and plenty of grain and water, the horses ridden by Bo and Scratch had no trouble keeping up. In fact, they had to hold the animals in a little, because the horses felt frisky and were ready to run.

They didn't see anyone on the way into the settlement. When the church steeple came into view, Bo relaxed a little. He considered it unlikely that Cole would spring an ambush this close to town. A few minutes later they reached the buildings. The night before, Bo and Scratch had noted that the undertaking parlor was near the church, so they knew they didn't have far to go.

Theresa brought the buckboard to a halt in front of the building. Scratch dismounted in a hurry so that he could take her hand and help her down from the seat. Bo tended to tying the horses to the hitch rack. Then Theresa led the way inside. Her head was held high, chin tilted in defiance. She was stubbornly maintaining control, thought Bo, taking pains not to reveal her emotions.

The tall, gaunt undertaker came into the front room from somewhere in the back. He still wore his black suit, although the top hat was nowhere in sight and his balding head was bare. Bo wondered fleetingly why so many fellows in that line of work looked like this gent.

"Good morning, Mrs. Kincaid," the man said. "My sympathy on your loss."

"Thank you, Mr. Sturdevant," Theresa replied formally. "We've come to pick up the body of Johnny Del Rio."

"Yes, ma'am. Everything is ready."

The undertaker led them into the back room, where a pine coffin rested on a table built for that purpose. The coffin had been varnished so that it looked fairly nice.

Sturdevant said, "My helpers are out back. I'll fetch them to load the deceased onto your wagon."

"Before you go," Theresa said, "perhaps we'd better settle up."

Sturdevant smiled solemnly and shook his head. "No need. The bill is all taken care of. This gentleman saw to it yesterday evening." He nodded toward Bo.

Theresa turned toward him. "Is that true?"

"Don't worry about it," Bo said with a shrug.

"I'll pay you back," Theresa insisted. "This is my responsibility."

"Worry about that later," Scratch told her. "Bo and me may be ridin' the grub line, but that don't mean we're completely broke."

Reluctantly, Theresa said, "Well, all right. For now."

Sturdevant called the two men who had helped him take Johnny's body from the saloon the night before. Bo and Scratch lent a hand, as well, and it didn't take long for them to get the coffin loaded onto the buckboard. As the undertaker stepped back, he said, "I suppose the deceased will be buried on your ranch, Mrs. Kincaid?"

"That's right," Theresa said. "There's a small burial ground out there."

"I'll make a note of it for my records. The state requires me to keep track of where all my, ah, customers wind up, you know."

"Does it require you to keep track of whether or not they were murdered by gunslingers?" Theresa asked coolly.

Sturdevant looked uncomfortable. "I try not to take sides in disputes, ma'am. A man in my line of work has to remain neutral, since I serve all parties."

Theresa might have said something else, but at that moment, a sudden flurry of gunshots sounded from the far end of the street. Bo and Scratch looked sharply at each other.

Trouble had come once more to Buffalo Flat.

Chapter 13

At the sound of the blasting guns, instinct took over in Matt Bodine and Sam Two Wolves. Both young men whirled around. Matt dropped the stack of advertising fliers, and the hammer Sam had been wielding dropped unheeded to the ground at his feet. Their hands flew to their guns.

They stopped their draws as they saw that the shots weren't directed at them. Four men stood in the street not far away, pouring lead into the post where Sam had just tacked up the flier. Bullets chewed into the wood and sent splinters flying through the air. In a matter of seconds, the flier was ripped to pieces by the slugs. It looked almost like a miniature snowstorm as tiny bits of paper fluttered to the ground at the base of the post.

The guns fell silent as the men were finally satisfied that their vandalism was complete. Laughing and joking among themselves, they began to reload.

"Hey!" Sam called. "What the hell was that all about?"

One of the men looked at him with a sneer. "You talkin' to us, breed?"

"You know we're talking to you," Matt snapped. "We just put that flier up!"

"Flier?" one of the other men repeated. "We thought it was a target and figured you put it up there for us to practice on!"

That brought another round of laughter from the men. They grew more serious as they closed the cylinders of their revolvers and slid the reloaded weapons back into their holsters.

"We know who you and the breed are, Bodine," said the first man who had spoken. "If you want to make somethin' outta what we did to your pretty little piece o' paper, you go right ahead."

Matt and Sam glanced at each other. It was obvious to them what was going on here. By now Junius Cole had to know that they had been released from jail the night before. Sheriff Branch had probably gone straight to the saloon to tell Cole about it like the good little lapdog he was. And this morning Cole had sent more of his crew of hired guns to seek out Bodine and Two Wolves and settle the score with them.

This time, though, the gunmen were trying to prod Matt and Sam into drawing first, just so everything would be nice and legal where Cole was concerned.

"Target practice, eh?" Matt drawled. "Sounds like a good idea. Sam, go put up another of those fliers, would you?"

"Sure," Sam agreed. He picked up one of the papers Matt had dropped, along with the hammer, and returned to the post. It was so splintered by bullets that he turned to Matt and asked, "All right if I use another post?"

"Go right ahead," Matt told him.

The previous shots had drawn some attention. A

small crowd of townspeople was gathering as Sam nailed the flier to another post. He moved quickly out of the way as Matt backed off to put a respectable distance between himself and the target. When he was ready, Matt smoothly palmed out the right-hand Colt and fired from the hip.

The shots rolled out in one seemingly continuous roar—one, two, three, four, five. Then, before the echoes had even had a chance to die away, Matt's other revolver leaped into his left hand and added five more shots in a wave of thundering noise.

The advertising flier was still on the post, seemingly intact.

"Did he even hit it?" one of the gunmen muttered. "I saw splinters flyin' in the air while he was shootin'. Leastways, I thought I did."

Matt holstered the left-hand gun and started to reload the one in his right hand. "Sam?" he said.

Grinning, Sam poked his finger at the first letter O in the word SALOON. "One," he said as the tip of his finger sunk into the bullet hole in the middle of the letter. He moved on to the next letter O and repeated the process, saying, "Two . . . three . . . four . . . five . . ." and on down the line as he pointed out the hole in the middle of each O, until he got to the tenth and final one, which also had a clean shot right in the middle of it. "That's all of them."

Matt had his second Colt reloaded by this time. He pouched it, smiled coolly at the gunmen, and said, "You're right, it was good practice for the next time I have to shoot at something that's empty in the middle . . . like a pack of gutless cowards. Like, say, you boys."

The faces of the gunmen twisted with anger. Matt

had shown them up and flung their challenge right back in their faces. They could take it—or they could draw.

The sheriff hadn't come to see what all the shooting was about, Matt noted as the tense moment stretched out. That came as no real surprise to him. Given Branch's connection to Junius Cole, the sheriff might have known that another attempt on the lives of Bodine and Two Wolves would be made this morning. Or maybe he'd just guessed as much when he heard the shots. Either way, he didn't have the stomach for finding out what was going on until it was over.

The gunnie who seemed to be the spokesman for the group of hired killers breathed, "You son of a bitch."

Matt stood facing them calmly. He and Sam were separated by several yards, which was a good thing with the odds four against two. With the instincts born of riding many a long and dangerous trail with his blood brother, Matt knew which pair Sam would take and which would be left to him if it came to a shoot-out.

And that was what it was going to come to, no doubt about that.

"Talk's cheap," Matt said.

He saw the telltale flick of the eyes as the man snarled and grabbed iron. Both of Matt's hands swept down and then up, filled with the butts of his Colts. Shots blasted from the guns as they bucked against his palms. Off to his left, Sam's gun was roaring, too.

Cole's gunslingers were good at their work. They got their weapons out of their holsters and even triggered off a few rounds. But they were no match for

Bodine and Two Wolves. Matt saw both of the men he had targeted stagger backward as his bullets slammed into them. He felt a slug jerk at his sleeve and heard the wind-rip of another past his ear. Then the two gunmen were folding up like puppets with their strings cut. Near them, one of the other men had doubled over and pitched forward on his face as a bullet from Sam's gun punched into his midsection.

The fourth man, even though he was wounded, had managed to stay on his feet and was struggling to lift his gun for another shot. As Matt's Colts fell silent, he saw that and briefly considered whether he ought to angle his left-hand revolver in that direction and take the man down. Before he could do anything, though, Sam's gun spoke again and the final gunslinger flew backward off his feet to land in a limp sprawl.

It was over.

But as another pair of shots suddenly rang out behind him, Matt wasn't so sure about that.

When the roar of gunfire sounded from the other end of the street, Bo and Scratch turned instantly in that direction, seeking the cause of the trouble. Theresa Kincaid stiffened as if expecting the bullets to come toward her, and Sturdevant and his helpers disappeared quickly back into the undertaking parlor.

As the blasts died away, Bo said quietly, "Doesn't seem to be anybody shooting at us, ma'am. Maybe we'd better get you out of here—"

"No," Theresa said. "You and Scratch go find out what's going on. Junius Cole runs this town. It's probably something to do with him."

Scratch was like an old fire horse hearing the bell. Obviously, he wanted to go loping down the street to see what all the commotion was about. But he said, "Are you sure you'll be all right, ma'am?"

Theresa reached to the driver's seat of the buckboard and picked up the Winchester lying there. "I'll be fine," she said. "I want to know what Cole's up to now."

Any knowledge of the enemy might prove to be useful, Bo thought. He said to Scratch, "Let's go."

Side by side, the old-timers strode down the street toward the eastern end of town. That was where the public watering trough and corrals were located. Quite a few townspeople were on their way down there, too.

When they got closer, Bo's still-keen eyes saw two men facing four others in an obvious confrontation. It didn't take him but a moment to figure out the sides in this conflict. He didn't have any idea who those two strapping youngsters were, but the four hard-faced gunnies facing them were exactly the sort of hired scum who worked for Junius Cole.

On second thought, the two young men looked vaguely familiar, Bo decided. The one in the flat-crowned black hat and black vest had Indian blood in him, despite wearing white man's clothes and packing iron on his hip like a white man. The other hombre, in buckskin shirt and tipped-back brown Stetson, wore two guns, and as Bo watched, he was the one who put on an impressive display of shooting skill over the next few minutes, drilling a bullet into the middle of each letter O on some sort of sign tacked up on a corral post.

Then both young men faced the four gunslingers, clearly ready to do battle if that was necessary.

The townspeople started to edge away, knowing that they had better get out of the line of fire. Bo said quietly to one of the townies, "Who are those two fellas?"

"You don't know? Mister, that's Matt Bodine and Sam Two Wolves. And those gents facin' 'em work for Mr. Cole, so I'd hunt a hole if I was you!"

Scratch had a shoulder propped against one of the posts holding up the awning over the board-walk in front of a saddle shop. He grinned at Bo and asked, "You figure on runnin' and hidin'?"

"No, I want to see this," Bo said calmly. He had heard of Bodine and Two Wolves, although he couldn't recall ever seeing them before. They had reputations as being fast on the draw, but unlike many gunfighters, they were known to be honest men, not hired killers. Bodine had even done quite a bit of scouting work for the army. Bo wanted to see how they handled themselves against Cole's men.

Townspeople went diving for cover as the hired guns slapped leather. Matt Bodine was a two-gun man, Bo noted as Bodine brought both weapons into play with blinding speed. Sam Two Wolves was almost as fast, and both youngsters were cool under fire and exceedingly accurate with their shots. Bo knew that a man could win most gunfights just by keeping his wits about him and not panicking, taking his time and aiming his shots. With Bodine and Two Wolves, though, their skill rose to an en-tirely different level. They combined amazing speed with those other attributes, and Bo wasn't surprised when the four gunmen who worked for Cole were cut down by the deadly fire from Bodine and Two Wolves.

Then Scratch nudged Bo with an elbow and

nodded toward a two-story building across the street. A flicker of movement drew Bo's eye to the second floor. He saw a rifle barrel being poked through an open window up there, and it took him only an instant to realize that the rifleman was drawing a bead on Matt Bodine's back.

Bo and Scratch drew and fired in the same instant, directing their shots at that second-floor window. They didn't know who was up there, but the son of a bitch was a backshooter and that was enough to make the drifters take a hand in this game.

Matt and Sam whirled around to see who was shooting at them now, only to realize that the shots hadn't been aimed at them. Two older men stood on the boardwalk about thirty feet away from them, each holding a revolver with smoke curling from the barrel. The guns were tipped up and pointed toward a building on the other side of the street.

As Matt and Sam watched, a rifle dropped from a half-open window, hit the awning below, slid off, and fell to the street. It was followed by a man who crashed through the raised pane, toppled forward, and plunged to the ground. He landed with a heavy thud, raising a puff of dust from the street, and then didn't move again.

Matt looked at the old-timers. The one who wore a dark, dusty suit and black hat nodded in friendly fashion as he lowered his gun. "Hombre was drawing a bead on you from behind," he explained.

"And if there's anything we hate," the other man drawled in an unmistakable Texas accent, "it's a backshooter." He opened his gun to replace the spent round. His partner did likewise.

Matt and Sam shrugged and took care of that chore, too. When all the guns were reloaded, the blood brothers holstered their weapons and walked over to join the older men. All along the street, people were starting to emerge from the hiding places they had ducked into when the shooting started. Matt figured it was only a matter of time now before Sheriff Branch came blustering up.

He held out his hand to the man in the dark suit. "Matt Bodine," he introduced himself.

"Bo Creel. I've heard of you, Bodine." Creel gripped Matt's hand, then turned to Sam. "And you'd be Sam Two Wolves."

"That's right," Sam said. "We're much obliged for the favor, Mr. Creel."

"I'm Scratch Morton," the other old-timer said as he shook hands. "Maybe you've heard of me."

Matt hated to disappoint the man, but he had to shake his head and say, "No, I don't believe I have. But I'm mighty glad to meet both of you. You sure enough saved our bacon here today."

"Like Scratch said, we don't like backshooters," Bo replied.

"Especially when they work for that varmint Cole, like that fella probably did," Scratch added as he gestured toward the bushwhacker who had fallen from the second-floor window.

That added to Matt and Sam's interest. "You know about Cole?" Matt asked.

Both old-timers nodded. "One of the towns-people told us those men you were facing worked for Cole," Bo explained, "so it stands to reason the backshooter did, too. And we don't have any use for Mr. Junius Cole. One of his men killed a friend of ours last night, and he's trying to steal a ranch from the lady we work for."

None of that surprised Matt. He knew that Cole owned quite a few of the businesses in Buffalo Flat, and it stood to reason that the man might have a cattle spread, too. And knowing what they did about how ruthlessly Cole tried to wipe out his competition, it was easy to believe that he would want to crush anyone who owned a neighboring ranch.

"We ought to get together sometime and have a drink," Sam suggested, "maybe compare notes on what this fellow Cole has been up to around here."

"No good, that's what he's been up to," Scratch said. With a grin, he nodded toward the bodies sprawled in the street. "Looks like you boys are whittlin' down his forces, though. Bo and me accounted for a few of 'em ourselves yesterday."

Matt chuckled grimly and said, "That's just the latest bunch we've had to ventilate. How many of those skunks have we shot in the past twenty-four hours, Sam?"

"I make it at least fourteen," Sam replied. "Maybe a few more."

Scratch let out a low whistle of admiration. "That's a mighty fine job of work. Pretty soon Cole won't have any gunnies left."

"I wouldn't count on that," Bo said. "Men like that always flock to where the blood money is."

"Speakin' of blood money," Scratch said, "here comes the sheriff."

"You know he's in Cole's back pocket, too, eh?" Matt asked.

Bo said, "You don't have to be around here long to figure that out."

Carrying a shotgun as usual, Sheriff Branch hurried

up after all the shooting was over, also as usual. He was clearly upset, especially when Judge Ashmore stepped out of the crowd and said, "Don't bother taking anybody to jail, Sheriff. I've already been collecting affidavits stating that Bodine and Two Wolves acted in self-defense after those other gents drew on them first."

"I don't appreciate you sticking your nose into this without being asked, Ambrose," the sheriff snapped. Matt knew what Branch meant—*Cole* wouldn't appreciate the lawyer getting involved. But even though it was somewhat reluctantly, Ashmore seemed resolved to do the right thing.

Red-faced with anger, Branch warned Matt and Sam that if they kept getting involved in gunfights he would lock them up and throw away the key, self-defense or not. Then he turned to Bo and Scratch and said, "If you two old-timers are thinkin' about getting mixed up with these two killers, you'd better think again."

"We won't stand by and let anybody be gunned down from behind," Bo said.

The sheriff shook a finger at him. "Just remember what I said!"

As the lawman stalked away, Matt looked at Bo and Scratch and said, "Some friends of ours run a saloon. How about coming down there with us for a drink?"

Scratch licked his lips like he wanted to say yes, but Bo shook his head. "Can't," he said. "We have to get back to the ranch. Like we said, we came in with Mrs. Kincaid to pick up the body of one of her hands, so we have to get back to the Half Moon and see about giving him a proper burial."

"Tell the lady we're sorry to hear about that," Sam said.

"And come back to the Silver Belle any time you want," Matt added. "We'll either be there, or the ladies who run it will know where we are."

"Maybe tonight," Scratch suggested.

"We'll see," Bo said. "Come on, Scratch."

As the older men walked away, Matt waited until they were out of earshot and then said, "I'll bet those two were pretty salty hombres in their time."

"The way they spotted that bushwhacker and drilled him, I'm not sure I'd want to cross them even now," Sam replied. He and Matt stood on the boardwalk as the undertaker's wagon rumbled past. Sturdevant and his helpers hopped out of the vehicle to start loading up the bullet-riddled corpses.

Sam suddenly reached out and gripped Matt's arm hard. "Look," he said between clenched teeth.

Matt turned his head and followed Sam's gaze. His blood brother was looking along Main Street with a surprised stare. Close to the far end of it, Bo Creel and Scratch Morton had reached their horses and swung up into the saddles. They sat there as a blond woman on a buckboard turned the vehicle around to head west out of the settlement.

Even though the woman was several blocks away, Matt felt a shock of recognition go through him that was almost like a physical blow. "Terri," he said.

The woman on the buckboard might be calling herself something different now, but her real name was Terri Kelly.

And the last time Bodine and Two Wolves had seen her, she had been cursing them both and threatening to hunt them down and kill them.

Chapter 14

"What was all the shooting about?" Theresa asked as she got the team moving at a brisk walk on the edge of town. "Some of Cole's men were involved, weren't they?"

"They sure were," Scratch replied. "They were tryin' to hooraw a couple of young fellas who got on Cole's bad side. They found that they'd bit off more than they could chew, though. What they wound up chewin' on was some hot lead."

"Cole's men were killed?"

Bo nodded. "That's right. Even though it was four against two."

Theresa looked sharply at him. "Four against two . . . and the two won?"

"Yep," Scratch said. "They were fast and slick on the draw."

"Do you think they might want to work for me? Cole might decide to leave me alone if I had a couple of fast guns on my side. Besides you two, I mean."

"Don't worry, you didn't offend us," Bo assured

her. "We can handle our irons pretty well, but we've never considered ourselves gunfighters."

Scratch said, "Speak for yourself. I'm known far and wide as a dangerous man."

Bo chuckled and said dryly, "Yes, folks are always speaking your name in the same breath as that of Smoke Jensen, John Wesley Hardin, and young Bodine back there."

Theresa's head jerked toward the two old-timers. "Bodine!" she repeated. "Matt Bodine is in Buffalo Flat?"

"Yes, ma'am. It was Bodine and his partner, Sam Two Wolves, who had that gunfight with Cole's men just now."

"Were either of them hurt?"

Scratch said, "No, but they got me and Bo to thank for that. After they dropped Cole's gunnies, another polecat with a rifle in a second-floor window tried to ventilate them from behind. We spotted that varmint in time to settle his hash for him."

"You saved the lives of Matt Bodine and Sam Two Wolves?" Theresa sounded like she could hardly believe it.

"I don't know about that," Bo said. "Those two are good enough so that at least one of them might have survived once that bushwhacker opened up on them. But he probably would've gotten one of them."

"Bo's just naturally too modest," Scratch added. "I reckon we *did* save the lives of those two young hellions, if I do say so myself."

Theresa had kept the buckboard moving, but she was obviously surprised to hear that Bodine and Two Wolves were in Buffalo Flat, and that they shared a mutual enemy with her in Junius Cole. "I reckon you must've heard of those two," Bo said.

She nodded. "Yes, I certainly have."

"They asked us to have a drink with them later," Bo went on. "Scratch and I figured we might ride into town this evening and take them up on it; that is, if everything is quiet at the ranch. If you like, maybe we can bring up the idea of them working for you."

"Let me think about it," Theresa said. She sighed. "Right now, we have to concentrate on getting poor Johnny laid to rest properly."

"Sure," Bo agreed. He thought that Theresa didn't seem as interested in getting Bodine and Two Wolves to work for her now that she knew who they were, but he supposed he could have been wrong about that.

He didn't really think any more about it as they traveled on to the ranch. He scanned the skies for smoke and listened intently for the sound of distant gunshots, two signs that could indicate trouble on the Half Moon. But the day seemed quiet and peaceful, if a little hot. They reached the spread in early afternoon.

Hardy, Mort, and Hector met the buckboard as Theresa brought it to a stop in front of the bunkhouse. All three of the hands carried rifles and wore grim expressions, but when Theresa asked if there had been any trouble while she and Bo and Scratch were gone, Hardy shook his head.

"No, it was plumb peaceful," he said. "We went up on the hill and got the grave dug. Hope that's all right with you, ma'am."

"Of course it is," Theresa told him. "Where did you put it?"

"Off to one side a little, facin' the valley, where that big aspen tree'll give Johnny some shade of an afternoon. That boy pure-dee hated to get too hot."

Theresa nodded and smiled sadly. "That sounds perfect. Shall we go on up?"

"Might as well," Hardy said.

"*Un momento,*" Hector said. "I will get my guitar, so I can play a hymn."

A short time later, Theresa drove the buckboard up the hill to the burial ground while the five men rode along behind the vehicle. When they reached the grave site, they dismounted and lifted the coffin from the buckboard. Using lassos, they lowered the pine box into the grave, which was already starting to get a little shade from the aspen tree nearby.

As they gathered around and the men took off their hats, Hector strummed his guitar. The soft, plaintive notes drifted out over the ranch headquarters below and on into the valley to the east. Hardy pulled a battered New Testament from the hip pocket of his jeans and read a few passages of Scripture. Then he looked at Theresa and asked, "Is there anything you want to say, ma'am?"

She shook her head. "You're doing fine, Hardy. Thank you."

"All right. In that case, I reckon I'll lead us in prayer." A breeze sighed across the hillside, softly rustling the leaves of the aspen and causing the sunlight and shadows to shift as the foreman spoke. "Lord, we ask that You welcome our pard Johnny Del Rio into Your heavenly bunkhouse. We didn't know him well or for all that long, but he was a good hand and never let nobody down. He rode for the brand, and to my way of thinkin', that's just about the best thing anybody can say about a fella. We pray now that You'll take Johnny on and let him ride for Your brand forever and ever. Amen."

"Amen," Bo echoed, and Scratch, Mort, and

Hector did the same. Theresa didn't say anything, but she dabbed at her eyes with a handkerchief she had slipped out of a dress pocket.

Hardy put away his New Testament, turned to her, and said, "We'll take care of the rest of this, Miz Kincaid. Why don't you go on back down to the house and rest for a spell? I know this has been a tryin' day."

She nodded and said, "Yes . . . yes, it certainly has." She turned to the buckboard and started to step up to the seat. Scratch quickly moved toward her to help her.

He hadn't even had a chance to touch her arm yet when his hat suddenly leaped off his head, something thudded into the back of the buckboard seat, and an instant later the sound of a shot echoed through the foothills.

Even before that echo began to roll across the slopes, Scratch had grabbed Theresa and none too gently had borne her to the ground beside the buckboard. He shoved her underneath the vehicle as Bo and the ranch hands leaped for their horses to drag Winchesters out of saddle boots.

As soon as the rifle was in his hands, Bo leaped back to the buckboard and dropped to one knee beside a rear wheel. Knowing that the bullet had knocked Scratch's hat off before striking the seat, he was able to figure out the path it must have followed and use that rough estimation to locate the probable location of the bushwhacker. His gaze settled on a rocky knoll a couple of hundred yards distant, and sure enough, as another slug smacked into the buckboard, Bo saw a puff of powder smoke rise from the rocks.

"Over there!" he called as he snapped the

Winchester to his shoulder and began spraying the top of the knoll with bullets as fast as he could work the rifle's lever. Hardy, Mort, and Hector had scattered around the buckboard, and they put their rifles to work, too. Even at this distance, Bo heard the high-pitched whine of slugs ricocheting from those boulders.

"Need a hand?" Scratch asked from under the vehicle.

"No, just keep Mrs. Kincaid under there," Bo replied between shots. The buckboard didn't provide great shelter, but it was the best cover up here.

A moment later, Bo said, "Hold your fire!" As the guns fell silent, he listened carefully. The drumming of hoofbeats came to his ears. Someone was riding away in a hurry. The hoofbeats diminished to nothing.

"I think that damn drygulcher lit a shuck," Hardy said.

"Sounded like it," Mort put in.

Bo nodded in agreement, but warned, "Better keep your heads down for a few minutes anyway, just to make sure he's not trying to trick us."

"You mean I can't get out from under here?" Theresa asked.

"You just stay right where you are for the time bein', ma'am," Scratch told her. He lay beside her with a protective arm over her shoulders. With his other hand he reached out from under the buckboard and picked up his hat where it had fallen. "Dadgummit! That bustard put a bullet hole in my Stetson!"

"That's not the first hat you've had shot off your head," Bo reminded him. "Better a hole in your hat than in your skull."

"Yeah, I reckon."

"That bushwhacker was aiming at *me*," Theresa said. "Scratch, you stepped forward at just the wrong time. You almost took a bullet meant for me."

"Well, since that slug didn't hit either of us, I'd say I moved just at the right time. Must've thrown off that polecat's aim."

"I think he must be gone," Bo said as he came to his feet. "After his first shot missed, he tried one more time, but we were making things so hot for him over there that he didn't want to stick around."

The other men stood up as well, making targets of themselves if the bushwhacker was still hidden in the rocks. But no shots sounded, and when it became obvious the ambush was over, Scratch and Theresa crawled out from under the buckboard.

"Hardy, you and the boys get Mrs. Kincaid back to the ranch house," Bo ordered. If Hardy was bothered by the fact that Bo had taken charge, he didn't show it. He just nodded his agreement. Bo went on. "Ma'am, you should stay inside where it's safe. Scratch and I will ride over to that knoll and take a look around the place where the bushwhacker was hiding. Might be able to pick up a clue as to who he was."

"I can tell you who he was," Theresa said. "Not his name or anything like that, but I'm sure he was one of Cole's hired killers."

"Yes, ma'am, more than likely."

Theresa climbed onto the buckboard seat. Hardy stepped up beside her and took the reins. He turned the vehicle around and drove quickly down the hill, so quickly that he and Theresa bounced quite a bit on the seat. Mort and Hector rode right behind them, with Hector leading Hardy's horse.

Bo and Scratch mounted up and headed for the

rocky knoll. "The lady won't want to stay cooped up in the house for very long," Scratch predicted.

"I know," Bo said, "but for right now, that'll be safer. Hard to believe somebody would take a shot at her here on her own property."

"Fellas like Cole don't stop at anything to get what they want."

Bo nodded. "I know."

It didn't take them long to reach the place where the rifleman had hidden. They found a few hoofprints among the boulders to show where the man had left his horse, and behind one of the rocks the butt of a quirly lay on the ground where the would-be killer had dropped it, along with a couple of shell casings from a Winchester. The Texans didn't find anything else, certainly not anything that would tell them the identity of the bushwhacker.

Bo and Scratch checked the hoofprints again, looking for any telltale nicks in the horse's shoes. They memorized the few markings they found, even though it was very unlikely that they would be able to identify the rifleman that way.

"I'll bet a hat Miz Kincaid was right," Scratch said as they mounted up and started toward the ranch house. "That drygulchin' son of a bitch was one of Cole's men."

"Your hat's got a bullet hole in it," Bo reminded him with a smile. "I don't think I want to take that bet."

Scratch took off the Stetson and wryly poked a finger through the hole in the crown. "Anyway, I got to grab the gal and roll around on the ground with her," he said. "I reckon maybe that was worth nearly gettin' my noggin ventilated."

Bo just shook his head.

When they got back to the house, Theresa came

out onto the porch to greet them. She had her rifle in her hands and a grim, angry expression on her face. "Did you find anything?" she asked.

"Nope, just some horse tracks and what was left of a cigarette," Scratch replied. "Just enough to tell us the fella was there, and we already knew that."

Bo said, "If Cole's so anxious to get rid of you that he'll try a stunt like this, you'd better lie low for a while, ma'am. Is there any place you could go, some relatives who'd take you in?"

Theresa shook her head. "I didn't have any family except William, or any home except this place. And I won't be run off of it by a greedy scoundrel like Cole. I'm staying put."

Her tone didn't brook any argument, but Bo tried anyway. "We could hold down the fort here. Maybe you should go to Denver and talk to the governor. Cole's pet sheriff isn't going to do anything to protect you, so the state authorities may have to step in."

Again, Theresa gave a stubborn shake of her head. "I'm in the right. I don't need the sheriff or the governor."

"Bein' in the right won't stop a bullet," Scratch said bluntly. "Right or wrong don't mean a thing to a piece of lead."

"I'm not leaving," Theresa said. "We'll just have to think of a way to deal with Cole."

"It's hard to deal with a man like that short of killing him," Bo pointed out.

With a hard stare, Theresa looked levelly at him and said, "Then maybe that's exactly what we should do."

Chapter 15

Matt and Sam gathered up the fliers advertising the reopening of the Silver Belle Saloon. The gunfight with Cole's men had been an ugly interruption, but they still had a job to do. Folks watched them warily, though, as they walked around town tacking up the fliers. Even though these two young men had been in Buffalo Flat for only a short time, it was already obvious that they attracted trouble like a lodestone pulled iron filings.

As they worked, Matt asked quietly, "Are you sure that was Terri Kelly?"

"You saw her with your own eyes," Sam replied. "What do you think?"

Matt sighed and nodded. "It was her, all right. It's been a few years since we've seen her, but she hasn't changed all that much." He rubbed at his chin. "You reckon she knows that we're here?"

"I don't know. If we spotted her, it stands to reason that she could have spotted us. I guess it's a good thing she hasn't started shooting at us yet, like the last time."

Despite the situation, Matt had to chuckle. The

last time they had seen Terri Kelly, she had been standing on a wagon and banging away at them with a pistol, despite the fact that they were out of handgun range. She had been cussing a blue streak at the time, too.

The blood brothers had first met Terri while they were doing some scouting for a cavalry patrol. She had stumbled into their camp, claiming to be the only survivor of an Indian attack on the small settlement where she had served as the schoolteacher. The story was, in a way, true, but Terri Kelly was hardly the innocent schoolmarm she claimed to be. She had a long history as a criminal and swindler, and once she was back in what passed for civilization on the frontier, she had reverted to type pretty quickly. Eventually, she had thrown in with an outlaw and killer named Tom Thomas and a Texas gunfighter called Walker, both of whom were mortal enemies of Matt Bodine and Sam Two Wolves. After Thomas and Walker bit the dust, Terri had been run out of the town she had taken over with the help of her hired gunslicks, and that was the last Matt and Sam had seen of her.

Until now.

"Those two old-timers didn't seem like the sort of hombres Terri usually had working for her," Matt commented.

"You think maybe she's reformed?"

Matt frowned at his blood brother. "Terri Kelly reformed? That's one gal I can't ever imagine walkin' the straight and narrow!"

"Yes, that's pretty much the way I feel, too," Sam agreed with a nod, "but how can we rule out the possibility? They said that she owns a ranch now.

Maybe she's finally settled down and trying to lead a decent life."

Matt snorted. "I'll believe it when I see it . . . and even then I'll figure I'm just imagining things!"

"If Creel and Morton ride into town later to have that drink with us, we'll have to be careful what we say. Maybe they already know what sort of woman she is, maybe they don't. If they don't, they might not appreciate hearing how low-down she really is."

"But if they don't know the truth, they ought to," Matt argued. "They might not want to ride for her anymore if they did."

Sam considered that and nodded. "We'll try to find out more before we talk to them."

When they finished putting up the fliers, they walked back to the Silver Belle. As they approached the saloon, the strains of tinny music floated past the batwings to their ears.

"Sounds like one of the gals got that player piano working," Matt said with a smile.

"And they have some customers, too," Sam added.

It was true. The sounds of conversation and laughter blended with the music. As Bodine and Two Wolves entered the saloon, they saw about a dozen men lined up at the bar, and an equal number were sitting at the tables. A poker game was going on at one of them.

Charity and Lydia were behind the bar serving drinks. Janie, Wilma, Becky, and Kathy worked the tables. All of the women were smiling as they delivered buckets of beer and trays of whiskey-filled glasses.

Charity saw Matt and Sam and lifted a hand in greeting. As they came over to the bar, she said, "I don't believe it! People started streaming in here about half an hour ago, after all that shooting." Her expression grew more serious. "Some of the customers mentioned that you two were involved in that. Are you all right?"

"We're fine," Matt assured her. "But four more of Cole's men aren't."

Charity nodded. "That's what I heard. I know I should feel sorry about anyone dying, but it's hard to do when you're talking about those hard cases who work for Cole. They knew what they were getting into. At least, they should have."

"They called the tune," Matt said. "They had to dance to it."

"But you're sure you weren't hurt?"

"Not a bit," Sam told her.

"Would you like a drink?"

"Still a mite early in the day for that," Matt decided. "But if there's any coffee left in the pot from breakfast, I wouldn't mind having a cup of it." Sam nodded in agreement with that.

"We can do better than that," Charity said. "Lydia put on a fresh pot a while ago. I'll fetch some cups."

Sam was looking around the room. He spotted Judge A.A. Ashmore sitting at one of the tables near the stage in the rear of the room and told Charity, "We'll be over there with the lawyer." She nodded.

The blood brothers went over to the table, and Matt asked Ashmore, "Mind if we join you, Judge?"

Ashmore grunted. "Might as well. I'm already in Dutch with Cole for taking your side last night. He won't be happy when he hears about me drinking in here, so I might as well talk to you boys, too."

The lawyer had a bottle and a glass on the table, and judging by his flushed face and a slight slur in his voice, he had already filled and emptied the glass more than once. He tipped up the bottle and splashed more amber liquid into the glass.

Matt and Sam pulled out chairs and sat down. "How come you're worried about what Cole will think, Judge?" Matt asked. "You don't work for him like the sheriff does, do you?"

Ashmore tossed back the drink and licked his lips in appreciation. He scowled and said, "Sheriff Branch works for the county, not Junius Cole."

"But Cole is the more important man in the county," Sam said. "Probably the richest, too."

"No probably about it."

"And yet he wants to get richer still, even if he has to break the law to do it. Even if he has to resort to hired killers and murder."

Ashmore reached for the bottle again. "How much money is enough? As far as I know, no one has ever come up with a satisfactory answer to that question, have they?"

Matt took hold of the bottle at the same time Ashmore did. "Hold on, Judge," he said. "We need to have some straight palaver here. Just where do your loyalties lie? Because if they're with Cole, maybe you shouldn't be here in Miss Charity's saloon."

Ashmore drew himself up and tried to look dignified, which wasn't that easy to do with his nose swollen and red. "My loyalties lie with the law," he said, "not with any individuals. But at the same time, I've always been a practical man. Perhaps in the spirit of that practicality I've sometimes turned a blind eye to many of Cole's excesses. But when he starts ambushing women and setting his gunslingers on men like yourselves . . ."

"In other words," Matt said, "you're going to try to do the right thing, whether you really want to or not."

"Let go of that bottle, you young whelp," growled Ashmore. "Growing a conscience is damned thirsty work. It needs to be watered frequently."

Matt chuckled and let Ashmore have the whiskey bottle. "That ain't water," Matt said.

"It'll do." Ashmore filled the glass again, but he didn't drink it right away. Instead, he sat there staring at it.

Sam asked, "What about the sheriff? Any chance that *he'll* grow a conscience, too?"

Ashmore took a deep breath. "Sherman and I are old friends. I hate to speak ill of him. But his wife is . . . not well. Her needs sometimes outstrip the wages that the county is able to pay. Sherman has been forced to take help from various sources."

"Namely Cole," Matt said. "So the sheriff is in debt to him."

Ashmore shrugged. "We're all indebted to someone, aren't we, from the moment we first draw breath until the dirt is shoveled over us."

"What it comes down to is that anybody who crosses Cole can't expect any help from Sheriff Branch, whether they're in the right or not," Sam said.

Ashmore finally picked up the glass and swallowed the whiskey. His brooding silence was all the answer Sam's question needed.

"There's something else I'm wondering about," Sam went on after a moment. "Do you know a woman named Theresa Kincaid?"

The sudden switch in the conversation's direction took Ashmore by surprise. He stared owlishly at Sam. Before he could answer, Janie came up to the table carrying a tray with two cups on it.

"Charity said for me to bring this coffee to you, Matt," she told him as she bent over to set the tray on the table. Despite the fact that the dress she wore wasn't the usual low-cut saloon-girl get-up, the top couple of buttons were unfastened and she leaned over far enough so that Matt could see the creamy swell of her breasts and the top of the dark valley between them. He didn't think for a second that the exposure was accidental, either.

"Uh, one of those cups is mine," Sam said.

Without looking at him, Janie shoved a cup toward him and said, "Here." She kept smiling at Matt.

"Thank you," he told her.

"Any time. And anything you want, Matt. You just let me know."

"Janie!" Charity called from the bar. "Get back over here. You've got work to do."

Janie sighed, but kept smiling. "Anything, Matt," she said. "You remember that, hear?"

When the blonde had finally left the table and returned to the bar, Judge Ashmore cleared his throat and said, "That's a rather attractive young woman, Bodine, and she appears to have set her cap for you."

"I know, Judge."

"You should remember her former and perhaps future profession, though."

Matt shook his head. "I'm not one to look down on folks for doing whatever it takes to survive, as long as they're not breaking too many laws to do it."

"Speaking of which," Sam said, "I just asked you about Theresa Kincaid."

Ashmore frowned in puzzlement. "Are you imply-
ing that Mrs. Kincaid is some sort of criminal?"

"We just want to find out what you know about
her," Matt said.

Ashmore thought it over for a moment before
answering. "Not a great deal. Will Kincaid brought
her back with him from Denver about a year ago.
He'd gone up there on business. They were already
married when they got here. Will said she was a
schoolteacher, but she'd given it up to come down
here and be his wife."

Matt and Sam exchanged a glance. This wasn't
the first time Terri Kelly had claimed to be a
teacher.

"They seemed happy enough together," Ashmore
went on, "even though Will was considerably older
than her. He was a widower, lost his wife some years
ago when she died in childbirth. Baby didn't make
it, either. That left Will alone with nothing to care
about except his ranch. He worked hard and made
the Half Moon into a fine spread."

"He had to be pretty lonely, though," Sam said.

"If you're saying that Mrs. Kincaid took advantage of him and tricked him into marrying her, I
wouldn't know a thing about that," Ashmore said.
"Like I told you, they were already married when
Will came back from Denver with her. He and I
weren't close friends, you understand, but I talked
to him fairly often, and he never said anything
about being unhappy in his marriage."

"Most men wouldn't say anything," Matt pointed
out. "They'd keep something like that to themselves."

"You two know something you're not telling me,"
Ashmore snapped.

"What happened to Will Kincaid?" Matt said.

Ashmore hesitated as if he didn't want to answer any more questions, but then he grudgingly said, "He was killed. Shot in the back while he was out riding on his range."

"Does anybody know who did it?"

"The killer was never found. Will had already had trouble with Junius Cole, though. Cole wanted to buy him out and add the Half Moon range to the spread he already owned. So at least some people figured that Cole had something to do with Will being ambushed."

"Is the Half Moon such a good spread that Cole would kill for it?" Sam asked.

"It's a fine ranch, as I mentioned before," Ashmore said. "But the main reason Cole wanted to get his hands on it is because the spring that feeds the creek that's the main water supply on Cole's spread rises on the Half Moon."

"So whoever owns the Half Moon could cut off the water to Cole's ranch any time they wanted to," Matt said.

Ashmore nodded. "That's right."

"But Kincaid didn't want to sell out."

"He flatly refused to even consider it."

"Maybe Cole thought that if Kincaid was dead, his widow would be easier to deal with."

Ashmore looked uncomfortable. "No one could prove that. And there had been some rustling going on around here, too. The sheriff decided that Will Kincaid was probably shot by rustlers."

"Of course he did," Sam said. "That left Cole in the clear as far as the law was concerned. Not even Sheriff Branch could do anything about people suspecting him, though."

Ashmore shrugged. The conversation seemed

to have sobered him up considerably. "I've answered your questions," he said. "Now tell me why you're so curious about Mrs. Kincaid."

Matt looked at Sam, who nodded. Matt said, "We got a look at her earlier and thought we recognized her. If she's who we think she is, we've run into her before. She was mixed up with some pretty shady characters. Ever hear of a man named Tom Thomas?"

Ashmore's eyebrows rose in surprise. "The outlaw? He's dead now, isn't he?"

"Yeah, and so's Walker, the gunfighter from down Texas way. But Terri Kelly was tied up with both of them at one time or another."

"Terri Kelly?" the lawyer repeated. "That's Mrs. Kincaid's real name?"

Sam said, "For all we know, her name really is Theresa. Terri could be short for that. As for the Kelly part, who knows?"

Ashmore nodded slowly as he thought over what the blood brothers had told him. "Even if all this is true," he said, "even if Mrs. Kincaid really is this Kelly woman, you have no way of knowing if she's currently involved with anything illegal or even unsavory. She might have met Will Kincaid in Denver, fallen in love with him, and married him with the best and most honest of intentions."

"I suppose it could be true," Matt said with a shrug, "but we're havin' a hard time believing it."

"Good God, man, can't you give the lady the benefit of the doubt?"

"Hard to do when she's been responsible for the deaths of good men in the past." Something occurred to Matt. "When Will Kincaid was bushwhacked, who found his body?"

"Why, I believe his wife—" Ashmore's eyes

widened again. "Good Lord! You suspect she might have murdered her own husband?"

"I wouldn't put it past her," Matt said bluntly.

Ashmore shook his head. "I have a hard time believing *that*. In the days after Will's death she certainly seemed like a grieving widow to me."

"Terri always was a good actress," Matt said.

Ashmore shoved his chair back and lumbered to his feet. "I want nothing to do with this," he declared. "And before you set out to make trouble for the woman, you should ask yourselves—what if you're wrong about her?"

"Nobody said anything about making trouble for her," Sam replied. "But it might be a good idea to keep an eye on her and see if she's up to any mischief."

"What she's up to is fighting for her life and the survival of her ranch against Junius Cole . . . just like Miss MacKenzie and her friends have to worry about hanging onto this saloon. Perhaps you should be more concerned with that."

"Oh, we're concerned with Cole, all right," Matt said. "But just because you step on one rattlesnake doesn't mean there's not another one coiled up around the next rock."

And that was just about the best way he could think of to describe Terri Kelly, he thought—a rattlesnake, poised to strike.

She was that deadly.

And one of the questions he and Sam had to answer was whether or not those old-timers from Texas, Bo Creel and Scratch Morton, knew just what sort of serpent they had coiled their twine with.

Chapter 16

Theresa didn't say anything more about killing Junius Cole, nor did she explain her comment concerning that possibility. Bo had been able to tell that she meant it, though—she wanted Cole dead. And considering everything he had done, who could blame her for feeling that way? He was probably responsible for the death of her husband, as well as at least two attempts on her own life.

She rustled up a late lunch for the men, and after they had eaten, Hardy offered to show Bo and Scratch around the ranch.

"If you're gonna be ridin' this range, you might as well know where you're goin'," he said.

The Texans agreed and saddled a couple of horses from the remuda, since their own mounts had made the trip into Buffalo Flat and back already today. They rode out with the foreman while the sun was still high in the sky.

"The spread's too big to show you all of it today," Hardy said as the three men headed north, paralleling the line of the Prophet Mountains. He waved a hand toward the peaks and went on. "The boss lady's range runs way the hell and gone that way, back up in all those canyons. Only time they're a problem is durin' the spring roundup when we have to comb those breaks for any cows that've strayed up in 'em. Most of the stock's kept lower down, but some ol' mossyhorn's bound to stray from time to time."

"That's what I keep tellin' Bo here," Scratch said, "but he just don't listen."

"Yeah, but you're the ol' mossyhorn," Bo replied.

Hardy said, "Miz Kincaid told us about that gunfight in Buffalo Flat this mornin'. Was it really Matt Bodine and Sam Two Wolves who went up against four o' Cole's men?"

Bo nodded. "It was. We talked to them after the ruckus was over." He didn't mention the fact that he and Scratch had played a small part in the affair, stepping in when that backshooter had tried to kill Bodine and Two Wolves. "Did she say anything to you about trying to get them to come to work for the Half Moon?"

"Bodine and Two Wolves, you mean?" Hardy shook his head. "I'd love to have a couple of ringtailed rannihans like those two sidin' us, but Miz Kincaid never said nothin' to me about it."

Bo nodded. Clearly, Theresa had changed her mind, scared off maybe by the reputation that Bodine and Two Wolves had. Bo might not agree with that, but he would respect the lady's decision.

They saw quite a few head of stock during the afternoon, and to the experienced eyes of the Texans, the cattle appeared to be fine animals. They ought to be, thought Bo, since the graze was good here and there was plenty of water. There had been a time when all he wanted was a good ranch—and a family to raise on it along with the stock—but those days were far in the past.

And the life he'd led instead hadn't been a bad one, he reflected. At his age, a man did a lot of pondering on where he had been and where he was going. He and Scratch had seen a lot of sights, had some mighty good times, and helped a lot of folks who had gotten themselves in one sort of trouble or another. It might not be the life he would have chosen for himself, but as he looked back on it now, he thought it could have been a hell of a lot worse.

"What sort of deviltry has Cole been up to lately?" Scratch asked. "From the sound of it, he's been tryin' to run Miz Kincaid off this spread for a while."

"Those varmints who ride for him have stolen our cattle, poisoned our water holes, set fires, and tooken potshots at us," Hardy replied hotly. "None of the boys was killed, but a few got creased and decided they'd rather ride for somebody else. So did most of the rest of the crew. Only a handful of us were mule-headed enough to stick, and now with Johnny bein' gone, we're whittled down that much more. 'Course it helps that you two fellas are here now. You wouldn't happen to have ten or twenty amigos who'd like to sign on with the Half Moon, would you?"

"I wish we did," Bo said. "As fiddle-footed as Scratch and I have been all these years, though, we haven't made many lasting friends."

"Well, you've made some here by steppin' in to help the boss lady yesterday, that's for damn sure."

Late in the afternoon, still not having reached the limits of the Half Moon range, they turned around and rode back to the ranch headquarters, arriving there just as the sun was setting behind the Prophets. As they unsaddled, Scratch asked Bo, "Are we ridin' to Buffalo Flat this evenin' to have that drink with Bodine and Two Wolves?"

Bo nodded. "I thought we would, since everything appears to be peaceful here."

"What about askin' them to work out here? Seems like Miz Kincaid don't really want that anymore."

"That's what it seems like to me, too. But I don't reckon it'll hurt anything to sort of feel them out about it. The worst they can do is say that they're not interested."

It was a subdued supper. Everyone who had known Johnny Del Rio was still mourning his untimely death. Theresa turned in not long after the meal was finished. Bo and Scratch strolled out to the bunkhouse with the other hands.

"I'm thinkin' we ought to post a guard tonight," Hardy said as they paused outside.

Bo nodded. "That's a good idea. Scratch and I will take our turns standing watch, but it'll have to be later. We're going into town."

Hardy's voice was like flint as he asked, "Goin' to kill Junius Cole, like Miz Kincaid said?"

"We ain't hired killers," Scratch said as he took out the makin's and started to roll a quirly.

"We're going to talk to Matt Bodine and Sam Two Wolves," Bo explained. "They asked us to ride in and have a drink with them."

"Oh." Hardy shrugged. "Be careful, then. Trouble seems to congregate around hellions like those two."

Scratch licked the cigarette paper and rolled it

shut. "Folks have said pretty much the same thing about us," he said with a chuckle.

"We'll be back by midnight," Bo said. "We can re-lieve whoever's on guard duty then."

They saddled their own horses this time, and soon were on the way to Buffalo Flat. They had been on this trail earlier that day, so it wasn't hard for them to follow it, even by starlight.

"We've sure spent a heap of time ridin' back and forth between the ranch and town," Scratch commented.

"I've got a hunch that'll change after tonight. Between us and Bodine and Two Wolves—*especially* Bodine and Two Wolves—Cole has been hit pretty hard the past couple of days. But it won't take him long to regroup, and then he'll come after the Half Moon again. We'll probably have to hunker down out there until we figure out what to do about him."

"Somethin' to be said for stompin' on a snake when you see one."

"Like you told Hardy, we're not hired killers. I wouldn't hesitate to put a bullet in Cole's mangy carcass if he ever came out of his hole and tried to do his own dirty work, but a man like that usually hides behind the guns of other men."

"Well, maybe we can think of a way of drawin' him out in the open."

Bo nodded. "That's something to ponder on, all right."

By the time they saw the lights of Buffalo Flat looming in front of them, they hadn't come up with any other ideas. That would have to wait until after they had talked to Bodine and Two Wolves, Bo thought.

The settlement was small enough so that they

didn't have any trouble finding the Silver Belle Saloon. Judging by the number of horses tied up at the hitch racks in front of the saloon, the place was doing pretty good business. Not as good as the Colorado Palace down the street, which was full, Bo noted as he and Scratch rode past, but still not bad. They dismounted in front of the Silver Belle and wrapped their reins around the rack.

Scratch drew in a deep breath as they stepped through the batwings and said, "I love the smell of a good saloon."

"You like stale smoke and whiskey?"

"Not so much the smells themselves, but the good times they recall."

Bo could understand that. Sometimes when he smelled coffee brewing and biscuits cooking, that combined aroma transported him back for a moment to a different time, a time when his wife and kids had still been alive, and mornings with his family had been special. A time that was long gone now, but would never be forgotten.

The Texans' spurs jingled as they walked over to the bar. Behind the hardwood, a young, pretty woman with long, thick red curls was tending bar. She smiled at them and asked, "What'll you have, gents?"

"Beer for both of us," Bo said. He and Scratch needed to keep clear heads while they were in Buffalo Flat. The settlement was the headquarters of their enemy, after all.

While the redhead was drawing their beers, they looked around. The Silver Belle's customers were a fairly even mix of townsmen and cowboys from the ranches in the area. Several attractive young women worked the tables, delivering drinks and flirting a little with the customers. Bo looked for Bodine and Two Wolves, but didn't see the two young men. He turned back to the bar as the redhead set a pair of full, foaming mugs on it. "Matt Bodine and Sam Two Wolves asked us to meet them here tonight," he said. "Have you seen them around?"

The redhead smiled. "You're those two fellas from Texas who gave them a hand this morning, aren't you? I thought I recognized the accent." Without waiting for either Bo or Scratch to answer, she went on. "Those beers are on the house. Matt and Sam went upstairs a while ago, but they should be back down soon. Why don't you have a seat at one of the tables, and I'll let them know you're here?"

"We're much obliged for your kindness, ma'am," Scratch said. He and Bo picked up their beers and walked over to an empty table toward the back of the room, while the redhead turned her bartending duties over to one of the other young women and went upstairs.

She came back down a couple of minutes later, followed by Bodine and Two Wolves. They came over to the table. Bo and Scratch both stood up politely since the redhead was with them.

The men shook hands all around, then Bodine said, "This is Miss Charity MacKenzie. She owns the place."

Bo raised his eyebrows as he said, "Begging your pardon, ma'am, but you seem a mite young to be running a saloon."

"I inherited it from my great-uncle. I don't really own it by myself, though. All of us girls have a share in it."

Bo nodded. That was an unusual setup, but if it was the way the young women wanted it, that was no business of his. He said, "I hear Junius Cole isn't too happy about the situation, either."

"Why don't we all sit down?" Charity suggested. "I hear that you've had your own share of troubles with Cole, and any enemy of that skunk is a friend of mine."

Once the five of them were seated and one of the other women had brought over a beer for Bodine and a cup of coffee for Two Wolves, Bodine said, "Why don't you fellas start by telling us how you got mixed up with Cole?"

"Pure-dee luck," Scratch said. "I reckon whether it was good or bad depends on your point o' view. It was bad for those fellas who were tryin' to bushwhack Miz Theresa Kincaid."

Bo noticed that Bodine and Two Wolves exchanged a glance at the mention of Theresa's name. They didn't say anything, though, as Scratch went on to describe the fight with Cole's men in typically colorful terms.

"After we ventilated three of the polecats and sent the other one runnin'," Scratch concluded, "we rode back to the Half Moon with Miz Kincaid and agreed to sign on with her. Poor woman needs all the help she can get, what with Cole and his hired killers gunnin' for her."

"I'm sure Mrs. Kincaid would like to hire some more good hands," Bo put in. "And it would help if they were handy with their guns, too."

Bodine and Two Wolves didn't take the hint, but Charity understood what Bo and Scratch were getting at. She said, "I don't know what my friends and I would have done without Matt and Sam helping

us. I don't think we ever would have made it alive
to Buffalo Flat." And Charity didn't want to lose
their help now, Bo reflected. She was at war with
Cole every bit as much as Theresa was.

And it sure as hell made sense that Bodine and
Two Wolves would rather stay here, living in a
saloon with six beautiful young women, than be
holed up on a ranch with one beautiful young
woman and five scruffy ranch hands.

Bodine said, "I know there's trouble between the
spread you ride for and Cole. What's that all
about?"

Bo took up the story, filling in the details, as far
as he knew them, of the ongoing clash between the
Half Moon and Cole's riders. "It makes sense that
William Kincaid was murdered by one of Cole's
gunmen," he finished.

"You'd think so," Two Wolves said, and Bo wondered just what the young man meant by that.

"You don't put any stock in Sheriff Branch's
theory about rustlers drygulching Kincaid, do
you?"

"That's not necessarily what I meant," Two
Wolves replied guardedly.

Bo frowned. "I get the feeling you two are trying
to work your way around to something. Whatever it
is, why don't you just spit it out?"

Bodine swallowed the last of the beer in his mug
and then took a deep breath. He looked at Two
Wolves again, who nodded encouragement. Bodine
leveled his gaze at Bo and Scratch and asked, "Just
how much do you really know about Mrs. Kincaid?"

"We know she's a widow woman in trouble,"
Scratch said. "What are you gettin' at, Bodine?"

Instead of answering directly, Bodine said, "Just

to make sure we're talking about the right person, Mrs. Kincaid was the woman driving the buckboard as you left town this morning, right?"

"That's right," Bo said. "We came to pick up the body of one of her hands, who was killed last night by Cole's pet gunfighter, Lucas Tate."

"We assumed that was the case," Two Wolves said. "You see, Mr. Creel, when Matt and I got a look at the woman who was with you, we recognized her. We've met her before."

"You're talkin' about Miz Kincaid?" Scratch asked.

"We're talking about Terri Kelly," Bodine said flatly. "That was the name she was using the last time we saw her."

Bo shrugged. "Theresa . . . Terri . . . could be the same woman. Where did you know her, in Denver?"

"No, the last place we saw her was a little settlement up in the Medicine Bows."

"Teaching school there, was she?"

Bodine shook his head. "Running a saloon. Running the whole town, in fact, with the help of a hard case named Walker and a bunch of other gunslingers."

The Texans stared at him in disbelief for a long moment before Bo finally said, "You must be mixed up. Mrs. Kincaid isn't that sort of woman."

"*I* run a saloon," Charity pointed out.

"And I mean no offense to you, ma'am," Bo said. "But from what young Bodine here is saying, the woman he's talking about was some sort of . . . outlaw queen or something."

Bodine nodded. "That's about the size of it, Mr. Creel. Before she was involved with Walker, Terri Kelly was mixed up with a hard case called Tom

Thomas. And before that she had a long history of being a criminal and swindler stretching back to when she was a girl in St. Louis."

"We crossed trails with her several times," Two Wolves put in, "and came close to getting killed because of her treachery nearly every time."

"Well, I just don't believe it!" Scratch burst out as he leaned forward in his chair. "Miz Kincaid's a fine young woman, and she's had enough bad luck without lies bein' spread about her by a couple o' young rapscallions who don't know any better!"

Bodine's face tightened with anger as Scratch's words lashed at him, but Two Wolves remained calm. He said, "I can understand why you feel that way, Mr. Morton. Terri Kelly is a consummate actress, and she's had a great deal of experience at getting people to believe what she wants them to believe about her. Especially men."

"Damn it, boy, I'm not some old geezer who'll get taken in by the first pretty face that comes along—"

"Take it easy," Bo said to his partner. That was exactly what Scratch was, he thought, but it wouldn't do any good to point that out now. As Scratch sat back reluctantly, Bo went on to Bodine and Two Wolves. "Maybe you're mistaken. Maybe Mrs. Kincaid just looks like this Kelly woman."

"We thought about that," Bodine admitted, "but we both got a good look at Mrs. Kincaid. She's the same woman, all right. She's Terri Kelly."

Bo couldn't help but think about the way Theresa had looked when she heard that Matt Bodine and Sam Two Wolves were in Buffalo Flat. Whether he wanted to believe it or not, her reaction could have been one of recognition. He had to admit that to himself.

"Even if you're right," he said, "that doesn't mean she's still up to no good. People can change, you know."

"I reckon they can," Bodine said.

"Where Terri's concerned, we'd have to see it to believe it, though," Two Wolves added.

"Well, by God, you're wrong this time," Scratch said. "Come out to the ranch with us and see for yourselves."

"Maybe we'll just do that," Bodine replied coolly. "Could be you and Mr. Creel will be the ones who see for yourselves, though, Mr. Morton."

Scratch scraped his chair back and stood up. "Come on, then," he challenged. "No point in sittin' here flappin' our gums any longer."

Bo put out a hand to stop him. "Hold on. Mrs. Kincaid has had a hard couple of days. She'd already turned in before we started to town. We're not going to ride out there and roust her out of her bed just on your say-so, Bodine."

The young man shrugged. "It wasn't my idea," he reminded Bo. "Your partner came up with it."

"Why don't you come to the Half Moon tomorrow?" Bo suggested. "Then we can clear the air once and for all."

Bodine nodded. "We'll be there. If you want to get an honest reaction from Terri, though, you'd better not tell her that we're coming. If she knows she's about to be exposed, she'll hatch some scheme to get out of it."

"Unless you're lyin' through your teeth about the whole thing," Scratch snapped.

Bodine stood up at that. "I don't like being called a liar, even by a gent I ought to respect because he's old enough to be my granddaddy."

"I'm not too old to handle you, you young skalleyhooter!"

Bo and Two Wolves both came to their feet, as did Charity. The loud, angry voices had gotten some attention from the saloon's other patrons, and the noise in the place had quieted down considerably as men turned their heads to watch the confrontation and wait to see what was going to happen next.

"Let's all settle down," Bo said. He wasn't sure how he had gotten appointed to be the voice of reason, but somebody had to do it. "There's no point in anybody getting all riled up until we know for sure that this isn't just a simple mistake."

"It's no mistake," Bodine said.

"We'll find that out tomorrow. And we won't say anything to Mrs. Kincaid about it."

"But that ain't fair," Scratch protested. "I don't like ambushin' her that way."

"If we're mistaken, it's not really an ambush, is it?" Two Wolves said.

"Just let it go until tomorrow," Bo said again. He nodded politely to Charity. "It was nice to meet you, Miss MacKenzie, and we're obliged to you for the beers. Good luck with your enterprise here."

"Thank you, Mr. Creel. I hope—" Charity stopped short and shrugged her shoulders. "Come to think of it, I don't really know what I hope."

Bo felt sort of the same way. He knew the friction that had sprung up, pitting him and Scratch against Bodine and Two Wolves, was unfortunate, though. He had hoped that they would all be friends.

As the hum of conversation and laughter in the saloon resumed its normal level, Bo steered a still-angry Scratch out of the place. As they mounted up and turned their horses toward the Half Moon, Scratch said, "Those boys were either lyin' or plumb out of their heads."

"They don't strike me as the sort who'd lie," Bo said.

"Well, then, they're just crazy. Miz Kincaid's a fine young woman."

"Who we haven't known for even two days yet."

Scratch glared over at him. "Don't tell me you think they're right about her!"

"I don't know. I'd like to find out, though. That's why we're going to do like Bodine asked and not say anything about this to her."

Scratch muttered quite a bit, but didn't continue the argument. After they had ridden a ways through the darkness, he said, "Even if Bodine and Two Wolves are tellin' the truth about who Miz Kincaid used to be, that don't mean she's like that now. Like you said, folks can change, can't they?"

"We'll see," Bo said.

Chapter 17

The conversation with the two old-timers from Texas hadn't gone as well as Matt and Sam had hoped it would, but neither of them were really surprised by that. All Bo and Scratch had seen of Terri Kelly was a plucky young widow beset by troubles and menaced by a man who was undoubtedly really out to drive her from her ranch and grab the spread for himself.

But the fact that Junius Cole actually was a ruthless son of a bitch didn't mean that Terri was innocent. Matt was still mighty curious about the way William Kincaid had really met his death.

The rest of the night passed quietly. Matt and Sam were both convinced that Cole would make another move against Charity and the Silver Belle sooner or later, but after the violence of the past couple of days, he might wait a while before trying anything else. For one thing, he had lost quite a few men and probably needed to come up with some more hired guns, and for another, even though he controlled Buffalo Flat, he had to be careful not to be too blatantly lawless. There were still some honest folks who lived here, and if Cole ran too roughshod over the citizenry, some of them might take it on themselves to go to Denver and complain to the governor. With his tame sheriff backing him up, the last thing Cole would want would be for outside authorities to come in and start poking around.

So he would bide his time until he was convinced it was the right moment to strike again. That might be a day from now, or a week, Matt reflected, but the one thing you could count on was that sooner or later that moment would come.

And when it did, the air would once again be filled with the smell of gun smoke. . . .

In the meantime, after another fine breakfast prepared the next morning by Lydia, the blood brothers saddled their horses and took the western trail out of Buffalo Flat, heading for the Prophet Mountains and the Half Moon Ranch.

As they rode out of the settlement, they weren't aware of the eyes watching them from inside the Colorado Palace. Even though it was fairly early in the morning, Lucas Tate already had a drink in front of him on the bar. He never slept much. A barely contained rage was banked within him, and that heat was fueled by the whiskey he consumed almost nonstop. It kept him awake most nights. That, and the ghosts of the men he had killed, going all the way back to the first one when Tate had been only sixteen years old.

Sixteen or not, he'd been a man full growed. A man capable of jerking iron and pulling trigger faster than most men.

A couple of decades had rolled past since then, and Tate had lost track of exactly how many men had fallen to his gun. He wasn't vain enough to care about numbers. He just cared about staying alive and earning enough money for whores and poker and whiskey.

He threw back the drink and then strolled over to the stairs. As he went up them, he thought about Bodine and Two Wolves. Both of them were fast, but Bodine was special, the sort of gunman who drew comparisons to Smoke Jensen, who was said to be the fastest of them all. Tate had never crossed trails with Jensen, but destiny had brought Matt Bodine to Buffalo Flat.

And who was Lucas Tate to argue with destiny?

Tate went down the second-floor hallway to the door of Junius Cole's room. He knocked on it. A moment later Cole's sleepy voice called, "Who the hell is it?"

"It's Lucas, Boss," Tate replied.

He heard Cole's footsteps approach the door. Cole jerked it open. He was dressed in a pair of long underwear. His usually carefully combed hair was disheveled from sleep, and his eyes were red. Tate glanced past him at the bed and saw Anna Malone lying there, still asleep, the sheet twisted so that the smooth, bare expanse of her back was revealed down to the swell of her buttocks.

Cole stuck an unlit cigar in his mouth and chomped down on it. "What do you want?" he asked.

Tate inclined his head toward the street. "I just saw Bodine and Two Wolves ride by," he said. "Looked like they were on their way out of town."

Cole grunted. "So?"

"They were headed west, toward your spread—and the Half Moon."

Cole shook his head, indicating that he didn't know what the gunfighter was getting at.

"Didn't you say that Bodine and Two Wolves were talking last night to those two old codgers who ride for Mrs. Kincaid now?"

Cole rubbed at his jaw and grimaced in thought. "Yeah," he said. "Yeah, that's true." He was an important man, and there were plenty of people in Buffalo Flat who wanted to curry favor with him. One of the townies who had witnessed the conversation in the Silver Belle between Bodine and Two Wolves and the two Texans had come to the Colorado Palace later to pass along the information to Cole.

"What if Bodine and Two Wolves are going out there to sign on with Mrs. Kincaid?" Tate said. "That'll make getting your hands on her ranch that much harder."

"The gent who told me about it said it looked like they weren't getting along too well with those old-timers."

Tate shrugged. "Maybe not, but that still doesn't mean they won't get mixed up with Mrs. Kincaid. She's a fine-looking woman, after all."

"She's a damn stubborn woman, that's what she is," Cole said with a scowl. "I thought sure after her husband was killed, she'd take whatever I offered her and sell out. Hell, before it was over I even offered to give her a fair price, and you know how I hate to do that! I figured it was a real stroke of luck when somebody bushwhacked Kincaid, but it didn't work out that way."

Tate nodded. He knew what most people in Buffalo Flat thought. Folks assumed that Cole was behind the ambush that had taken Will Kincaid's life. As a matter of fact, though, Cole hadn't had a thing to do with it, at least not as far as Tate knew, and he didn't think Cole was keeping any secrets from him. Cole had tried to take advantage of the situation, of course, but somebody else had murdered Kincaid.

"What about Bodine and Two Wolves?" Tate asked. "You want them stopped before they get to the Half Moon and talk to the Kincaid woman?"

"I want 'em stopped, period," Cole snapped. "Those women at the Silver Belle will fold up pretty quickly if they don't have those two bastards to protect them. Take care of it, Lucas."

Tate nodded.

"You'll have to move fast, though," Cole went on. "If they already left town, they've got a lead on you."

"They weren't hurrying," Tate pointed out, "and they don't have any reason to get in a lather. I can get ahead of them."

Cole nodded curtly. "Do it, then."

With that, he turned to go back to his bed, where a nude Anna Malone waited for him. Tate pulled the door closed and thought about Anna, about how smooth and fine her bare back looked. Cole didn't know it, but Tate had been with Anna a time or two, and he figured he would be again. Maybe even tonight. If he succeeded in killing Bodine and Two Wolves, his employer would be in a celebratory mood and would probably drink too much. Booze put Cole to sleep, and once he was passed out, Anna could do pretty much what she wanted.

Smiling faintly, Tate went to get his rifle from his room.

* * *

One of the customers in the Silver Belle had told Matt and Sam how to get to the Half Moon, something they hadn't thought of the previous night until after Bo and Scratch were gone. The man, a cowhand on one of the other area ranches, had told them that they would be riding across the Diamond C first. That was Cole's spread.

"But don't worry, there aren't any fences or gates or anything like that," the cowboy had explained. "Not even Cole would mess with the road. Better not get off the trail, though. Cole's riders get a mite gun-happy when they find anybody just wanderin' around."

"We'll keep that in mind," Sam had promised.

Now, as the blood brothers followed the trail across the Diamond C, Matt commented, "This looks like a fine spread. Seems like Cole would be satisfied with it."

"You know how some men are. They're never satisfied, no matter how much they've got. And there's the matter of the water, too."

"If I controlled the spring where a neighbor's creek came up, and that neighbor started giving me trouble, I'd be more likely to close it off and stop the creek from flowing instead of leaving it alone."

Sam shook his head. "No, you wouldn't. You grew up out here in the West. You'd never interfere with someone else's water, no matter what the provocation."

"Well, maybe not," Matt admitted. "But I'm surprised Terri hasn't thought of threatening Cole with it before now. She never hesitated to resort to whatever it took to get what she wanted."

"Remember, she's pretending to be respectable

now," Sam reminded him. "Maybe she doesn't want to show her hand yet and reveal how ruthless she can be. Or maybe she's just trying to do the right thing."

Matt grunted, indicating just how doubtful he thought that proposition was.

By the time they figured they were off of Cole's range and onto the Half Moon, they hadn't seen any other riders, although they had spotted some cattle grazing in the distance. Matt's eyes narrowed as he gazed along the trail in front of them. He nodded in that direction and said, "Little dust in the air up yonder."

"I see it," Sam said. "Could be any number of reasons for it."

"Yeah, but I don't like the looks of that little ridge—"

Matt stopped short in voicing his suspicion when he saw the sun strike a reflection off something on top of the small, wooded ridge he was looking at. Instantly he shouted, "Ambush!" and yanked his stallion to the right, sending the horse lunging off the trail in that direction.

Sam went the other way, veering sharply to the left and kicking his paint into a run. At the same time, as the blood brothers were splitting up, the crack of a rifle and the whine of a bullet sounded practically simultaneously. The slug sizzled harmlessly through the air between Matt and Sam, but if not for their swift, instinctive reactions, it might have ventilated one of them.

Matt headed for some trees that represented the nearest cover. He leaned forward over the stallion's neck to make himself a smaller target, and as he did so he heard the sound of another bullet passing close by his head. That told him there were either two bushwhackers, or if there was only one, the hidden rifleman was concentrating on him and letting Sam go.

That might prove to be a mistake, Matt thought. He glanced over his shoulder and saw that Sam had disappeared. A grim smile tugged at Matt's mouth as a third bullet kicked up dust just in front of the galloping stallion. Sam must have found a gully or some other cover, and now he would be getting ready to turn the tables on the drygulcher.

The trees loomed up in front of Matt. He pulled his Winchester from the saddle boot, kicked his feet out of the stirrups, and left the saddle in a dive. He landed agilely and rolled behind the thick trunk of a pine. The stallion ran on to safety while Matt ended up lying on his belly behind the tree, his Winchester pointing toward the ridge where the would-be killer was hiding.

A couple of bullets struck the trunk of the tree above him and showered pieces of bark down on him. Matt's keen eyes spotted the puff of smoke that marked the bushwhacker's location. He cranked off three rounds in that direction, keeping the bushwhacker occupied while Sam snuck up on him.

A couple of hundred yards away, Sam had left his horse in a brushy arroyo that ran roughly parallel with the trail. He moved along it now on foot, getting closer to the ridge. When he reached a stretch of rugged terrain dotted with boulders and thick clumps of brush, he climbed out of the gully and began working his way around behind the hidden rifleman, who was still shooting at Matt on the far side of the trail.

Judging by the sound of the shots, Sam was pretty sure there was only one bushwhacker. The man was in a dense stand of trees on top of the ridge. Sam would have to approach him from the other side of the ridge. This side didn't have enough cover.

He heard the familiar sound of his blood brother's Winchester as Matt kept the man busy ducking. Sam took advantage of that distraction to come up in a crouch and sprint for twenty yards or so. That took him far enough so that the bushwhacker didn't have a good angle to spot him now. From that point he was able to move faster.

But not fast enough. The shooting from the top of the ridge stopped, and a moment later Sam heard the sound of hoofbeats. The bushwhacker must have figured out that Sam was trying to circle around him. That was the only explanation for his flight.

"Damn it," Sam grated as he threw his rifle to his shoulder and fired several times toward the sound of the horse, triggering the Winchester as fast as he could work its lever. He didn't expect to hit anything, but blind luck sometimes smiled in even the unlikeliest of circumstances.

Not in this case, though. The hoofbeats never faltered. Sam lowered the rifle and listened to them as they faded in the distance until he could no longer hear them.

Matt must not have realized that the bushwhacker had fled, because he was still shooting toward the top of the ridge. During a lull in the firing, Sam cupped his hands around his mouth and shouted, "Hold your fire! Hold your fire! You're just wasting lead!"

Matt bellowed back, "Did I get him?"

"Get him, hell! He's gone!"

Unless the whole thing was a clever trick of some sort. That possibility had occurred to Sam. Unfortunately, the quickest and surest way to find out whether or not that was the case was to step out into the open, figuratively painting a nice, big target on his chest.

That was what he did, moving from cover and walking straight toward the spot where the rifleman had been hidden. It was a tense few moments before Sam reached his destination, but no shots rang out.

Sam had been trained in reading sign by his father, Medicine Horse, and other warriors of the Cheyenne, so to his eyes the tracks left by the bushwhacker and his horse were blindingly obvious. He studied the prints for several minutes, but there was nothing unusual about them. As he turned and walked down the slope, he saw that Matt had emerged from the trees on the other side of the trail and was mounted once again on the big gray stallion. Matt had the reins of Sam's paint in his hand.

"I figured you must have found a gully over yonder and probably left this nag there," Matt said as Sam walked up. "So I found him and brought him back."

"Much obliged," Sam said as he took the reins from him, "but he's not a nag. Nor is he as crazy as that walleyed brute of yours."

Matt had started the exchange of insults out of habit as much as anything else. Since they were even, he didn't continue with it. Instead he asked, "Did you get a look at that bastard?"

Sam swung up into the saddle and shook his

head. "I'm afraid not. He took off for the tall and uncut before I could get close to him."

"Whoever he was, he's not that good with a rifle. He had a couple of pretty clear shots at me while I was lighting a shuck for those trees, and he missed 'em both."

"He probably would have drilled you with his first one, though, if you hadn't spotted him," Sam said as they resumed their journey toward the Half Moon Ranch. "Surely it wasn't just the dust he left in the air when he rode up on that ridge that tipped you off."

"No, I saw the sun glint off his rifle barrel." Matt grinned. "At least, I figured it was a rifle barrel and acted accordingly."

"And if it had turned out to be something harmless?"

"Well, I've always believed it's better to look a mite foolish than it is to look dead."

Sam chuckled. He couldn't argue with that.

"You think that was one of Cole's men?" Matt went on.

"Who else around here wants us dead?"

"What about the lady—and I use the term loosely—we're goin' to see?"

Sam glanced over at him and frowned. "Creel and Morton said they wouldn't tell Terri that we're coming out to the ranch today."

"Yeah, but you know how she is. She's got Morton wrapped around her little finger already."

"I'm not so sure about Creel, though. He seems like a pretty cagey old bird."

"Only takes one of them to give the game away," Matt pointed out.

"You really think Terri would send somebody to bushwhack us?"

"As much as she hates us, I'd say it's possible. And if we were dead, we couldn't foul up whatever scheme she's working on."

"That makes sense," Sam admitted. "Between her and Cole, we need eyes in the back of our heads."

"No reason this should be any different than all the other scrapes we've gotten ourselves into," Matt said.

They rode on in silence, and soon came in sight of the ranch headquarters. It was a good-looking place on the far side of a creek, up a little rise with a hill behind it. The sprawling log house looked sturdy, as did the bunkhouse and the other out-buildings and the corrals. As owners of their own ranches up in Montana, Matt and Sam knew a good spread when they saw one, and the Half Moon appeared to be a fine ranch, well worth fighting for.

"I wouldn't mind helping to defend this place from Cole," Matt commented as their horses splashed across the creek, "if only it wasn't Terri Kelly I'd be helping."

"I know what you mean," Sam agreed.

Their approach hadn't gone unnoticed. A couple of curs came bounding toward them, barking loudly. Matt and Sam didn't know how many hands were left on the place, or if they were here or out on the range, but the commotion was bound to attract the attention of anyone who was around.

Sure enough, a man came out of the barn carrying a rifle. He was short and middle-aged, with a brushy gray mustache.

At the same time, Bo Creel appeared on the porch of the main house. He lifted a hand in greeting as Matt and Sam reined to a stop in front of the house.

"Scratch has gone to fetch Mrs. Kincaid and tell her that we've got company," Bo said quietly. He nodded toward the man approaching from the barn. "In the meantime, this is Hardy Thomas, the Half Moon's foreman."

As Matt glanced at the rifle the man was carrying, he couldn't help but wonder if Thomas had been the ambusher on top of that ridge. The foreman gave him and Sam a friendly but wary nod of greeting and said, "Howdy, boys."

Bo started to introduce the newcomers. "This is—"

"Matt Bodine and Sam Two Wolves," a new voice finished for him as the woman stepped out of the house, followed by Scratch Morton. She fixed a cold, level stare on them as she added, "Hello, Matt."

"Terri," he said with a nod, itching to know which direction trouble was going to come from.

Because trouble always followed Terri Kelly.

Chapter 18

So she wasn't even going to deny it, Bo thought as he watched the way Theresa regarded the two visitors. He had been right when he suspected that her reaction upon hearing their names meant she knew them.

But that didn't necessarily mean what Bodine and Two Wolves had said about her the night before in the Silver Belle was true.

"Wait a minute," Scratch said with a surprised look on his weathered face. "You really do know these fellas, like they claimed?"

"I know them," Theresa said. She turned her head to glare at Bo. "And you knew they were coming out here today, didn't you?"

Bo shrugged. "They said something about it last night when we were having a drink with them in Buffalo Flat."

Theresa's voice was cold as she said, "I thought you two were my friends."

"We *are* your friends!" Scratch exclaimed. "I never believed a word of anything these varmints said about you!"

"But they were telling the truth about knowing you, ma'am," Bo pointed out. "I reckon your name really is Terri Kelly?"

"My name is Theresa Kincaid. I've been called Terri in the past, but my mother named me Theresa. And I was legally married to William, so Kincaid is my name, too." Her chin jutted defiantly. "And I don't see why I should have to dignify any other lies these two have spread about me by denying them."

Bodine rested his hands on the saddle horn and leaned forward. "It's not a lie that you swore you'd get Sam and me. The last time we saw you, you said you'd hunt us down and kill us. You would have ventilated us right then if we hadn't been out of handgun range."

Theresa sniffed. "That was years ago, and anyway, things are often said in the heat of anger that people don't really mean."

"But you did threaten them?" Bo said.

"And you took over a town up in Wyoming with the help of a bunch of outlaws?" Scratch added.

Theresa glared at all four of them, crossed her arms over her bosom, and heaved an angry sigh. "You're going to force me to defend myself, aren't you?"

Hardy Thomas spoke up. "You don't have to defend nothin' as far as I'm concerned, ma'am. You own the Half Moon, and I ride for the brand."

Theresa smiled faintly. "Thank you, Hardy," she said. "I appreciate that." The smile disappeared as she looked at Bodine and Two Wolves again. "As for you two, since this *is* my land, I'll thank you to get off of it. You're not welcome here."

Bodine gave a curt nod. "If that's what you want, Terri."

"And I'll thank you not to call me that. That part of my life is over."

"Come on, Sam," Bodine said. He started backing his horse away. The implication was obvious—he didn't want to turn his back on her. Theresa's face, already flushed with anger, grew even darker at the insult.

Two Wolves followed Bodine's example. When they were several yards away, they wheeled their horses and put the animals into an easy lope.

"Don't bother comin' out here again!" Scratch called after them. "You heard the lady! You ain't welcome!"

Bodine and Two Wolves didn't look back as they rode away.

Theresa sighed again, then turned toward Bo. "Was this your idea?"

Bo would have taken the blame for it, but before he could reply Scratch said, "No, ma'am, as a matter of fact, it was me."

She turned back to him, and there was a note of hurt in her voice as she said, "You, Scratch? I thought you trusted me."

He snatched his Stetson off his head and looked miserable as he said, "I do, ma'am, I surely do. When them two started spoutin' all that stuff about knowin' you before, and about how you used to run with outlaws, I told 'em they were either mixed up or crazy and said they ought to come out here and see for themselves. I didn't know—"

"That they were telling the truth?"

"*Were* they telling the truth?" Bo asked quietly.

"You don't believe me, either?"

"Before I get all the way into a shooting war, I like to know which side I ought to be on," Bo said.

"Like I said, I used to be known as Terri Kelly. I did some things to survive, things I'm not proud of, but that's the way it is on the frontier sometimes. It's hard to find anybody who's walked the straight and narrow every step of their lives."

"Yes, ma'am, we know that for a fact," Scratch said. "There have been times when Bo an' me have been in trouble up to our necks and had to cut a few corners, so we know just what you're talkin' about."

A tear welled from the corner of Theresa's right eye. "You mean . . . you mean you're willing to give me the benefit of the doubt and continue helping me protect this place from Cole, no matter what I might have done in the past?"

"Why, sure we are!"

She turned to look at Bo. "What about you, Mr. Creel? Will you stick . . . or would you rather abandon me?"

That was slick of her, putting the question like that, Bo thought. He said, "I don't turn my back on folks in trouble. Never have and never will. And we've seen plenty of proof that Cole is a skunk who wants to take over this spread any way he can." Bo took a deep breath and blew it out. "I'll stick."

Theresa smiled as another tear joined the first one. "Thank you," she said. She laid a hand on Scratch's arm. "Thank you both. And you, too, Hardy. Your loyalty means a lot to me." She straightened her back, squared her shoulders, and wiped away the tears. "Now, let's all get on about our business, and we'll pretend that this ugly little incident never happened. There'll be no need to speak of it to Mort and Hector when they get back from checking on the stock."

"No, ma'am," Hardy agreed. "No need at all."

Theresa nodded and turned to go back in the house. When the door had closed behind her, Scratch glowered at Bo and said, "Now, don't you feel like the biggest damn-blasted fool on the face of the earth?"

"Why should I feel like a fool?" Bo returned. "You were the one who suggested that Bodine and Two Wolves ride out here."

"Yeah, but that was because I didn't believe what they were sayin'."

"Which turned out to be true, more or less."

Scratch shook his head. "You just don't understand, do you? Folks can change. It don't matter what Miz Kincaid's done in the past, no more'n it matters what you and I done. And you *know* some o' that was a mite sketchy."

"I'm willing to give just about anybody the benefit of the doubt," Bo said. "We'll wait and see what happens."

"Hide and watch," Scratch said. "Just hide and watch."

"You believe her?" Sam asked as they rode away from the Half Moon's headquarters.

Matt snorted derisively. "If Terri Kelly told me that the sun was shinin', I'd reach for my rain slicker. I don't think she's capable of telling the truth."

"If it was anybody else, you'd probably be willing to believe that they might have changed."

"Yeah, but it's not somebody else. It's Terri."

"Morton believes her."

"Morton would believe anything a pretty woman

told him, and I've never denied that Terri's mighty pretty . . . until you get to know her." Matt grunted and shook his head. "She's probably back there right now telling them how we twisted everything around and how she was just some poor innocent gal who got taken advantage of by big bad men. She might even squeeze out a tear or two to make it all more convincing."

"I wouldn't be surprised if you're right," Sam admitted. "So what do we do now? Can we just sit back and do nothing while Cole tries to grab her ranch?"

"It's not our fight," Matt said stubbornly. "Anyway, we've got enough to worry about trying to protect Charity and Lydia and those other gals from Cole. He wants to run them out of business, just like he wants to stampede Terri and take over the Half Moon."

Sam mused, thought it over, then said, "Cole's fighting a war on two fronts, and he's had losses on both of them. He's going to have to regroup. But when he has . . ."

"He'll come after Charity again," Matt said. "Count on it."

Anna Malone was sitting at a table in the Colorado Palace, dealing a hand of solitaire, when Lucas Tate came into the saloon with an angry scowl on his face. He spotted her and stalked over to the table.

"Where's Cole?" he asked without any sort of greeting.

"It's good to see you, too, Lucas," she murmured.

"Damn it, Anna, I'm in no mood for games—"

"Sit down," she said. "Sit down and settle down.

Junius is in his office going over the books. I'm fairly sure he doesn't want to be disturbed. Whatever you have to tell him, it can wait."

"Who made you the boss around here?" he demanded in a surly voice, but she noticed that he pulled out a chair and sat down as she had told him to do.

"Take it easy," she said as she put a red queen on a black king and then moved a black jack onto the queen. "I know you rode out to ambush Bodine and Two Wolves before they could reach the Kincaid woman's ranch. I take it your mission didn't succeed as well as you'd hoped it would?"

"It didn't succeed at all," Tate snapped. "Those lucky bastards got away."

Anna doubted that luck had much to do with it. Tate was swift and deadly with a handgun, no doubt about that, but he was only an average shot with a rifle. Like most men, though, he believed that he was much better than he really was. She wasn't surprised to hear that Bodine and Two Wolves had escaped from his ambush.

If Junius really wanted those two troublemakers taken care of, he would do well to assign the task to her. After all, she had gotten rid of Archibald MacKenzie for him, hadn't she? It had been child's play for her to get a job in the Silver Belle when the old Scotsman was still alive and running the place. She had just arrived in Buffalo Flat in response to Cole's summons, and no one in the settlement knew there was any connection between them, had no idea that they had worked together in other places, on other schemes.

Once MacKenzie was smitten with her, poisoning him slowly was easy. He trusted her, just like any older man would trust a young woman who was willing to go to bed with him. He'd had no idea what was really going on until it was much too late to do anything about it. Then he was dead and the Silver Belle—the only real competition for the Colorado Palace—was closed down, just like Junius wanted.

It would have stayed that way, too, if not for that meddling lawyer and the redheaded whore and her friends from Kansas City.

And if their arrival in Buffalo Flat wasn't bad enough to start with, fate had also aligned Matt Bodine and Sam Two Wolves with them. With those two on their side, they wouldn't be nearly as easy to root out.

She would have to start thinking about ways to eliminate them from the game, Anna told herself.

Tate signaled for the bartender to send over a bottle. He turned back to Anna, leaned forward, and asked in a low voice, "Say, when are the two of us gonna get together again?"

"That's dangerous, Lucas, you know that," she replied coolly. "Junius wouldn't be happy if he found out about those other times."

"Cole pays me to keep him alive and do some of his dirty work for him. He doesn't pay me to keep him happy."

"Just be patient," she told him. "The more successful his business endeavors are, the less attention he pays to me. Once he's taken over the entire town, he may be content to let me go. Then you and I can be together all the time."

That would never happen, of course. Anna knew quite well how greed worked and how it could never be satisfied. Even if Cole ran the entire state of Colorado and not just the settlement of Buffalo Flat, he would still want more. He considered her his property, and he would never relinquish her, any more than he would give away the Diamond C or the Colorado Palace. But Tate didn't have to know that. The gunslinger was a useful weapon for Anna to have in reserve, a part of her arsenal along with her own amoral cunning and stunning beauty and utter ruthlessness.

She continued playing solitaire while Tate put away several drinks from the bottle of whiskey one of the bar girls brought over to the table. Then the door of the office opened and Cole came out, finished with his bookkeeping chores. He spotted Tate sitting at the table with Anna and came over to join them, an intent expression on his face.

"Well?" he demanded as he pulled out a chair and sat down. "Did you take care of that problem like you said you would, Tate?"

"I had some bad luck," Tate growled. "And Bodine and Two Wolves had all the good luck."

Cole's expression hardened. "Let me guess. They got away."

"Like I said, they were lucky." Tate poured another drink.

"Were either of them even wounded?"

Tate shook his head and lifted the glass to his lips.

In a burst of anger, Cole leaned forward and slapped it aside before Tate could drink. The whiskey spilled across the table, splashing a little on Tate's shirt. The glass clattered to the floor. Some of the customers in the saloon looked around at the commotion, but they looked away quickly when they realized what was going on. Nobody wanted to draw Cole's attention when he was this angry.

"You stupid son of a bitch," he grated. "You can't even handle a simple job like bushwhacking a couple of meddlesome bastards!"

"How many of your men have gone up against them the past few days?" Tate shot back, making a visible effort to rein in his own temper. "At least I'm still alive and can try again. That's more than most of the others can say. Anyway, I'd rather face Bodine man-to-man so I can prove that I'm faster than he is."

"I don't pay you good money to inflate your reputation," Cole snapped. "I pay you to take care of problems for me, and right now you're not earning your wages."

"I will," Tate promised grimly. "You can count on that."

"I'd better be able to." Cole sat back in his chair and took a cigar from his vest pocket. He used the moment it took to light the cheroot to calm himself. Then he said, "Bodine and Two Wolves will blame that ambush on me."

"And they'll be right, of course," Anna put in, the first comment she had made since the flare-up between the two men.

Cole nodded. "I think it's time to lie low for a while and let things settle down again."

"You're not gonna do anything about those whores over at the Silver Belle?" Tate asked.

"All in good time. I'm going to leave the Kincaid woman alone, too. Let everybody think that there's not going to be any more trouble. That'll give me a chance to send for some more guns."

"And then?" Tate prodded.

"And then, when the time is right, we'll strike so hard that none of them will know what hit them. Not the whores, not Mrs. Kincaid, and not Bodine and Two Wolves. One big cleanup, and I'll be well on my way to being the most important man in this part of the state. Hell, in the whole state!"

Tate nodded, but Anna could see the anger and resentment still smoldering in his eyes. The gunman wouldn't forget the way Cole had spoken to him, or getting that glass slapped out of his hand. Even though he would play along with Cole for now in hopes of a bigger payoff in the end, those insults would rankle and fester inside him and grow into an implacable hatred.

A hatred that someday she would put to good use, Anna thought. As Cole had said . . .

When the time was right.

Chapter 19

Three days later, as Matt and Sam sat at one of the tables in the Silver Belle playing a lazy game of poker for penny-ante stakes, Charity came over and joined them. As they started to stand up politely, she waved them back into their chairs and said, "No need to get formal on my account."

"My ma wouldn't take it kindly if we weren't polite to a lady," Matt said. "She sort of raised us both after Sam's ma passed on."

"And she insisted on good manners," Sam added.

"A couple of rugged frontiersmen you two are," Charity said with a laugh as she sat down. "If you're that worried about proper etiquette, why don't you stick your pinky finger out when you drink your coffee?"

"Don't think we can't," Matt told her. "Why, I've seen Sam there dressed up so fancy and talkin' so cultured-like, you'd think he was a gosh-darn Englishman!"

"There's nothing wrong with a little civility, you ruffian," Sam replied.

"You hear that?" Matt asked Charity with a grin.

"He called me a ruffian. I reckon I'm mortally offended. If I had me a white glove, I'd slap him across the face with it and challenge him to a duel. Maybe one of those fancy sword fights."

"You don't know the first thing about fencing," Sam said. "I, on the other hand, became an expert with the foil while I was a student at the university—"

Charity sighed in exasperation and shook her head. "Will you two just stop it? I swear, the way you go on at each other, a person would think you're enemies instead of, what do you call it, Brothers of the Wolf."

"Onihomahan," Sam supplied.

"Yeah, that. Anyway, the reason I came over here is to ask you what you think Cole is up to."

Matt shrugged. "It doesn't appear that he's up to anything. He's just sitting over there in his saloon not giving anybody a lick of trouble these days."

"I know," Charity said, "and that's got me worried."

Sam guessed, "You think he's planning something even worse than before."

"Well, what else could it be? He hasn't given up on getting rid of me and the girls. I'm sure of that."

"Maybe he's decided that he can live with some competition from the Silver Belle," Matt suggested.

"You don't really believe that, do you?"

Matt shrugged and then shook his head. "No, not really. Cole doesn't strike me as the sort of hombre who'd give up until he's got what he wants—or until he's dead."

"I agree with that assessment," Sam said. He thumbed his hat back and frowned. "You know, we haven't actually introduced ourselves to Cole yet. Maybe we should go down to the Colorado Palace and do just that."

Matt perked up at that idea. "You mean walk right in?"

Sam nodded. "Beard the lion in his den, so to speak. That might even give us a better idea what Cole is planning. If he gets angry enough, he might let something slip."

Matt tossed his cards onto the table. "Let's go," he said without hesitation. "It's about time we did something besides sit around."

"Wait a minute, wait a minute," Charity said quickly. "I didn't come over here and bring up the subject of Cole with the idea of you fellas going down there and doing something foolhardy."

"There's nothing foolhardy about it," Sam told her. "Consider it a scouting mission. We're trying to gauge the enemy's strength and intentions."

"You're liable to get in a shoot-out with Cole's gunslingers."

"I'm not sure he has any hired gunmen left other than Lucas Tate. He has some bartenders and bouncers and such, but I'd be willing to bet they're not that handy with their guns," Matt said. He stood up, unwilling to be dissuaded now that he had made up his mind.

"Well, if you're bound and determined to do this, at least be careful," Charity said.

"We always are," Sam assured her.

"Oh, yeah. Considering all the stories I've heard about you two, I'm going to believe *that*."

Grinning, the blood brothers left the saloon and strolled toward the Colorado Palace. As they approached Cole's establishment, Sam commented, "You know, this is a little like poking a hornet's nest with a stick."

Matt chuckled. "Yeah, and that was always one of my favorite things to do when I was a kid."

"I remember. I also remember you got stung more than once."

Matt lightly touched the butts of his guns. "I've got stingers of my own now."

They crossed the street and stepped up onto the boardwalk near the corner entrance of the Colorado Palace. Even though it was only early afternoon, quite a bit of noise came from inside the saloon, telling them that the place was doing good business. Over the past three days, the Silver Belle had been busy, too, although the novelty of having a new saloon in town was wearing off and some of the customers weren't returning as often. It was crazy for Junius Cole to be so worried about competition that he would resort to gunplay, Matt thought. There were enough people in Buffalo Flat and the surrounding area to support both saloons.

But evidently Cole wasn't the sort of man who was content to just do well enough. He had to crush his opponents and hog all the power and wealth for himself. Ambition was a good thing— nothing worthwhile would ever get done in this world without it—but in a man like Cole it had become something like a sickness.

Matt couldn't help but wonder how things were going out at the Half Moon. He didn't have any sympathy for Terri Kelly, or Theresa Kincaid, or whatever her name was now. But he had sort of liked those two old-timers from Texas, despite the fact that Scratch Morton was stubborn as all get-out. He wondered if Cole was leaving them alone, too, for the time being.

Then he and Sam were pushing through the

batwings, and Matt didn't have time to ponder anymore. Sam had referred to the Colorado Palace as
a lion's den, and that was just about right. The
blood brothers needed to have all their attention
focused on the here and now.

The bar was crowded and most of the tables in
the place were occupied. Judge Ashmore had
pointed out Cole to Matt and Sam one day on the
street, so they knew what the man looked like. As
their eyes searched quickly over the big room, they
didn't see him, which meant he was probably in his
office or upstairs.

Lucas Tate was lounging at the far end of the bar,
though. He stiffened and then straightened sharply
as he spotted Bodine and Two Wolves. Matt could
tell that the gunslinger was surprised they had ven-
tured in here.

Surprised—but not displeased. In fact, an ugly
smile tugged at Tate's mouth. He stepped away
from the bar, and some of the customers who were
in a potential line of fire began sidling away.

"Bodine," Tate said. "Two Wolves. What are you
doin' here?"

Matt's thumbs were hooked casually in his gunbelt. He shrugged and said, "Can't a man step into
a saloon for a cool beer on a hot afternoon?"

"Sure," Tate replied, still smiling. "In fact, the first
round's on me."

"That's mighty generous of you," Sam said.
"We're much obliged."

"Believe me, the pleasure's all mine." Tate snapped
his fingers at one of the bartenders. "Beer for these
two gentlemen."

Tate strolled along the bar toward them. Matt

kept his eyes on the man, watchful for any telltale sign that Tate was about to hook and draw.

"We haven't been introduced," Tate said when he was a few feet away. He came to a stop. "I'm Lucas Tate."

"We know who you are," Matt said, "and it's obvious you know who we are."

"Bodine and Two Wolves," Tate said. "A couple of big men with big reputations. I have to wonder if they're deserved. Those reps, I mean."

Using his left hand, Matt picked up one of the full mugs of beer the bartender placed on the hardwood. "It's up to other folks to decide about things like that," he said. He took a sip of the beer. It was cool and tasted good. "I never cared all that much about a reputation."

"Easy to say when you've won every gunfight you've been in . . . until now."

Sam picked up his beer and said, "We didn't come in here looking for trouble, Tate."

"Then why *did* you come?" Tate asked with a sneer.

Matt lifted his mug and smiled. "Like I said . . . hot afternoon, cool beer . . . Reckon I ought to draw you a picture, Tate?"

Tate's sneer turned into an angry snarl. Matt knew that the man was spoiling for a fight. Even though Sam was right about them not looking for trouble, neither would they back away from it. If Tate wanted to force the issue, he would find that neither of the blood brothers had an ounce of back-up in him.

"What's going on out here?" a new voice demanded. Junius Cole emerged from a door at the end of the bar and stalked toward the three men confronting each other. A few seconds earlier, Matt had noticed a swamper sneaking through that door, which undoubtedly led to Cole's office. He figured the man had alerted Cole that a showdown was rapidly developing in the saloon. As Cole came up beside Tate, he went on. "What's the trouble here?"

"No trouble, Boss," Tate said. "Just a couple of saddle tramps gettin' proddy."

"You're the one acting like he wants to start the ball, mister," Matt said.

"All three of you take it easy, damn it," Cole snapped. He frowned at Matt and Sam. "I don't want any shooting in here. Bloodstains are hell to get off the floor. Why don't you boys go back to the Silver Belle, since that's where you obviously belong?"

"Maybe we're thinking about switching sides," Sam said.

Tate started to laugh, but Cole silenced him with an outstretched hand. "If you're serious about that, Two Wolves, maybe we should have a talk."

Tate glanced at him. "What the hell—"

"I don't think so, Cole," Matt said. "There's not enough money in the world to get us to work for a skunk like you."

If Cole was offended, he didn't show it. He was smiling as he said, "You come in a man's place and drink his beer and then insult him. That's no way to be." His eyes glittered with hate as he spoke, though.

Matt shrugged. "Sorry. Just telling the truth."

"Maybe you and your half-breed friend should move on."

"If you plan on making us do that, you'd better

have somebody better than Tate here to back your play."

Tate's face reddened with fury, but before he could say or do anything, a flurry of hoofbeats sounded from the street, growing louder and louder until it sounded like a small army was riding up outside the saloon. Cole looked out through the windows and grinned smugly, triumphantly.

"I think I'm going to have all the help I need to do whatever I want," he said.

"Uh-oh," Sam muttered under his breath. "Now what?"

That's what Matt wanted to know. He turned toward the entrance as boot heels rang on the planks of the boardwalk and spurs jingled.

A couple of men pushed through the batwings and came into the saloon. They were followed by two more, then two more, and so on until fully a dozen men had entered the Colorado Palace. All of them were covered with dust from the trail. They were lean, hard-faced hombres, some clean-shaven, while others sported mustaches or beards. A couple were well dressed in suits and vests, while the rest wore typical range clothes, except for one gray-bearded gent in buckskins and a coonskin cap who looked more like an old-time mountain man than a range rider. All twelve of them were gun-hung, and it was clear they knew how to use those irons.

Matt and Sam knew they were looking at a wolf pack, a crew of hired killers.

Reinforcements for Junius Cole, more than likely.

One of the men ambled toward the bar. He was a little shorter than the others, wearing a black Stetson and a cowhide vest. His face was dark and pocked with old scars. When he stopped, he said, "We're lookin' for Junius Cole."

The saloon had gone quiet as the gunmen entered, so the man's voice carried to everyone in the room.

Cole took a step toward him and said, "I'm Cole."

"I'm Porter Wood," the gunman replied. He leaned his head toward his companions. "That's Lije Braddock, Norm Haney, Clint McGee, Warren Jones, Bart Hill, Ed Guidry, Ben Martin, Chuck Forrest, Jim Ketchum, and Thad Wilbur. The old-timer is Ike Davis."

Cole nodded eagerly. "I know who you are," he said. "I'm the one who sent for you, after all."

"Well, that's where we've run into a little problem," Porter Wood drawled.

"Problem?" Cole asked as a worried frown appeared on his face. "What sort of problem?"

"We're not going to be working for you after all," Wood said.

Cole looked surprised and began to bluster. "But I'm the one who asked you to come to Buffalo Flat," he said. "We had an agreement—"

Wood interrupted him by shrugging and saying, "Sorry. Something else came up."

"Then what are you doing here?" Cole demanded. "Why come all this way to tell me that you're not going to be working for me after all?"

A thin, humorless smile appeared on Wood's pockmarked face. "We thought maybe you could tell us how to find the Half Moon Ranch."

Matt laughed. He couldn't help it. He looked at the saloon owner and said, "Sounds like you got outbid, Cole."

Cole looked like he couldn't believe what he had

just heard. He glared furiously at the gunslingers as he asked, "You're going to ride for that Kincaid woman?"

Wood nodded. "That's the idea."

"We had an agreement, damn it!" Cole said again. He looked like he wanted to take a swing at Wood, but he suppressed the impulse.

Wood shook his head and said, "Actually, we didn't. We agreed to come here and talk to you, that's all. We never said for sure we'd take your offer."

"Want me to teach this hombre a lesson, Boss?" Tate asked. He stood there next to Cole in an apparently casual pose, but Matt could tell that Tate was anything but casual. The gunfighter had already been keyed up because of the way Matt and Sam had invaded Cole's domain. It seemed like he wanted to prove something to Cole and was willing to draw on anybody to do it.

Porter Wood tensed slightly at Tate's words. Without turning his head, he said to his companions, "This is my affair, boys. All of you stay out of it."

Cole said exasperatedly, "Damn it, there's no need for gunplay! Tate, back off."

"But, Boss—" Tate began.

"You heard me, back off," Cole grated. To Wood, he went on, "Whatever she's paying you, I'll better the offer."

Wood shook his head. "Sorry. Not interested."

Cole looked past him at the other gunslingers. "What about the rest of you?" he said. "Aren't you interested in making more money? I'll pay top dollar!"

"We ride together, mister," one of the men replied. "And what Porter says, goes."

Wood smiled that thin smile again. "We came by to talk to you first out of professional courtesy, I reckon you could say. Wanted to let you know what the situation was. But now we've got to be ridin'. And never mind the directions to the Half Moon. We know where it is."

Matt spoke up again, saying, "I'm not surprised that Terri would send for gents like you."

Wood's cold eyes swung over to him. "Who are you? Another of Cole's men?"

"Not hardly. Name's Matt Bodine." Matt hooked his thumbs in his gunbelt and inclined his head toward his blood brother. "This is Sam Two Wolves."

Several of the gunslingers stood up straighter and looked interested, including Porter Wood. "Bodine and the breed, eh?" he said. "I've heard of you two. They say you're fast, especially you, Bodine."

Matt shrugged. "They say a lot of things. The proof's in the doin'."

"Wouldn't mind seeing for myself someday," Wood said.

"Any time, mister. Any time you like."

Wood thought about it for a couple of tense seconds, then laughed softly. "Not today. We've got other things on our plate right now." He lifted a finger to the brim of his hat. "Another time."

Matt nodded.

Cole made one last try. "I'll double whatever she's paying you," he said.

Wood ignored him. He turned and said to the other gunmen, "Let's go." They filed out of the saloon, their movements casual on the surface. But

Matt could tell that they were ready to kill on an instant's notice.

When the gunslingers were gone, Matt said, "I reckon Sam and me will mosey on, too, Cole. You've had enough trouble for one day."

Tate said tensely, "You and me got unfinished business, Bodine."

Matt had to laugh again. "That's fine. There's enough of me to go around." He and Sam walked to the batwings, pushed through them, and stepped out onto the boardwalk.

"Well, that was a mighty interesting development," Sam said quietly as they started back toward the Silver Belle. "I wonder how Terri got enough money to hire Wood and his bunch."

"I don't know, but she just changed the balance of power around here. I've heard of quite a few of those boys, including Wood. They're supposed to be pretty fast."

Sam rubbed his jaw in thought. "I'm just wondering . . ." he said.

"Wondering what?"

"Maybe Terri's got her sights set a little higher than just hanging onto that ranch. Maybe with that many fast guns on her side, she's thinking about taking over from Cole. We could be talking about open warfare here."

Matt nodded, more solemn now. "And if that happens, Charity and her friends—and the rest of the folks here in Buffalo Flat, for that matter—will likely be caught right in the middle of it."

Chapter 20

For the past three days, things had been quiet on the Half Moon, almost quiet enough so that Bo was worried a gun storm of some sort was building. But at his age, and with the rambunctious history he and Scratch shared, he had learned to take respites from trouble wherever he could find them.

The two of them had ridden all over the ranch by now, committing the spread to memory with their frontiersmen's knack of knowing a trail for good once they had been over it. They had turned back Half Moon stock trying to wander onto Diamond C range; they had pulled cows and calves out of mud holes in the creek; they had straightened and tightened up the corral fences and patched holes in the barn roof. With five experienced hands on the place now, they were all rapidly whipping everything into shape.

And it felt good, too. There was nothing like a day of hard but honest labor to make a man feel worth his salt. Bo hated to think that a day might come when folks would look down on work and try to avoid it as much as possible, when people would rather take a handout than a job. Luckily, he didn't figure that would ever happen in his lifetime.

Despite the calm—or maybe because of it—Bo wondered when trouble would break out next. He said as much to Scratch as they were riding a couple of miles north of the ranch headquarters after hazing some strayed steers away from the boundary line between the Half Moon and the Diamond C.

"I swear, I never saw anybody as eager to hunt for a ruckus as you, Bo," Scratch replied. "Folks think *I'm* the one who's always on the prod because you look so much like a parson, but *you're* the one who gets restless if you don't smell gun smoke for a few days."

"I've just got a feeling that something's going on," Bo said. "You saw Cole's riders a while ago when we were chousing those cows back over here. They were in easy rifle range of us. Mrs. Kincaid and Hardy both warned us that Cole's men like to take potshots at anybody who comes close to the line. Why didn't they make a try for us?"

"I don't believe it! You're complainin' because you didn't get shot at!"

"No, that's not it," Bo insisted. "The only thing I can figure out is that Cole ordered his men not to shoot at folks on the other side of the line. Why's he changing his strategy now?"

"Maybe he finally figured out that he ain't gonna be able to run Miss Theresa off. Maybe he gave up."

"And maybe he's planning something even worse than he's done before."

"You're the most damn pessimistic son of a buck I ever did see. I swear, if you'd been on the ark with Noah, you'd've been worryin' that it was gonna stop rainin' too soon and cause a drought—"

Bo sat up straighter in the saddle and gazed off into the distance. "What's that?" he asked tensely.

"What's what? What're you—" Scratch stopped short in his question. "Hell. That's a lot of dust boilin' up over yonder."

"And it's heading for the ranch house." Bo leaned forward and dug his heels into his horse's flanks, sending the animal leaping forward in a gallop. "Let's go!"

As they hurried toward the Half Moon head-quarters, Bo wondered if Cole was launching an all-out attack on the spread. From the looks of the dust cloud rising into the sky, a large group of riders was bearing down on the ranch house. He listened for the crackle of gunfire, even though at this distance he might not be able to hear it over the pounding hoofbeats of his and Scratch's mounts.

As they drew closer, though, he still didn't hear any shots, and when they reached the top of the hill where the little cemetery was located, they could look down at the ranch headquarters and see that everything appeared peaceful. Something unusual was definitely going on, though. At least a dozen horses were tied up at the bunkhouse. Bo and Scratch couldn't see what was happening at the front of the house. They rode quickly down the hill and circled the sprawling log building.

Bo reined in as they came in sight of the long porch on the front of the house. The men who had ridden in on those horses were gathered there, and Theresa was talking to them, apparently calmly. She didn't appear to be frightened or upset at all. In fact, there was a pleased smile on her face, as if things were finally going her way at last.

Several of the men had swung around at the

sound of the horses. Bo didn't like the looks of them. He knew hard cases when he saw them, and these men sure as hell fit the description. One of them, an older man in buckskins and a coonskin cap, glared at the Texans as if he knew them.

"Son of a bitch!" Scratch exclaimed suddenly. "Is that ol' Ike Davis?"

"Morton!" the man in buckskins shouted before Bo could reply to Scratch's question. "I knew I'd run into you again sooner or later!"

With that, he launched himself off the porch in a diving tackle that drove Scratch right out of the saddle.

Bo backed his horse away and grabbed the reins of Scratch's mount as it spooked. He hauled the horse away from the men, who had fallen to the ground and started grappling there. The way they were trying to choke each other and gouge each other's eyes out, they appeared likely to do enough damage to themselves without getting stepped on by a horse.

Theresa stepped to the edge of the porch, looking startled by the fracas that had broken out with no warning. At her side was one of the strangers, a short, wiry man with a pockmarked face.

"Bo," Theresa said as she gestured toward Scratch and the man in buckskins, "what's this all about?"

"Just an old grudge," Bo said. "Best just let them work it out among themselves."

"Sounds good to me," said the man who stood next to Theresa. "I wouldn't want to try to get between those two old wildcats."

Scratch and his opponent were going at it pretty good, all right. Both of them were experienced in rough-and-tumble, no-holds-barred brawling. Dust rose around them as they flailed and kicked and bit. Finally, they broke apart, rolled to put a little distance between them, and came up onto their feet with fists clenched, ready to slug it out. They had lost their hats, their clothes were dirty and torn, and blood streaked their faces from various scratches and contusions. Scratch's left eye was swelling, and the other man had lost a tooth—and he didn't have so many left that he could easily afford to lose one.

"Bo, can't you stop this?" Theresa asked worriedly.

With a sigh, Bo slipped his gun from its holster. "Reckon I'd better," he said, "before they actually hurt each other."

He pointed the Colt into the air and fired.

The roar of the shot made the two combatants halt just as they started to advance on each other. The blast was followed an instant later by a second shot, this one fired by the man standing on the porch with Theresa. As the echoes died away, the man said, "Rein it in, Ike, you old curly wolf!"

The buckskinner pointed at Scratch and protested, "But, Porter, this here is the fella who stole that little Mex gal from me down in Santa Fe a few years back!"

"Like hell I did!" Scratch said. "*You* stole her from *me*! Broke her heart when you ran out on her, too!"

Bo holstered his gun as he said, "I remember that. And as I recall, the lady in question was no lady. Chances are her heart wasn't broken. I doubt she even remembered either one of you by the next day."

Scratch started slapping dust off his clothes. "Aw, hell, Bo, that ain't any kind of a way to talk. Ain't you got a romantic bone in your body?"

The man in buckskins said, "Yeah, Creel, you're

just jealous 'cause Rosita didn't want nothin' to do with *you*."

"You think whatever you want to, Ike." Bo extended a hand. "It's good to see you anyway."

Ike hesitated, but then reached up and gripped Bo's hand. Then he turned to Scratch and said, "Put 'er there, Morton?"

"Hell, why not?" Scratch said. He shook hands.

"Let me get this straight," Theresa said with a puzzled frown on her face. "You two *weren't* actually trying to kill each other?"

Scratch picked up his hat, knocked it back into shape, and put it on. "Naw, that was just our way of sayin' howdy, I reckon. Although I am still a mite peeved at this ugly ol' badger."

"Ugly old badger, is it?" Ike snorted. "You're uglier an' older than I am, Methuselah."

Still holding the reins of Scratch's horse, Bo swung down from the saddle. "I know Ike," he said to Theresa, "but who's the rest of the company?"

She took hold of the arm of the man standing next to her. "This is an old friend of mine," she said. "Porter Wood. And these other men are friends and associates of his. They've come to give us a hand."

Bo kept a friendly smile on his face, but inside he tensed with wariness. He recognized Porter Wood's name. The man was a gunslinger. More than that, he was a hired gun, and judging by their looks, the rest of the men with him might well be cut from the same cloth.

A few days earlier, Theresa had said something about having sent for some help. At the time, Bo had figured she meant some more cowhands to help run the ranch.

He hadn't expected a small army of gun-throwers to arrive instead.

It made sense, though. To deal with the threat she was facing from Junius Cole, Theresa needed men who were handy with their guns, not a rope and a branding iron. Probably the only ropes these men had any experience with were the hang ropes they had dodged, and any branding they had ever done had been with a rustler's running iron.

Those thoughts went through Bo's head as he gave Wood and the other men a polite nod and said, "Pleased to meet you, boys."

That was a lie. Bo wasn't pleased by this development at all. The fact that Theresa counted Porter Wood as an old friend and had brought him and these other gunmen in to help her made it all the more likely that Matt Bodine and Sam Two Wolves had indeed been telling the truth about her. She was no better than she had to be, and probably as bad as she could get away with.

At the moment, however, there wasn't anything Bo could do about it. He would have to talk to Scratch later. They might have to think about whether or not they had done the right thing by throwing in with Theresa. Bo had a feeling Scratch still wouldn't want to hear anything bad about her, even if she *was* well acquainted with a bunch of ruthless gunmen.

Bo went on. "If you're signing on to ride for the Half Moon, I reckon you'll want to head on over to the bunkhouse and settle in. It might be a little crowded, but there ought to be room for all of you."

"Porter will be staying here in the ranch house," Theresa said.

Scratch looked a little crestfallen, but Bo just

nodded and said, "Yes, ma'am." Theresa's personal life was none of his business, and she had been widowed for a while. It seemed like a waste for a gal as young and pretty as her to take up with a gunslinging snake like Porter Wood, but there was no accounting for taste.

Scratch said to Ike Davis, "Come on. I'll introduce you to the other fellas who work here."

Bo brought the horses along as he fell in step beside Scratch and Ike. In a quiet voice, he asked, "How'd you come to be riding with Wood and the rest of that bunch, Ike?"

"What do you mean by that, Creel?" Ike responded in a sullen voice. "You think I ain't good enough to be ridin' with them?"

"That's not what I mean at all. Wood's a hired killer," Bo said bluntly, "and those other hombres look like the same sort. You've been mixed up in some shady deals in the past, but in the old days you never sold your gun to the highest bidder."

"That's right, Ike," Scratch put in. "Even though I'd never trust you around a gal I liked, you'll do to ride the river with the rest of the time."

Ike scowled. "I ain't crossed trails with you two in quite a while. Things change, damn it. I ain't as young as I used to be. It's gettin' harder to find the kind of work that a fella like me can do. How the hell am I supposed to make a livin'? Can you honestly see me clerkin' in a dry-goods store or totin' bags at a railroad depot?" He shook his head. "I been ridin' with Porter for a while. The pay's good, and the work's always excitin'."

"Getting shot at, you mean?" Bo asked.

"I'd rather go out with my boots on and a gun in my hand, instead of a damn broom!"

Bo didn't say anything to that, and neither did Scratch. They both understood what Ike meant. After lives spent in action and adventure, the thought of fading away and finally dying in some lonely rented room held no appeal for them, either. It might have been different if they'd had families, if they could have looked forward to crossing over the divide with a passel of kids and grandkids and great-grandkids around to send them on their way. But as it was, maybe Ike was right.

Bo wasn't completely convinced, though. He didn't trust Porter Wood, and he was beginning to trust Theresa less and less.

Hector Ibañez was the only one of the regular hands at the ranch headquarters at the moment; Hardy Thomas and Mort Skaggs were out checking on stock, as Bo and Scratch had been earlier. They introduced Ike to the genial Mexican. The other men came into the bunkhouse and began claiming bunks. There were enough beds to go around with a few to spare, but one of the gunslingers went over to Hector's bunk, picked up the guitar lying there, and tossed it aside so that he could dump his war bag down in its place.

"Señor," Hector said to him, "my apologies, but that is my place."

"Not anymore, greaser," the man said. Several of the others laughed derisively.

Hector picked up his guitar and checked it for damage. Finding none, he set it carefully on Bo's bunk for the moment and then turned back to the man who had dispossessed him.

"I must insist—"

"Blow it out your Mexican ass," the gunman snapped. "Now get away from me before I make you sorry you ever left the land of the chili peppers, *comprende?*"

"Take it easy, Guidry," Ike put in. "Ain't no reason for you to be pickin' on this fella."

"There's the best reason in the world," Guidry said. "I don't like greasers. And if you got a problem with that, old man, that's just too damn bad."

Guidry was young, probably no more than twenty-four or twenty-five. A young, sleek, dangerous gun wolf. But Ike Davis had been surviving on the frontier for more years than Guidry had been alive. Ike muttered something that Guidry couldn't make out. The gunslinger stepped closer to him and demanded belligerently, "What'd you say to me, old man?"

Ike's right hand came up with blinding speed, and the sunlight that spilled through the open doorway of the bunkhouse glinted off the broad blade of the bowie knife he held. The razor-sharp tip dug into the flesh just under Guidry's chin.

"I said, would you rather me open you up from gizzard to gullet, you little piece o' shit, or should I just cut your throat and get it over with quicklike?" Ike asked between clenched teeth. "'Cause I got a problem, all right, and it's gonna be too damn bad for you."

Guidry's eyes bugged out in fear and surprise. "T-take it easy, old-t-timer," he stammered. "I . . . I didn't mean nothin' by it. Just p-put that knife down, all right?" His wide eyes rolled toward Bo and Scratch. "You two know him. Can't you talk some sense into his head?"

"Problem there is that Hector's our amigo, too," Scratch said.

"And we can't abide folks treating our friends rudely," Bo added.

"All right! I'm sorry! Is that what you want me to say? The greaser can have his bunk back! I don't care!"

Ike jerked his head toward Hector. "Tell him, not me."

"Look, mister, I'm sorry," Guidry forced out as he very carefully turned his head to look at Hector. A little trail of blood trickled down his throat from the spot where the knife rested.

Hector shrugged and said, "*De nada.* You must remember, though, to treat a man's guitar with respect."

"Sure thing," Guidry said.

A shadow crossed the bunkhouse door, and Porter Wood snapped, "What in blazes is going on here?"

Ike lowered the bowie. "Just gettin' a few things straight with young Guidry here. He hadn't figured out that an old wolf's generally the most dangerous varmint of all. Reckon he knows it now, though." Ike wiped the tip of the blade on his buckskin trousers and then sheathed the bowie.

"Damn it, Ike, don't get your back up so easy," Wood said. "We've got a job to do here, and I can't afford for you boys to start killing each other. We've got more important things to take care of."

"Like what?" Bo asked.

Wood frowned at him. "Excuse me? Creel, isn't it?"

"That's right," Bo said, "and I asked just what those important things are that you have to take care of."

Wood smiled. "I reckon you know that already,

Creel. We're going to make sure that Junius Cole never bothers Mrs. Kincaid again."

"And how are you going to do that?"

"However I have to," Wood replied.

Bo and Scratch exchanged a glance. Both of them knew what the boss gunslinger was talking about.

War was coming to Buffalo Flat.

Chapter 21

Junius Cole had heard the old saying about being stuck between a rock and a hard place, but he had never really understood it until now. The rough crew he had hired to run the Diamond C were still out there on the ranch, but most of the gunnies he'd had working for him here in Buffalo Flat had been killed off or seriously wounded by that damn Bodine and Two Wolves. Several of the others who hadn't been injured had drawn their wages and deserted him, riding away from the settlement rather than staying and running the risk of facing a gunfight with the two dangerous young men. The only fast gun Cole could still count on here in town was Lucas Tate.

Tate might be fast enough to take either Bodine or Two Wolves, but not both of them. Even facing them one at a time, the odds would still be against him.

That meant Cole had to leave those whores at the Silver Belle alone for the time being, no matter how much their presence in Buffalo Flat grated at him. He had gotten rid of his only real competition in Archibald MacKenzie, or so he had believed at the time. It rankled to have someone else come into town and become a thorn in his side.

But after the betrayal by Porter Wood and the other men Cole had hoped to hire, he didn't really have a choice in the matter. It was time to turn his attention to the Half Moon. Theresa Kincaid was a threat, and she would continue to be as long as she controlled the spring that fed his creek.

He was in his office at the Colorado Palace when Anna came in and said, "Roy Barlowe is here to see you, Junius."

Barlowe was the foreman of the Diamond C, the man whose job it was to see to it that Cole's orders were carried out. Cole had sent a rider out to the ranch that morning, with orders for Barlowe to come into Buffalo Flat and see him.

"Bring him in," he told Anna as he shoved some papers aside on the desk. He opened one of the drawers and brought out a bottle and a couple of glasses.

Anna led Barlowe into the office a moment later. The burly foreman watched the sway of her hips appreciatively as he came into the room. Cole noticed, but didn't take offense. If he was going to get upset every time some hombre eyed Anna, then he wouldn't have time to do anything except be mad all the time. Anyway, he liked the idea that other men wanted her when he was the only one who could have her, unless he said otherwise.

"Sit down and have a drink, Roy," Cole invited with a wave of his hand.

"Don't mind if I do, Boss," Barlowe said as he sank into a chair in front of the desk. He was a big, barrel-chested man in his forties with thinning brown hair under a thumbed-back Stetson. He possessed exactly the qualities Cole needed in a ranch foreman—he was good at handling both livestock and men, he was a deadly fighter with gun and knife and fist, and he could be utterly ruthless when he needed to be. Plus he was wanted for murder in Arizona, a fact that Junius Cole happened to know. The knowledge was a useful lever in case Barlowe ever got any big ideas, although that was unlikely to happen. As long as the money was good, Barlowe was glad to do pretty much whatever Cole wanted. Cole was confident the foreman would have bushwhacked William Kincaid if Cole had asked him to—and if somebody hadn't already beaten them to the punch on that score.

Cole poured the drinks and slid one of the glasses across the desk to Barlowe. Anna had left the room after showing Barlowe in. The man looked a little disappointed at her departure, but didn't say anything except, "Here's mud in your eye," as he picked up the glass. He tossed back the liquor, said, "Ah," as he set down the empty glass, then asked, "What can I do for you, Boss?"

"You've been steering clear of the Half Moon for the past few days, like I told you?"

"Yeah." Barlowe didn't sound happy about it, either. "Yesterday me and a couple of the boys had a good shot at those two old codgers who've gone to work for Miz Kincaid, but we didn't take it, just like you said."

Cole nodded. "That's good. But the situation is different now. All bets are off. Use your own best judgment, Roy."

Barlowe sat forward, clearly excited by the news. "You mean we're goin' after the Half Moon again?"

"That's right. Do whatever it takes to convince that stubborn woman it'd be in her best interests to sell me the ranch and get out of this part of the country."

Barlowe grinned. He knew that if Cole took over the Half Moon, the combined spreads would be the largest and best ranch in the entire state. And even though Cole would be the owner, Barlowe would be in charge of the day-to-day operations. Cole knew the idea of wielding that much power appealed to the foreman.

"Don't you worry, Boss," Barlowe said. "We'll have that gal convinced in no time at all."

"There's just one thing," Cole went on. "The Half Moon has some new hands riding for it now."

From the puzzled look on his face, Barlowe hadn't heard about that development while he was out on the Diamond C. But he shook his head and said, "Doesn't matter. We can handle anything that woman throws at us. How many men are we talkin' about?"

"A dozen. And they're led by Porter Wood."

Barlowe's expression turned into a frown. "Wood?" he repeated. "The gunfighter?"

"That's right."

"And I reckon the men with him are the same breed of hombre?"

"I'm afraid so," Cole said.

That put a new face on the situation, and Cole knew it. Barlowe sat there for a long moment, glaring. Finally, he said, "I've got twenty men, Boss, but not all of 'em are gun-handy enough to stand up to the likes of Porter Wood. I ain't sure that even half of them are."

"When you took over the Diamond C for me, I

told you to hire the saltiest cowboys you could find," Cole snapped.

"Yeah, and they're plenty salty," Barlowe said, "but they're still cowboys. They ain't professional gunslicks."

Cole leaned back and spread his hands. "You have the advantage of numbers," he said. "Plus you admit yourself that even the men who aren't professional gunmen are plenty tough. I think you can handle this problem, Roy. I have confidence in you."

"Well, I appreciate that," Barlowe said as he scrubbed a hand along his jaw. "Still . . . Porter Wood's got a heap of notches on his gun. If there's ten or eleven more like him on the Half Moon crew . . . I just dunno, Boss."

"I leave it in your hands. As I told you, use your best judgment." Cole's voice hardened. "But I want results, Roy, make no mistake about that. If you can't get results . . ."

"I never said that," Barlowe replied quickly. He gestured toward the bottle. "How 'bout another drink?"

"Sure." Cole poured it, and Barlowe slugged it down.

"Don't worry," the foreman said as he smacked the empty glass down on the desk. "Give me a chance, and it won't be long before that woman's gone from the Half Moon . . . or dead."

Cole smiled. "Like I said, Roy . . . I'll leave that up to you."

After the confrontation between Ike Davis and Ed Guidry, things were quiet on the Half Moon that night and the next day. If Bo, Scratch, and the other ranch hands had counted on getting some help around the place from Porter Wood's crew, they would have been disappointed. The gunslingers didn't budge from their bunks until late the next morning, and even when they woke up, they didn't offer to help out. Instead, they sat around the bunkhouse playing cards, rolling quirlies, and nipping from flasks. Ike was the only one who rattled his hocks to do something useful, and Bo suspected that was only because Ike was an old friend of him and Scratch.

Luckily, Bo and Scratch hadn't been expecting anything from the newcomers, except maybe the potential for more trouble.

As they rode out onto the range the next day, Bo brought up the subject. "Starting to look like Bodine and Two Wolves had Mrs. Kincaid pegged pretty accurately," he said.

Scratch's voice was worried as he replied, "Yeah, it don't look good, her bein' so friendly with Wood and the rest of his bunch. They're skunks, most of 'em, plumb skunks. But you got to remember that ol' Ike's ridin' with 'em, too, so they ain't all bad."

"Ike was never what you'd call a choirboy. I recall several loads of guns that got smuggled across the Mexican border a while back. He had a hand in that. And I wouldn't be surprised if he'd robbed a bank or two in his time."

"Hell, *we've* robbed a bank or two in our time!" Scratch objected. "Remember that time in Arroyo Rojo—"

"That was different. We had a good reason to rob that bank. Anyway, we gave the money back."

"And what about that stagecoach we held up?"

Scratch asked, warming to his subject. "And that fella we kidnapped?"

Bo took off his hat and sleeved sweat from his forehead. "That's not the same thing. We weren't breaking the law in those cases so much as we were trying to see that justice was done. I reckon you could say we just bent the law a little."

"Still, it ain't that much different. Ike probably figured he had a good reason every time he strayed across the line, too."

"Yeah, like filling his own pockets with loot. That's why he's riding with Wood's bunch. He admitted that much himself yesterday, remember?"

"So what are you sayin', that we ought to ride off and abandon Miss Theresa?" Scratch shook his head. "I ain't one to cut and run, Bo. You know that. Once I start somethin', I finish it."

Bo couldn't argue with that. A lot of the trouble in the world was caused by people giving up too soon, just because the task they had set for themselves was a difficult one. But the hard jobs were often the most worthwhile.

"All I'm saying is that Mrs. Kincaid's hooked up with a bunch of hard cases again, just like Bodine and Two Wolves said she has before, most recently at that settlement up at the Medicine Bows. Maybe, considering what she's up against in a varmint like Cole, what she's doing is justified. But we just have to think about it, that's all I'm saying."

"I ride for the brand," Scratch responded stubbornly. "That's all *I'm* sayin'."

Of course, it helped if that brand was owned by a pretty young woman, Bo thought wryly.

They didn't discuss the situation any further because at that moment both of the Texans spotted a tendril of gray smoke curling into the sky ahead of them, a couple of hills away. As they reined in to study it, Scratch said, "That looks like the smoke from a brandin' fire."

"The only branding going on right now is the running-iron kind," Bo said. "Come on."

He heeled his horse into a trot. Scratch fell in alongside him. Both men reached down and made sure their Winchesters were loose in the saddle sheaths.

They had just reached the top of the first hill when they saw another rider heading over the next rise. "Ain't that Mort?" Scratch asked.

Bo had recognized the lone horseman as Mort Skaggs, too. "He must've spotted the smoke just like we did and decided to investigate."

"By himself?" Scratch said. "If there's a bunch o' rustlers over there, he'll get his head shot off!"

"That's what I'm worried about," Bo replied as he urged his mount to an even faster pace.

They galloped through the little grassy valley between hills and up the wooded slope. Mort Skaggs was out of sight by now, and they couldn't see the smoke from where they were, either. But no shots had rung out yet, and the longer that condition lasted, the better, Bo thought.

As they topped the rise, he hauled back on the reins and signaled for Scratch to halt, too, so that they could get the lay of the land before charging into possible trouble. The trees along the ridge concealed them for the moment.

Sure enough, a couple of cowboys had kindled a small fire at the bottom of the hill, and they had a running iron heating in it while a hog-tied calf struggled on the ground nearby. The calf's mama stood several yards away, glaring belligerently at the rustlers. She had to be a Half Moon cow, but that wasn't going to stop the men from slapping a different brand on the calf. A Diamond C brand, more than likely, Bo thought.

Mort Skaggs had almost reached the rustlers' fire. He had drawn his gun and was riding openly toward them. The rustlers must have heard him approaching, but they didn't turn to face him. They acted like they didn't even know he was anywhere around.

"Something's wrong," Bo said. "It's some sort of—"

He was about to say "trap" when Mort shouted at the rustlers, "Hey, you bastards! What the hell do you think you're doin'?"

That was when the two men hit the dirt, and Bo felt sick horror twist his guts as he realized what was about to happen.

There was no time for him to even shout a warning to Mort. From a stand of trees on the opposite side of the rustlers' fire, a volley of shots rang out. At least half-a-dozen rifles blasted almost as one. Bo and Scratch saw Mort jerk in the saddle as bullets slammed into him, saw his horse falter and then fall as the animal was fatally wounded, too. Mort pitched forward out of the saddle as his mount collapsed. He fell in a bloody heap. More shots roared as the hidden riflemen poured more rounds into him. Mort had to be dead already. He was drilled through the body three or four times, maybe more. But that didn't stop the bushwhackers from savagely mutilating his body with their lead.

"Them two rustlers were just the bait," Scratch said between clenched teeth as the rolling thunder of rifle fire finally died away. The rustlers pushed themselves to their feet and grinned at what was left of Mort Skaggs.

Bo knew his fellow Texan was right. The smoke was just to draw in one or more of the Half Moon hands so that the hidden riflemen could mow them down. Rage welled up inside Bo as the full extent of the viciousness sunk in on him. He pulled his Winchester from its sheath and brought it to his shoulder. The rifle boomed twice, as fast as he could work its lever, and the unsuspecting rustlers were knocked off their feet by the slugs that sizzled through the hot air.

One of the men fell hard, drilled cleanly and mortally, but the other one was only hit in the hip. He tried to crawl away. Scratch had unlimbered his rifle by that time, however, and drawn a bead. The weapon cracked, and the wounded man slumped as Scratch put a bullet through his brain.

Bo raised his sights to the trees where the bushwhackers were hidden and opened up on them. He and Scratch were in the cover of some trees, too, but that didn't stop the hidden riflemen from putting up a fight. They returned the Texans' fire. Bullets thudded into tree trunks and clipped branches as the long-distance duel continued for a good thirty seconds. Then, running low on ammunition, Bo and Scratch had to wheel their horses and light a shuck before the bushwhackers came after them.

"I don't like leavin' Mort there!" Scratch called over the pounding of hoofbeats.

"Neither do I," Bo replied, "but maybe we can fetch some of the other boys and catch those bastards before they get off of Half Moon range!"

They didn't run into anyone on their way back to

the ranch headquarters. If Wood and his men had been out riding the range like they should have been, Mort might not have had to face the rustlers alone. Of course, that would have meant that even more men might have died in the trap. . . .

"Cole was behind this," Scratch said as he and Bo neared the bunkhouse.

"Yeah, I imagine you're right," Bo agreed. "He'd called a truce for a few days for some reason, but it's over now."

Ike came out of the bunkhouse, accompanied by Hardy Thomas. The Half Moon foreman had hit it off fairly well with the buckskin-clad gunfighter, since they were nearly of an age. Hardy saw the way Bo and Scratch were hurrying, and must have figured that something was wrong. He ran forward to meet them. "What is it?" he called. "Thought I heard shots a little while ago!"

"You did," Bo said with a grim nod as he reined in. "Mort tried to jump a couple of rustlers and got himself killed."

"Mort? Dead?" Hardy looked stricken.

"That's not all of it," Bo went on. "It was all a trap." He quickly described the way Mort had been drawn in and executed. Because that was what his death had amounted to—an execution.

Hardy turned toward the bunkhouse, but Ike was already moving in that direction. "I'll roust the fellas," he said. "We'll ride out there and have a look."

"Not everybody," Bo called after him. "Cole's men could be trying to draw us away from the ranch."

Theresa heard the commotion and came onto the porch of the ranch house. She waved Bo over to her while the men spilled out of the bunkhouse and hastily saddled their horses. "What's happened?" she asked tensely.

Bo told her, and she looked genuinely saddened and angered by the news of Mort's death.

"Cole again," she practically spat.

Bo nodded. "I reckon so."

"You're riding back out there to get Mort's body?"

"Yeah, and to see if we can find out anything for sure about those bushwhackers. I know it's pretty much a lost cause hoping for any help from Sheriff Branch, but it won't hurt anything to try."

"If you capture any of the men responsible for Mort's death, don't shoot them," Theresa ordered.

Bo frowned. "What do you want us to do?"

"Hang them," she said coldly.

Chapter 22

They didn't find anybody, not even the two so-called rustlers Bo and Scratch had killed. Bo wasn't surprised the bushwhackers had taken the dead men with them. They hadn't wanted to leave anybody behind who could be positively identified.

The only body lying on the ground near the burned-out fire was that of Mort Skaggs, and it was so shot to pieces that it barely resembled anything human. The calf had been untied and left to run off after its mama. Bo would have bet that the bushwhackers hadn't even taken the time to brand it.

Porter Wood and six of the other gunslingers had ridden back out here with Bo, Scratch, and Hardy. The other gunmen had remained back at the Half Moon headquarters, just in case the crew from the Diamond C tried a sneak attack there.

Wood studied the tracks left by the bushwhackers and declared, "We could follow them, but I don't really see any point in it."

"No point in it?" Hardy said angrily. "The bastards killed one o' my friends! They killed a man who rides for the same brand you do! How can you not go after 'em?"

Bo said, "I reckon Mr. Wood looks at things a mite different than we do, Hardy."

"I don't believe in wasting time or energy," Wood said. "They did what they came over here to do— they murdered a Half Moon rider. If they think that's going to scare off the rest of us, they're sadly mistaken." He turned his horse and added to his men, "Let's get back to the ranch."

Hardy stared after the gunmen, fuming. Bo, Scratch, and Ike sat their horses alongside his. After a moment, Hardy looked over at Ike and asked, "Do you agree with him?"

Ike shrugged bony shoulders. "Whether I agree or disagree don't matter. Porter calls the shots." He jogged his horse into motion and started to follow the others. A few more seconds went by before Hardy sighed and started to dismount.

"Help me get Mort over my saddle, will you?" he said to Bo and Scratch. "We got to take him back to be laid to rest proper. We'll put him beside Johnny."

"That's the least we can do for him now," Bo agreed as he swung down from the saddle.

Hardy's horse tried to shy away from the smell of blood and the weight of the corpse as they lifted Mort's body onto the saddle. It was a gruesome task, but the men got it done fairly quickly. They used Hardy's lasso to tie Mort onto the horse; then the foreman climbed up behind the saddle. Deep lines of sorrow and anger were etched into Hardy's weathered face as he took up the reins.

The three men started back toward the ranch headquarters with their grim burden, but they hadn't gotten far when the sound of shots suddenly came to their ears. "Blast it," Bo grated, "Cole's men must've jumped the ranch headquarters, just like I was afraid they would."

"Come on," Hardy urged. "Let's get in on the fight!"

Bo understood the foreman's enthusiasm. Hardy not only wanted to protect the spread he rode for, but he wanted vengeance on the men who had killed his friend Mort. But Hardy already had a job that couldn't be neglected.

"Scratch and I will ride ahead and see what's going on," Bo said. "You bring Mort's body but stay out of the fight."

"Damn it, Bo, *I'm* the ramrod on this spread! I give the orders!"

"I know, but you've got Mort's body you're responsible for. It's up to you to see to it that he receives a proper burial."

Hardy seethed, but clearly he understood the importance of what Bo had just said. "All right," he bit out. "But hurry up—and ventilate some o' those bastards for me!"

Bo nodded; then he and Scratch put their horses into a gallop as they headed for the ranch headquarters as swiftly as they could.

Across valleys, over ridges, around outcroppings of rock, they raced toward the sounds of battle. The booming shots grew louder, and not surprisingly, when Bo and Scratch came within sight of the ranch house, they saw clouds of powder smoke hazing the air around the buildings. Bo reined in and Scratch followed suit. They studied the layout intently.

"Got men holed up in the bunkhouse and the main house," Scratch said after a moment. "Riflemen across the creek in them trees and up on the hill behind the house, so they got the place in a cross fire."

Bo nodded. "Those buildings are plenty sturdy, though. It'd be hard for anybody to root out the defenders short of putting the place to the torch. And you know Wood and his men have to be pretty good shots. If they just rushed the buildings, Cole's bunch would have to pay a mighty high price to get to them."

"So why do it?" Scratch wanted to know. "Why attack the place now?"

"The crew from the Diamond C—if that's who bushwhacked Mort—probably thought they could circle around and get here while our forces were still split. From the looks of it, though, I'll bet Wood and the others got back here just about the same time Cole's men did."

"And once they'd opened the ball, they were too stubborn to back out." Scratch nodded. "I reckon you're right, Bo. Question is, what're we gonna do about it?"

"From here we can reach both the hill behind the house and the trees across the creek," Bo pointed out as he drew his rifle from its sheath. "Let's give Cole's gunnies something else to think about."

Scratch grinned as he pulled his Winchester. "I like the way you think, partner."

The Texans lifted their weapons and opened fire. By unspoken agreement, Bo targeted the hillside while Scratch peppered the trees on the other side of the creek with lead. The men from the Diamond C were already under fire from the defenders in the house and bunkhouse. This new attack from a different direction must have been more than some of them could stand, because a moment after Bo and Scratch opened up, they heard the sound of hurried hoofbeats.

"They're lightin' a shuck!" Scratch called exuberantly as he levered his Winchester.

"Some of them, anyway," Bo agreed. His rifle ran dry. He took a box of .44-40 cartridges from his saddlebags and started thumbing fresh rounds into the Winchester's loading gate.

A slug ripped through the air near his head and then thudded into a tree trunk. Another bullet hit a rock and whined off, spooking the Texans' horses. An oath leaped from Scratch's mouth as a third round whistled past his ear.

"You're right, Bo, they ain't all runnin'!"

In fact, a group of horsemen burst from the trees along the creek and started toward Bo and Scratch, firing from their saddles as they came. Ignoring the bullets buzzing around him, Bo dismounted quickly, turned his horse around, and slapped the animal on the rump with his hat, sending it running away, hopefully out of the line of fire. Scratch did likewise; then both of the drifters hunkered behind rocks and resumed the fight. They were under heavy fire now, from the riflemen hidden in the trees as well as from the riders who were thundering toward them.

Luckily, this wasn't the first time they had found themselves in a tight spot. Not hardly, in fact. Coolheaded, they kept their wits about them and took their time as they drew beads on the men charging them. Bo's rifle spoke and then a second later Scratch's cracked as well, and two of the riders jerked in their saddles. The men dropped their guns and sagged, but they managed to stay mounted as they veered their horses away. The other men stopped and furiously slung lead at Bo and Scratch for several long seconds, filling the air with gun thunder and forcing the Texans to hug the dirt behind the rocks. Then Cole's men whirled their mounts and galloped off in the other direction, evidently knowing that if they pressed their attack, in all likelihood more of them would be hit, probably fatally.

The firing died away, and more hoofbeats sounded as the hidden gunmen broke off their attack and got out of there while the gettin' was good. Their trap had claimed the life of Mort Skaggs, and for all Bo and Scratch knew at the moment, some of the other men on the ranch might have been hurt or killed during the initial moments of the raid.

But by and large, this thrust against the Half Moon by the Diamond C had failed. Theresa Kincaid and the men who worked for her were still in firm control of the ranch. If Junius Cole had hoped that his men could drive them out, he was going to be disappointed when he found out what had happened.

Scratch started to stand up, but Bo said, "Better stay down for a little while longer, just in case they left some sharpshooter behind."

"Yeah, I reckon you're right." Scratch suddenly swiveled his head and looked over his shoulder. "Somebody comin' up behind us!"

Bo rolled onto his back and drew his six-gun, figuring the Colt would be more effective in a close-range fight. But a second later he recognized the man riding toward them through the trees, as well as the limp, bloody shape carried across the horse's saddle.

"Stay back, Hardy!" Bo called.

Hardy reined in quickly. "What hap—" he began.

Then, with a distant whip-crack, a rifle went off, and Hardy grunted in pain as a bullet thudded into his chest. Bo saw the little puff of dust from Hardy's shirt as the slug struck the breast pocket.

"Hardy!" he shouted as the foreman began to sway in the saddle.

Nearby, Scratch's rifle blasted three times, fast, followed by a heartfelt curse. "He got away, damn it!" Scratch burst out. "I just got a glimpse of him ridin' hell-bent for leather through them trees!"

Bo was already on his feet, disregarding any further threat as he leaped toward Hardy's horse. He got there just in time to catch the foreman as Hardy toppled from the horse's back. Bo staggered, but remained on his feet. Carefully, he lowered Hardy to the ground as gently as he could.

Scratch ran over to join them, and dropped to a knee on the other side of the wounded man. A jagged crimson stain spread quickly on the front of Hardy's shirt. He looked up at Bo and Scratch with lines of pain tugging at his face as he gasped, "Looks like . . . you'll be diggin' . . . two graves now."

"Don't talk like that, Hardy," Scratch said. "You're gonna be fine."

"Look at your . . . partner's face," Hardy forced out. "He knows the . . . truth . . . and so do I. I'm . . . done for." His hand caught hold of Bo's arm. "The ranch . . . Is the ranch . . . all right?"

"Yeah," Bo told him. "We got here in time to help drive off Cole's men."

"Did you . . . drill any of 'em?"

"We got a few of them," Bo told him. "I don't know if anybody on our side was hit except for Mort and—"

"And me," Hardy broke in. "Damn, it . . . hurts. Put me on the hill . . . with Johnny and Mort. It sure is pretty there . . . of a mornin' . . ."

His head fell back and his last breath came out of him in a long sigh.

"Damn it," Scratch said softly. "Damn it to hell."

Bo lowered Hardy's head to the ground. "Stay here with these poor fellas," he said. "I'll go fetch a wagon for both of them and see if everybody's all right at the house."

He straightened and whistled for his horse. The animal came to him and bumped its velvety nose against his shoulder, but the grim look remained on Bo's face as he took up the reins, grasped the horn, and swung into the saddle. Scratch handed him his Winchester. Bo jammed the rifle into the boot and then rode toward the ranch house.

Hector Ibañez came running from the bunkhouse to meet him. "Señor Bo! Señor Bo! You are all right?"

Bo nodded as he reined to a halt in front of the house. "Yeah. What about everybody here?"

"A crease or two in the bunkhouse," Hector replied. "Nothing serious. I do not know about Miss Theresa and the others." Hector looked back in the direction Bo had come from. "Where are Hardy and Señor Scratch?"

"Scratch is back over yonder in those trees." Bo took a deep breath. "Hardy's there, too. He was hit. I'm afraid he's dead."

"*Dios mío!*" Hector made the sign of the cross. "I am the only one left."

Bo knew what he meant. Hector was the last of the ranch hands who had been on the Half Moon before all the trouble began.

Before William Kincaid brought back a new and unexpected wife from Denver. . . .

Theresa hurried out onto the porch, followed by Porter Wood and a couple of Wood's gunslinging companions. "Did I hear you right, Bo?" she asked with a taut look on her face. "Hardy is dead?"

Bo nodded. "I'm afraid so. What happened here?"

"They hit us just as the boys and I got back," Wood drawled. "We barely made it to the buildings in time. If they'd been a little faster getting here, while the bunch of us were split up, they might've succeeded in wiping us all out." He went on. "I reckon it was you and Morton who finally spooked them into running."

"But not before one of them took a last shot that hit Hardy," Bo said.

Wood shrugged. "He knew the risks. You can't get in the middle of a war like this without taking a chance on getting hurt."

"Well, this war isn't going to go on," Theresa snapped. "It's crazy, and I'm going to put a stop to it."

"Begging your pardon, ma'am, but how do you intend to go about doing that?" Bo asked.

"Get all the men together," Theresa said. "As soon as all the little wounds are patched up—and as soon as we've buried Hardy and Mort—we're all going to town."

"Now you're talkin'," Porter Wood breathed.

"What do you intend to do there?" Bo said to Theresa.

"I'm going to see Junius Cole," she declared, "and I'm going to put a stop to this madness, once and for all.'

Chapter 23

Since the day of the confrontation Matt Bodine and Sam Two Wolves had witnessed in the Colorado Palace between Junius Cole and the group of gunslingers led by Porter Wood, things had been quiet in Buffalo Flat. Neither Matt nor Sam expected things to *stay* that way, of course. Trouble was just taking a breather.

They were in the Silver Belle, sitting at a table with Charity and Judge Ashmore, when Casey McLennan, the editor of the local newspaper, came into the saloon. He spotted them and started across the room toward them.

"The representative of the press approaches," Judge Ashmore muttered under his breath. "I wonder what he wants."

"You can bet it'll be something he thinks will sell more papers," Matt said. "I never knew a newspaperman yet who cared about anything else, much less the truth. Why, if you take what most of them write as gospel, I'm nothing but a bloodthirsty lunatic just because I pack a gun and stick up for myself."

Sam took a sip of his coffee and said quietly, "Funny how folks who think there's always a peaceful solution to everything have usually never been shot at."

"Casey's not quite that bad," Ashmore said. "He's a Westerner, so he's got *some* sense." He nodded to the editor as McLennan came up to the table. "How are you, Casey? Sit down and join us."

"Thanks, Judge," McLennan said as he pulled back one of the empty chairs and sat down. He nodded politely to Charity and said, "Miss MacKenzie."

"Hello, Mr. McLennan," she replied with just a hint of coolness in her tone. "Did you decide that the grand reopening of the Silver Belle was worth a story in your paper after all?"

"As a matter of fact, I did. This establishment has been open for a while now and proving to be quite popular, so I convinced my wife we ought to at least mention that fact in our columns."

"I see. You mean, it's newsworthy that Cole's hired killers didn't murder me and my friends and shut down our saloon right away."

Matt saw a flash of anger in McLennan's eyes, but the newspaperman kept his temper under control. "I don't like Junius Cole much more than you do, Miss MacKenzie. It's no secret that he has political ambitions. I can't think of much worse for the state than to have a man like Cole as governor or senator."

Sam said, "You don't really think that people would elect a saloon keeper of questionable character like Cole to such an office, do you?"

"Hey, I'm a saloon keeper," Charity objected.

"You're not running for office," Sam pointed out,

"and anyway, your character is above reproach compared to a man like Cole."

"You *do* realize I used to be a whore, don't you?"

Matt grinned and said, "I'd vote for a good honest soiled dove over some of the chicken thieves who've held office in this country."

"Amen, my young friend," Judge Ashmore put in. The lawyer had been spending more and more time in the Silver Belle recently. If he had ever been under the thumb of Junius Cole, he seemed to have wiggled out from that position.

"Anyway," McLennan said to Charity, "I'd like to put something in the paper about your and your friends and the way you've taken over running this place. I'll have to be a little circumspect, of course—"

"And not say anything about us being a bunch of former prostitutes, even though everybody in town already knows about it?"

"I promise you, I mean no offense, Miss MacKenzie." The newspaperman looked over at Matt and Sam. "I'd also like to interview the two of you—"

Matt shook his head. "Not a chance, mister. Sam and I have enough people gunnin' for us without getting our reputations inflated even more by a bunch of highfalutin words in some newspaper."

"Do you honestly think that people don't already know who you are?" McLennan argued. "It didn't take long for the word to spread around town that Matt Bodine and Sam Two Wolves were in Buffalo Flat. You're famous, whether you like it or not."

"Never set out to be famous," Matt growled.

Sam added, "We just want to be left alone to live our lives."

"Then you shouldn't have been born so fast on the draw," McLennan said.

"I'm afraid he has you there, boys," Ashmore said. "Once you have a reputation as a fast gun, there's only one way to get over it."

"And that's to meet someone faster," Sam said. "We know, Judge."

"Boy, howdy, do we know," Matt said.

McLennan turned back to Charity, abandoning his efforts to persuade Matt and Sam to agree to an interview, at least for the moment. "What about it, Miss MacKenzie?" he said. "Will you go along with me doing a story about you and your friends and the Silver Belle?"

Charity had wanted that all along, Matt knew, so he wasn't surprised when she nodded. She just hadn't wanted to agree with the newspaperman without first pricking a few little holes in the pomposity that went along with his profession.

"I think that would be fine," she said, but before she could go on, a sudden outbreak of commotion from the street interrupted her. People started shouting and running, and that usually meant only one thing.

Trouble.

Matt and Sam came smoothly to their feet. "Stay here," Sam said to Charity, Ashmore, and McLennan as he and Matt started toward the batwings. "We'll see what's going on."

"I have to come, too," McLennan said as he stood up. "It's my job to know what's happening in Buffalo Flat."

"Well, stay back a mite," Matt advised him, "just in case any bullets start flyin'."

The two young men reached the saloon's entrance and stepped out onto the boardwalk. They peered down the street toward the Colorado Palace, which seemed to be the center of the commotion.

Most of the people hurrying along the street were headed in that direction.

"What the hell?" Matt muttered as he spotted the buckboard and the large group of riders coming up the street toward Junius Cole's saloon. "Is that—"

"It is," Sam said. "Terri Kelly is driving the buckboard, and those men with her are Porter Wood and his gunslingers, along with those two old Texans."

"My God," Casey McLennan said from behind them as he stood up on his toes trying to see past the broad shoulders of the two tall men. "Is there going to be a gun battle?"

"I don't know, but I wouldn't rule it out. Terri and Cole are mortal enemies."

"You mean Mrs. Kincaid?"

Matt glanced over his shoulder at the newspaperman. "There's a lot you don't know about the woman, mister."

McLennan pulled a pencil and a pad of paper from his pocket. "I'm listening," he said.

Matt ignored him and looked toward the Colorado Palace again. As he stepped down from the boardwalk into the street, he said, "I'm going down there. I want to see this for myself."

"Wait up," Sam said quickly. "I'll go with you."

McLennan swallowed hard, then followed them. All hell might be about to break loose in Buffalo Flat, and if that was the case, it was his duty to report it.

And try not to get killed in the process.

Cole sat at a table in the saloon with Anna, Roy Barlowe, and Lucas Tate. His face was dark with anger. He had listened to the report that Barlowe had just given him and gotten angrier with every word that the Diamond C ramrod spoke. Once again, Cole had sent an attack against his enemies, and once again, it had failed miserably.

"Were you able to kill any of those gunslingers?" he demanded.

Barlowe grimaced. "I can't say for sure, Boss. I know we winged a couple of them while they were scramblin' to get inside the buildings, but I ain't sure how bad they were hit. They were still movin' like they were pretty spry. But Mort Skaggs is dead, I'm damned certain of that."

"Skaggs was probably the least dangerous man out there," Cole said scathingly. "If you think knowing that he's dead makes me feel better about this fiasco, Barlowe, you're wrong."

"Maybe I should have ridden out there to give the Diamond C boys a hand," Tate suggested.

"You already tried to ambush those old-timers and failed just as miserably as Barlowe did," Cole pointed out. The harsh words made Tate scowl, but Cole ignored him. "I'm starting to think that if I want anybody dead, I'm going to have to kill them myself."

"You're not a gunslinger, Junius," Anna said. "What you do best is think and plan and provide the driving force for us all. You don't want to risk everything you've built here in Buffalo Flat by engaging in personal combat . . . especially one that you're not likely to win."

"You forget that I've won plenty of fights in my life," he snapped. "I grew up in Natchez-Under-the-Hill. Nobody survives there without being tough."

Anna might have said something else, but at that moment an old drunk who worked for Cole as a swamper came running into the saloon. He spotted Cole and the others at the table and veered toward them.

"Boss! Boss! Trouble comin'!"

Cole stood up and glared. "What are you talking about, Mose? Are you drunk again?"

The man shook his bald head, making the turkey wattles under his chin sway back and forth grotesquely. "No, Boss. I was just down the street, and I seen that woman who owns the Half Moon comin' into town on a buckboard. She had all them gunslingers with her, the ones who were in here the other day!"

"Wood," Cole breathed. "You say his whole bunch is with him?"

The swamper bobbed his head. "Yessir. And they's all loaded for bear, too!"

Cole glanced at Tate and Barlowe. The ranch foreman had gone a little pale under his tan, but Tate still lounged in his chair, seemingly unbothered by the prospect of violence.

"I've got a few of the hands in town with me," Barlowe said, "but not enough to stand up to Wood's whole gang!"

"The men who work here in the saloon for me will fight," Cole said. He was worried, and he couldn't keep from showing it. The timing was bad, and he had never expected Theresa Kincaid to bring the war to him. He had assumed that she would stay holed up on her ranch and that sooner or later he would figure out a way to either destroy her or force her to flee from this part of the country.

Now it looked like she intended to turn that around on him. It was a daring, audacious move. He had to give her credit for that much, anyway.

"Get your men," he said to Barlowe.

"They're all here in the saloon already."

Cole nodded. "Good." He raised his voice. "Everybody who doesn't work for me, get the hell out of here. *Now!*"

Customers scattered, realizing from the tone of Cole's voice that something was wrong. Nobody wanted to be in the line of fire if a full-scale battle broke out between Cole's men and the gunslingers who had come into town with Theresa Kincaid.

Cole turned to Anna and jerked his head curtly toward the staircase. "Get upstairs," he told her.

She began, "Junius, I'd rather stay—"

"Do what I told you," he grated. "I can deal with this better if I don't have to worry about you getting hit by a stray bullet."

She blinked and stared at him for a second, evidently surprised by the concern he had just expressed for her. Then she nodded and stood up. "All right. If that's the way you want it." She went to the stairs and straight up to the second floor.

Lucas Tate had gotten to his feet, too, and strode over to the saloon entrance. He peered over the batwings for a moment and then turned to look at Cole. "It's the Kincaid woman, all right," he announced. "And Wood and his bunch are with her."

Roy Barlowe had gathered the Diamond C hands together in a compact group near the bar. There were five of them, counting Barlowe. The two bartenders reached under the hardwood and came up with sawed-off shotguns. Those weapons weren't much good except at close range, but within a few feet they were devastating. Two bouncers were on duty, too, but they were armed only with short, thick clubs, perfect for breaking up a brawl, but not much use when it came to dealing with gun-throwers like Porter Wood and his companions.

The odds might not be overwhelming, Cole thought as he glanced around the room, but they were still pretty damn bad.

"They're here," Tate said quietly from the entrance. He moved back until he stood next to Cole. His hands hovered over the butts of his guns.

The arrival of Theresa Kincaid, accompanied by Wood and the other men, had drawn quite a bit of attention in Buffalo Flat. Cole could hear the uproar outside the saloon as townspeople crowded around, eager to see what was going to happen.

But as soon as they determined that violence was about to erupt, they would vanish in the blink of an eye, scurrying off to their holes like frightened rabbits, Cole thought bitterly. He had seen enough in his hardscrabble life to come to the conclusion that the human race was a lot of sorry sons of bitches, and the only way to get ahead in life was to be a bigger son of a bitch than everybody else. So far, that course of action he had steered for himself hadn't let him down.

But he had never faced odds quite like these today, either. Where the hell was the sheriff? What good was Sherman Branch if he couldn't prevent situations like this from happening?

Cole glanced around the room and growled, "Be ready to open fire when I give the word—but not before."

He heard boot heels thud on the planks of the boardwalk just outside. Keyed up the way he was, Cole almost shouted for his men to shoot as soon as a shadow fell over the batwings. The words choked to a halt in his throat as he saw Theresa

Kincaid's blond hair. The woman pushed through the entrance and stepped brazenly into the saloon. Respectable women weren't supposed to set foot in places like this. Cole supposed that Theresa had been pushed to the point that she didn't care anymore about being respectable.

She wore boots, a brown, divided skirt, and a white shirt with a buckskin vest over it. A cream-colored Stetson hung on the back of her shoulders by its chin strap. Her long blond hair was loose. If Cole hadn't hated her for standing in the way of his plans, he would have thought that she was breathtakingly beautiful.

Porter Wood was right behind her. The pock-marked gunslinger was small in stature, but he reminded Cole of a small but highly venomous snake. Several more of Wood's gunfighters followed him and Theresa. The rest of the bunch stayed outside on the boardwalk, visible through the windows of the saloon.

The way Theresa had walked right into the Colorado Palace told Cole that she didn't want a battle. But he was at a loss to figure out what she *did* want.

There was only one way to find out, he told himself.

"Mrs. Kincaid," he said, his voice rough but civil. "I don't believe you've been here before. What can I do for you?"

"I've come to put an end to the trouble between us," she replied, her words equally cool and controlled.

"And how do you suggest that we do that?"

"It's simple," Theresa said. "I think we should call a truce, Mr. Cole. We should be on the same side, instead of trying to kill each other."

Chapter 24

Bo still wasn't sure he and Scratch were doing the right thing by accompanying Theresa Kincaid and her crew of hired gunnies to town. Theresa had insisted that everybody on the Half Moon come with her, though. Bo had brought up the possibility that if the spread was deserted, some of Cole's men might ride in and take over the buildings—or even set fire to them. He hoped that Theresa would decide to leave some of the hands at the ranch to protect it, and if that was the case, he intended to see to it that he and Scratch were among the contingent remaining on the Half Moon.

If Theresa planned to force a showdown with Cole, Bo wanted no part of it, and he didn't want to see his old friend Scratch cut down by flying lead, either. It was enough that Hardy Thomas and Mort Skaggs had already died today, for a cause in which Bo no longer fully believed.

But Theresa had shaken her head and said flatly, "No. We're all going. Everyone saddle up."

As they rode out, with Bo, Scratch, and Hector bringing up the rear behind the buckboard and the group of gunslingers, Bo cast a glance at the hillside where Hardy and Mort lay in their freshly dug graves, next to Johnny Del Rio.

That little burial ground was liable to get mighty crowded before this was over, he thought.

On the way into town, Hector asked, "What do you think the señora plans to do, Señor Bo?"

"From the way she talked, she intends to have a showdown with Cole, maybe even ride in shooting," Bo replied.

Scratch said, "Innocent folks'll get hurt if we do that, sure enough."

Bo nodded. "I know. But I reckon Mrs. Kincaid has been pushed as far as she'll be pushed. Today's raid was the last straw."

Scratch rasped a thumb over the silvery stubble on his jaw. "You know," he said, "maybe a showdown ain't such a bad idea. Cole can't have too many men left in town, not after all the damage those young hellions Bodine and Two Wolves have done to his bunch. We might be able to wipe 'em out, and then that'd just leave the gunnies on the Diamond C. With Cole dead, chances are they'd give up the fight. Cut off the head of a rattler and the body dies, as the old sayin' goes."

"I still don't like the idea very much."

Scratch shrugged. "I didn't like helpin' to bury Hardy and Mort, neither. And they wouldn't be dead if Cole wasn't such a greedy, high-handed bastard."

"There is that," Bo agreed grimly.

The distance between the Half Moon and Buffalo Flat seemed to be covered quicker than usual today. The settlement soon came into view, with the church steeple being the first thing visible, as always. The buckboard being driven by a coldly impassive Theresa Kincaid rolled past the house of worship, followed by the fifteen men on horseback. The large group of hard-faced, gun-hung riders attracted attention immediately, and good-sized crowds were forming on both sides of the street as they approached the Colorado Palace Saloon.

Bo cast a glance toward the Silver Belle and wondered if Matt Bodine and Sam Two Wolves were in there. It would be a big help to Bodine and Two Wolves, as well as the ladies they had befriended, if Junius Cole was dead. Maybe Theresa *was* doing the right thing by seeking a showdown.

She brought the buckboard to a stop in front of the saloon. The men with her all reined in. Porter Wood dismounted first, and quickly stepped over to the wagon to help Theresa climb down from the seat. By the time she stepped onto the boardwalk, all the other men had swung down from their saddles and looped their reins around one of the hitch rails lined up in front of the building.

Bo, Scratch, and Hector were the last ones in the bunch to move onto the boardwalk. By the time they did, Theresa, Wood, and several more of the gunslingers had pushed through the batwings and gone into the saloon. However, the Texans and the Mexican ranch hand were close enough to the entrance to hear Cole's voice as he greeted Theresa.

And they heard her plain as day a moment later as she said, "I think we should call a truce, Mr. Cole. We should be on the same side, instead of trying to kill each other."

Bo stiffened, taken completely by surprise by Theresa's declaration. Beside him, Scratch muttered, "What the hell?" Hector just looked confused. All three of them pushed closer to the batwings. Hector was too short to see over them, but Bo and Scratch were able to watch as the tense confrontation inside the saloon continued.

"A truce?" Cole repeated, for a moment unable to believe that he had heard her correctly.

Theresa nodded. "That's right. Neither of us have the upper hand right now. We can go ahead and start shooting at each other, and maybe one of us will live through it. But there's an even better chance we'll both die, and neither of us will get what we want."

Cole's eyes narrowed. "And just what is it you want, Mrs. Kincaid?"

"To be left alone," she answered. "I know you want my ranch, Cole, but you can't have it. I've worked too hard for it. I won't let anyone take it away from me. You might as well accept that and let me help you get what *you* want." She gestured, taking in their surroundings. "The town of Buffalo Flat."

"Buffalo Flat is already mine," Cole declared bluntly.

Theresa shook her head. "Not all of it. What about the Silver Belle Saloon?"

Cole felt his pulse slug angrily in his head as he snapped, "What about it?"

"You let a bunch of whores come in and defy you, Cole." There was a sly light in Theresa's eyes now, as if she were mocking him. "I'm sure not everybody in this town likes you or is scared of you. They've seen Charity MacKenzie and her friends open up that saloon to compete with you, and you haven't done a thing about it because they've got a couple of gunslingers like Matt Bodine and Sam Two Wolves backing their play."

Something extra came into her voice at her mention of Bodine and Two Wolves, something very much like the raw edge of hatred. She went on. "People are going to look at that and decide that maybe you're not as important and powerful as you'd like to think you are. Maybe somebody else will decide that it's all right to cross you."

Cole's breath hissed between his teeth. "They'd damned well better not."

"How are you going to stop them?" Yes, she was definitely mocking him now, and he didn't like it. Not one damned bit.

"So how does leaving the Half Moon alone help me?"

"It's hard to fight two wars at once. And if I don't have to worry about you trying to take over my ranch anymore . . ." She smiled. "I think my friends here could be persuaded to help you tighten your grip in town."

Cole looked at Porter Wood, who also smiled thinly and gave a slight nod.

"With Porter and his friends working for you," Theresa went on, "I don't think even Matt Bodine and Sam Two Wolves would be able to stand up against you for very long!"

She was right, damn her eyes, Cole thought. He still hated her, but she was right. The truce she was offering would help solve some of his problems. With Wood and the other gunslingers on his payroll, as he had thought they would be originally, nobody in Buffalo Flat would ever dare to defy him again.

But he didn't trust her, and he wasn't crazy enough to believe that she would trust him. She had to have something else up her sleeve.

"Once I've dealt with the problem of the Silver Belle, what's to stop me from coming after you again?" he wanted to know.

"Because we'd be partners," Theresa said smoothly. "I'm not talking about just a truce. I'm talking about a permanent alliance. We'll have papers drawn up to make it all nice and legal. I'll give you a share in the Half Moon in exchange for a share in the Diamond C. That way, neither of us will be able to work against the other one without hurting ourselves in the process. And you can stop worrying about me doing anything to block the spring that feeds your creek."

The setup could work, Cole realized. He didn't think he would ever fully trust Theresa, but under the plan she'd outlined, he would at least have some influence over the Half Moon without giving up a controlling interest in his own ranch. And most of all, he would gain what he needed to take care of his other problems—the services of Porter Wood and the rest of his gunslinging crew.

Besides, who knew what the future might bring? One of these days, an unfortunate accident could still befall Theresa Kincaid. . . .

He pondered the proposal for a moment longer, then finally drew in a deep breath and stepped forward. He extended his right hand and said, "You've got yourself a deal, Mrs. Kincaid."

She smiled again and held out her hand. "Call me Theresa," she told him.

But before they could shake hands, a new voice called from the balcony, "Maybe first you should know just what sort of crook you're partnerin' up with, Cole."

Theresa's eyes jerked upward, and she hissed, "Bodine!"

Matt and Sam reached the edge of the crowd as Theresa, Wood, and several of the gunmen were entering the saloon. Jerking his head toward the alley that ran alongside the building, Matt suggested, "Let's go around back and see if we can get inside."

Sam nodded. Carrying out Matt's idea would be easier than trying to push their way through the crowd gathered around the batwings at the saloon's corner entrance.

They hurried along the alley to the back of the building, listening for the sudden eruption of shots they halfway expected to hear coming from inside the saloon. It was hard to believe that Terri and her gunslingers could confront Cole without a corpse-and-cartridge session breaking out.

But it was still quiet as they reached the sunbaked lane at the rear of the Colorado Palace. The door there was locked and probably barred on the inside, but an outside staircase led up to a landing and another door on the second floor. The blood brothers ascended those stairs, and when Matt grasped the doorknob, it turned easily. He swung the door open and they stepped into a short hallway. In front of them, at the end of the corridor, was a balcony overlooking the main room of the saloon.

They walked out onto the balcony. Movement to Matt's left caught his eye. When he looked in that direction, he saw a sleek, attractive brunette in a low-cut gown that molded itself daringly to the sensual curves of her figure. She glanced at Matt and Sam with some small measure of alarm, but she didn't move from where she stood looking down into the saloon, with her hands tightly gripping the railing along the edge of the balcony.

Matt and Sam arrived in time to hear Theresa Kincaid suggest her bargain with Cole, the arrangement that would have them exchanging shares in their ranches and working together, instead of being at odds with each other. And as Cole accepted the deal and stepped forward to shake on it, Matt said, "Maybe first you should know just what sort of crook you're partnerin' up with, Cole."

Theresa's head tilted back sharply as she looked up at the balcony and said in a voice filled with venom, "Bodine!"

Beside her, Porter Wood tensed, and so did the other gunmen who had accompanied them into the saloon. Matt said softly to Sam, "Watch Terri," as he kept an eye on Wood. He thought the other gunnies would follow Wood's lead and doubted that they would try to draw unless their leader did.

"I've got her," Sam returned quietly. It was unlikely that Theresa would try to take direct action against them—in the past her usual method had been to try to get someone else to do her dirty work for her—but Sam would keep his attention focused on her just in case she lost her head and tried to grab a gun.

The stairs were to Matt's right. As Matt and Sam started toward them, Cole said angrily, "You and the breed aren't welcome here, Bodine. This is between me and Mrs. Kincaid. It's none of your business."

No one tried to stop the blood brothers as they started downstairs. Matt waited until he reached the bottom of the staircase before he said, "We've run into Mrs. Kincaid several times before, Cole. I reckon we know her a mite better than you do. Well enough to know that you'd be a damn fool to trust her."

Matt's brain was working quickly. An alliance between Cole and Theresa would be the worst thing for Charity and her friends at the Silver Belle, as well as for anybody else in Buffalo Flat who opposed Cole's plans. Having his forces split as he tried to deal with the distraction of running Theresa off the Half Moon was probably the only thing that had prevented Cole from tightening his grip on the settlement. If Cole made peace with Theresa, it would be only a matter of time until he owned everything and everyone in Buffalo Flat. Then he would rule the town with an iron fist, and there was no telling where that might lead. As Judge Ashmore had said, Junius Cole was an ambitious man.

"I think I can handle my own business arrangements, Bodine," Cole said with a sneer.

"Don't listen to a word he says," Theresa added. "He and that obnoxious half-breed are both damned liars."

"If a *man* said that about me, he'd have a fight on his hands," Matt rasped.

Porter Wood squared his shoulders and moved his hand a little closer to his gun. He said, "My boys and I handle the lady's fighting for her. Start the ball any time you're ready, Bodine."

"Not in here," Cole said quickly. The confines of the saloon were too close, the odds too great that somebody—like him—might get hit by a stray bullet.

Sam said, "This isn't the first time the *lady* has gotten someone else to do her fighting for her. Ever hear of Tom Thomas, or a gunfighter from Texas called Walker?"

"They're both dead now," Matt put in.

Sam nodded toward Theresa and went on. "She's like a spider spinning a web. Men get caught in it like flies, and they die like flies, and she just keeps on spinning. That's what she'll do to you, Wood, and you, too, Cole."

"Kill them," Theresa said in a low voice that trembled slightly with emotion. "Somebody kill those bastards."

Before anybody could do anything, a burly figure pushed through the crowd on the boardwalk and into the saloon. Bystanders and gunmen alike moved aside from the twin barrels of the shotgun that threatened them. Sheriff Sherman Branch bellowed, "Everybody freeze! There's not gonna be any gunfight here, damn it!"

As Branch stalked up, Cole said, "There's no need for that scattergun, Sheriff. We're all friends here."

"That ain't the way I heard it," the lawman snapped. "All the talk on the street is about how you're all gonna try to kill each other in here."

"Don't be ridiculous, Sheriff," Theresa said. "Mr. Cole and I are just about to conclude a business arrangement that should make things in Buffalo Flat more peaceful than ever." Once again she held out her hand toward him. "Isn't that right . . . Junius?"

Cole didn't hesitate. He gripped her hand and grinned. "That's right, Mrs. Kincaid."

"Please, since we're going to be working together, you should call me Theresa."

"Of course . . . Theresa."

Matt and Sam both wore grim looks on their faces as Cole and Theresa shook on the deal. Sheriff Branch just looked confused. He had to be aware that as recently as a few minutes ago, Cole and Theresa had been bitter enemies.

Cole looked over at Porter Wood and asked, "Are you all right with this, too?"

Wood nodded. "What the boss lady says, goes."

A few feet away, Lucas Tate stood negligently with one hip propped on a table. His arms were folded across his chest now. But his eyes smoldered, Bodine noticed. Tate had been Junius Cole's top gun. Now, with the arrangement between Cole and Theresa, Porter Wood had probably taken his place. Tate wasn't too happy about that, either, although he seemed to be making an effort to keep the reaction from showing on his face.

Matt glanced up at the balcony. The brunette who had been standing there when he and Sam came in was still there, and her grip on the railing hadn't loosened any. In fact, it appeared to be tighter than ever now as she looked down at Cole and Theresa. The daggers in her eyes were even more obvious than the ones in Lucas Tate's gaze. Tate wasn't the only one who wasn't pleased with this new alliance. The brunette, whoever she was, was pretty upset about it, too.

"If you want to carry out your duties, Sheriff," Theresa said to Branch, "what you should be doing is running these two men out of here." She pointed at Matt and Sam. "All they've done since they rode into Buffalo Flat is try to stir up trouble."

Branch nodded grimly. "You're not tellin' me anything I don't already know, ma'am. I had 'em locked up in my jail once, and I reckon I should've kept 'em there no matter what anybody else said." He angled the Greener toward Matt and Sam. "Move along, you two. If you're still in here a minute from now, I'll run you in for disturbin' the peace."

"We're going, Sheriff," Sam said. He put a hand on Matt's arm to steer him away from the confrontation. "But if it's a disturbance of the peace that has you worried, I believe you're due for a lot more than you bargained for."

"In other words," Matt grated with a nod toward Cole and Theresa as he and Sam started toward the saloon entrance, "when a pair of devils makes a deal, sooner or later all hell's gonna break loose."

Chapter 25

Outside on the boardwalk, Scratch cursed bitterly as Theresa Kincaid made her deal with Cole. "This is crazy!" he said to Bo. "Hell, it's only been a couple of hours since we was buryin' Half Moon riders who'd been gunned down by Cole's men!"

"And now she's going into business with him," Bo said, his face even more grim than usual. "I reckon I ought to be surprised, but somehow, I'm not."

"Señores," Hector said, "what is going on? What is the señora doing in there?"

"Betrayin' the memory of those cowboys who got killed ridin' for her, that's what she's doin'!" Scratch snapped. Some of Porter Wood's gunslingers were starting to cast angry glances in his direction, but Scratch ignored them as he reached over to grip Ike Davis's arm. "Ike, damn it, this ain't right. You know it ain't."

Ike shook free and glared. "As long as Porter agrees, I reckon I'll go along with him. He's always played square with me."

"There's nothing square about this deal," Bo said. "It's all as crooked as a dog's hind leg."

Hector said, "I do not understand. Are we not going to fight Señor Cole's men?"

"Cole and Miz Kincaid are partners now," Scratch said heavily. "They just agreed to stop fightin'."

Hector's dark eyes widened in amazement. "But . . . but what about Hardy and Mort and poor Johnny? They are dead because of Señor Cole! How . . . how can the señora do such a terrible thing?"

Ed Guidry growled at Bo, "You'd better shut that pepperbelly up, old man, or I'll shut his greasy Mex mouth permanently."

Bo put a hand on the agitated Hector's shoulder and said, "Take it easy, amigo. We're as thrown for a loop by all this as you are, but I reckon we'll have to just wait and see how it plays out."

Even as he spoke, Bo *knew* how it was going to play out. Bodine and Two Wolves had been right all along about Theresa Kincaid, right all the way about how treacherous and not to be trusted she was. The drifters from Texas had put their faith in her, as they would have in any rancher they rode for. So had Hardy and Mort and Johnny.

And by shaking hands with Cole and agreeing to work with him instead of against him, Theresa had figuratively spit on those graves on the hill behind the Half Moon ranch house. That betrayal was like a knife in the hearts of the still-living men who had been loyal to the brand.

Bo and Scratch were still in a state of stunned anger as Matt Bodine and Sam Two Wolves made their entrance on the balcony. A few minutes later, the sheriff arrived and pushed his way through the crowd into the saloon. When that confrontation was over and Bodine and Two Wolves started out of the Colorado Palace, the men gathered on the boardwalk moved aside to let the two young men pass. As Bodine stalked past, Bo caught his eye and nodded. He hoped Bodine caught his meaning.

You were right about her all along.

Bodine returned the nod, and there was a friendlier light in the young man's eyes than there had been the last time they'd talked with the Texans. As the blood brothers headed for the Silver Belle, Scratch asked Bo, "What are we gonna do now?"

"I don't reckon there's but one choice, is there?" Bo replied. He turned to Ike. "Go in there and tell Mrs. Kincaid we'd like to talk to her, would you?"

Ike frowned. "Whatever you got in mind, Creel, you better think twice about it."

"We could think a dozen times about it," Scratch said. "Wouldn't make no difference. We'd still feel the same."

Scowling, Ike shook his head and then sighed. He slapped the batwings aside and walked into the saloon. A moment later Theresa appeared in the entrance, followed by Porter Wood. A worried frown was on her face.

"You wanted to talk to me, Bo?"

"That's right, ma'am." Even knowing what he did about her, Bo's ingrained chivalry still made him speak to her politely. "Scratch and I are drawing our time."

"You mean you're quitting?" Theresa looked surprised.

"That's right," Scratch said. "We can't ride for you no more."

"*Es verdad, señora,*" Hector added. "I, too, am drawing my time."

Guidry said, "You'll draw a bullet if you don't watch it, greaser."

Wood made a small motion with his left hand, telling Guidry to stay out of this for the time being. Then he turned a baleful glare on Bo, Scratch, and Hector.

"A man who runs out on the brand he rides for is yellow," Wood said.

Scratch stiffened with anger. Bo said, "It's got nothing to do with being yellow. We won't ride for a spread that turns its back on what's right."

"How have I done that?" Theresa asked.

"I think you know," Bo replied coolly. "Men died to defend you and your interests from Cole, and now you've gone and partnered up with him. That's not right, ma'am. It's just not right."

"Isn't it better to stop the fighting any way that I can?"

"Not when it means shaking hands with an enemy and forgetting all about those who gave their lives for you," Bo said.

Theresa's face hardened. "I'm doing what's practical, what's best for all concerned."

"Except those who'll be crushed by Cole in the future." Bo shook his head. "No, ma'am, we just won't have any part of it. We can't, not and live with ourselves."

Wood and most of the other gunmen looked like they would have been happy to slap leather at that moment. Only Ike Davis wore an uneasy expression. Bo knew that he and Scratch and Hector couldn't count on any help from the buckskin-clad old-timer, though. Ike had aligned himself with Theresa and Wood, and he was too stubborn to change his stripes now.

"All right, then," Theresa said coldly after a long, tense moment. "I hate to see you go after the help you've given me, but I won't try to force you to stay. You all have wages coming. You'll be paid when you go back to the Half Moon to collect your gear."

Bo nodded curtly. He wasn't going to say thank you. What Theresa had just agreed to was only right.

"We'll head on back to the ranch and wait for you."

"I'll be there a little later," Theresa said. "I still have some things to arrange with Mr. Cole."

Like how to finish the job of taking over Buffalo Flat completely, Bo thought but didn't say. He figured that was Theresa's ultimate goal. Just like with that settlement up in the Medicine Bows, she would wind up running the whole place if Cole didn't look out. Even if he did, she was cunning enough that he might not be able to stop her.

Feeling hostile eyes boring into their backs, the three men turned and went to get their horses from the hitch rail. No one tried to stop them as they mounted up and rode west out of town.

"Where do we go after we've been paid?" Scratch asked.

"Back to Buffalo Flat," Bo decided. "I want to have a talk with Bodine and Two Wolves."

A grin tugged at Scratch's mouth, the first smile that had appeared on his weather-beaten face in quite a while. "You thinkin' about throwin' in with those two young hellions for a spell?"

"Maybe," Bo said. "If Cole comes after them with Wood and the rest of those gun-wolves, they're liable to need a hand."

"I am with you and Señor Scratch, Señor Bo," Hector declared, "if you will have me."

"Of course we will," Scratch said. "Glad to have you along for the ride, Hector."

"We are three amigos, eh?"

More like three fools who are liable to find themselves on the wrong side of a shooting war, Bo thought. But again, he didn't say it.

Casey McLennan fell in step beside Matt and Sam as they started back toward the Silver Belle. "What happened in there?" he asked eagerly. "I tried to see past the crowd, but I couldn't hear anything and all I saw was a glimpse of Mrs. Kincaid talking to Cole."

"She made a deal with him," Matt said bitterly. "I'm not surprised. Betraying folks and seeing to it that she comes out on top is what she does."

"A deal?" the newspaperman repeated. "What kind of deal?"

Sam said, "They're partners now. Each will get a share in the other's ranch. And Porter Wood and his crew of gunslingers will go to work for Cole here in town."

McLennan's eyes widened. "But Wood and his bunch are even worse than the gunmen who were working for Cole before . . . before . . ."

"Before we killed nearly all of them, you mean?" Sam asked with a humorless smile. "We know. Everything will get cranked up a notch higher now. Cole won't be satisfied to bide his time any longer. He'll come after everyone who opposes him, starting with Miss MacKenzie."

"Good Lord," McLennan said in an awed voice. "There'll be shooting."

"Yeah," Matt said dryly. "A mite."

Charity, Lydia, and the other women were waiting anxiously on the boardwalk in front of the Silver Belle, along with a worried-looking Judge Ashmore. "What happened down there?" Charity wanted to know.

Matt and Sam quickly filled her in on the new alliance between Cole and Theresa Kincaid. The faces of the women fell as they heard the news.

"We might as well pack up and leave," Janie said.

"Better that than getting killed," Kathy agreed.

Charity made a sharp gesture and said, "Nobody's going anywhere. Damn it, this saloon is rightfully ours, and we're not going to let anybody run us off."

"The saloon is yours," Wilma pointed out. "You're the one who inherited it, not us."

"Judge Ashmore is drawing up papers to see that you all get a share—"

Becky said, "You never asked us if we wanted shares in a war."

"Damn it!" Lydia burst out, obviously angry and no longer able to contain it. "What's the matter with you ungrateful bitches? Charity offers us all a chance to get out of the whorehouse for good and you complain because there are some risks involved? Since when did life ever hand you anything without asking for payment in return? You've got to take some chances to get anywhere in life!"

The other women looked embarrassed, but not completely convinced by her tirade. Charity shook her head as she moved between Lydia and the others and said, "No, that's not the way I want it. Anybody who'd like to leave can just go right ahead, and there won't be any hard feelings on my part, I swear. I never meant for things to work out this way. I never meant to put any of you in danger."

Janie glanced at Matt and said, "I'm not leaving. I'm staying right here in Buffalo Flat."

"I reckon I will, too," Wilma said. "I didn't mean nothin' by what I said, Charity."

Becky and Kathy chimed in, also declaring their willingness to stay and help run the saloon and defend it from Cole's men if necessary.

Charity turned to Matt and Sam, saying, "What about you two? There's nothing holding you here."

Matt laughed. "You think you could drag us out of here with anything less than a team of wild horses? Shoot, things are just startin' to get entertaining."

Charity laughed and shook her head. "Then all I can say is that you have a strange notion of entertainment."

They all went back into the saloon. As evening approached, the place grew busier. Most of the talk among the townspeople concerned the new alliance between Cole and Theresa Kincaid. No one was really sure what it might mean, but the feeling was that no good could come of Cole having a whole gang of gunfighters at his disposal.

After night had fallen and all the lamps had been lit, Matt and Sam sat at one of the rear tables with cups of coffee and a deck of cards, which Matt laid out in a game of solitaire without paying too much attention to what he was doing. Out of long habit, both young men sat with their backs toward the wall. A few years earlier, up in Dakota Territory at a mining camp called Deadwood, Bill Hickok had made the mistake of not doing the same thing and had paid for it with his life. Matt and Sam both knew that the odds were good they would come to a violent end, but they wanted to do it standing on their own two feet, their guns in their hands, fighting to their last breath. No fate could be worse than being gunned down by some craven backshooter.

The buzz of conversation in the room suddenly died down as three men pushed through the batwings and came into the saloon. Matt recognized them immediately as some of Porter Wood's crew. He could even put names to them: Lije Braddock, Chuck Forrest, and Warren Jones. Braddock was tall and skinny, wearing a black vest and flat-crowned hat. Forrest's hat sported a Montana pinch, and his sharp-nosed face resembled that of a fox. Jones was the shortest and least impressive of the trio. The only thing unusual about him was his soup-strainer of a mustache. All three of them had numerous killings to their credit, Matt knew, and he also knew why they were here. As he exchanged a glance with Sam, he saw that his blood brother was well aware of the situation, too.

It hadn't taken Cole long to make his first move.

The gunnies swaggered over to the bar. Janie was working behind the hardwood, and Forrest leered at her as he said, "Three beers, pretty little lady."

Matt could tell that Janie was nervous, but she kept it under control as she drew the beers and set them in front of the three gunmen. "That'll be six bits, whichever of you boys is paying," she said.

"Might as well run a tab for us, darlin'," Jones told her. "We figure on bein' here for a while."

Charity was also behind the bar. She moved along it toward them in time to hear what Jones said. She replied, "It's pay as you go in the Silver Belle, mister."

Braddock drew himself up to his full height, which was impressive. "What do you mean by that?" he demanded. "We ain't good enough for you, sister?" He half-turned and gestured with his mug of beer toward the table where Matt and Sam sat. "Hell, you let a filthy half-breed Injun drink in here, and you tell us we ain't good enough?"

"Nobody said that," Charity replied tautly. "I just asked you to go ahead and pay for those beers."

"Fine." Braddock took a coin from his vest pocket and slapped it on the bar. "But since I paid for it, I'll damn well do what I please with it."

He turned the mug on its side and slowly poured the beer on the floor in front of the bar. Forrest and Jones did likewise, tossing coins onto the bar and then pouring their beers on the floor so that a good-sized puddle formed at their feet.

The saloon was completely quiet now, so that the splashing of the beer sounded unnaturally loud. So did the scraping of chair legs as Matt and Sam stood up and faced the three gunslingers.

The customers who were in the line of fire scrambled to get out of the way.

Braddock sneered at Matt and Sam and said, "What's the matter, Bodine? Something botherin' you?"

"You're making a mess there," Matt said.

"Yeah?" Braddock looked down at the spilled beer as if he hadn't seen it until now. "Somebody ought to mop that up. Be a good job for that half-breed. Sorry-ass Injun ain't fit for bein' anything more'n a swamper."

Sam said, "I could mop up that spilled beer, but I'm afraid that wouldn't help the smell."

"Yeah, it does stink of redskin in here," Chuck Forrest put in with a chuckle.

"No, I was referring more to the inevitable result of the relaxation of the sphincter muscle."

The three gunslingers frowned at him, obviously confused by what he had just said.

"He means you boys are gonna crap your pants when we shoot you," Matt informed them.

The frowns disappeared, replaced by outraged glares. "Why, you—" Braddock began. He didn't bother finishing the insult. His hand stabbed toward his gun in a blinding draw. Beside him, Forrest and Jones slapped leather, too.

The saloon erupted in gun smoke and death.

Chapter 26

Matt and Sam both pulled iron faster than the eye could follow. Matt's Colts cleared the holster just a hair ahead of Sam's gun. The twin revolvers bucked against his palms, blasting as soon as they came level. Tongues of flame darted wickedly from the muzzles.

The bullets smashed into Chuck Forrest's chest and threw him against the bar. The impact of the slugs was so powerful that he was bent backward over the hardwood from the waist. He had drawn his gun but never fired it. The weapon slipped out of suddenly nerveless fingers and flew up in the air, seeming to hang there for a second before thudding to the floor.

Even as Forrest was dying, Matt had shifted his aim and triggered again, this time at Warren Jones. The bullet from Matt's right-hand gun shattered Jones's left shoulder, turning him halfway around in that direction. The slug from the left-hand gun ripped through both of the ugly little hardcase's lungs, entering through the right side of his body and exiting from the left to smack into the front of the bar behind him. Jones stumbled and coughed.

Blood poured from his mouth. He pitched forward on his face, and Forrest slid from the bar behind him to land sprawled on top of him. Both men twitched a little in their death throes, but other than that, they didn't move.

At the same time as the shots from Bodine's guns were ringing out, Sam Two Wolves opened fire on Lije Braddock. Braddock got off a shot that scraped across the top of the table where Matt and Sam had been sitting, ripping the green felt that covered it. But Braddock didn't fire again, because two slugs from Sam's gun had torn into his belly, knocking him back a step and doubling him over. He staggered to one side and struggled to stay on his feet. It was obvious he wanted to lift his gun and take another shot at Sam, but he lacked the strength to do so. Finally, he dropped the gun and pressed both hands to his belly instead, but he couldn't stop the crimson tide that welled out over his fingers. With a groan, he took a couple of careening steps and fell headlong on a vacant table. The table's legs snapped, making it collapse under him.

Except for the dying echoes of the shots, the Silver Belle was silent again.

Matt holstered his left-hand gun and started replacing the expended rounds in the other weapon he held. "Sorry about the damage, Charity," he said to the stunned redhead standing behind the bar. "We'll go through those fellas' pockets, and if they don't have enough money on them to take care of it, Sam and I will make up the difference."

"That's right, ma'am," Sam said as he followed his blood brother's example and began reloading his gun. "Maybe if I'd hit Braddock a little cleaner, he'd have gone down before he got a chance to bust up that table."

Charity took a deep breath and blew it out. "Don't . . . don't worry about it," she said. "They didn't give you any choice."

"Oh, we had a choice," Matt said. "We could've let 'em buffalo us."

"We could've tucked our tails between our legs and run," Sam added.

"But that ain't like us."

"No," Sam said with a solemn shake of his head. "It's not."

Not surprisingly, the undertaker got there before the sheriff did. By the time Sherman Branch came in toting his ubiquitous shotgun, the bodies had already been hauled off and the blood and beer mopped up from the floor. "What happened here?" the lawman demanded anyway.

"A clear-cut case of self-defense—again," Judge Ashmore told him. "You can go down to the Colorado Palace and tell Junius Cole that the odds have been whittled down by three."

Branch glowered at Matt and Sam, who were sitting calmly at one of the tables again, and sputtered, "You . . . you can't keep on killin' people!"

"Then they should stop trying to kill us," Sam said.

"Yeah," Matt added with a smile, "because we don't cotton to it."

He knew, though, that Cole wouldn't stop. Neither would Terri Kelly—or Theresa Kincaid, as she called herself now—or Porter Wood or Lucas Tate. The lines had been drawn in the sand.

The killing was just getting started.

* * *

The sun was touching the tops of the Prophet Mountains as Bo, Scratch, and Hector rode toward the Half Moon. It had been a long, eventful, and pure-dee rotten day, filled with death, disappointment, and betrayal.

And it wasn't over yet, Bo thought. They had to collect the wages they had coming to them from Theresa, then ride back to Buffalo Flat and talk to Matt Bodine and Sam Two Wolves. Bo intended to throw in with Bodine and Two Wolves to help protect those women at the Silver Belle from Cole— that is, if Bodine and Two Wolves were willing to accept their help. It was possible the two young men might not trust the Texans and Hector, knowing that they had once ridden for Theresa.

They weren't far from the ranch when a shot rang out and muzzle flame stabbed through the dusky gloom ahead of them. Hector yelped in pain and started to topple from his saddle. He would have fallen if Scratch hadn't grabbed his arm and steadied him. More gun flashes lit up the twilight. Bullets ripped through the air around the heads of the riders.

"Get out of here!" Bo shouted at Scratch and Hector as he palmed out his Colt and returned the fire, triggering several shots toward the places where he had seen muzzle flashes. "Go! Ride for Buffalo Flat!"

Scratch grabbed the reins Hector had dropped when he was hit. The wounded man held himself in the saddle by tightly gripping the horn. As Scratch wheeled his mount around, he hauled Hector's horse with him. His spurs raked his horse's flanks and sent the animal lunging into a gallop.

Bo felt a bullet tug at the sleeve of his coat as he

finished emptying his six-gun at the ambushers. There had been an awful lot of bushwhacking going on in this part of the country, dating back to William Kincaid's murder, he thought as he whirled his mount and kicked it into a run after Scratch and Hector. He blamed that on Cole's influence. Things always went to hell when somebody like that tried to come in and take over.

More shots rang out as Bo pounded back along the trail. He didn't know if he had wounded any of the bushwhackers or not. Probably not, considering the poor light and the fact that he had been blazing away with a handgun.

He knew Hector had been hit by that first shot, but he didn't have any idea how bad the injury was. Bo hoped the little Mexican wasn't mortally wounded.

The firing died away behind them. The fading light was too uncertain for any long-range shooting. The bushwhackers had had one good chance to drop their targets, and they had failed at that. Bo intended to see to it that they didn't get another chance.

"Bo?" Scratch's voice called out through the gathering darkness. "That you?"

"Yeah," Bo replied as he reined in. "Where are you?"

"Over here at the side of the trail. Since the shooting stopped, I figured I'd better have a look at Hector and see how bad he's hurt."

Bo dismounted and led his horse toward the shadowy figures he could now make out to one side of the trail. Hector had taken a seat on a fallen log. Scratch leaned over him, pulling the Mexican's shirt aside.

"It is nothing, Señor Scratch," Hector protested. "The bullet, she barely touched me."

"It touched you hard enough to knock a chunk

of meat out of your side," Scratch informed him. "Bo, keep an eye out just in case them bush-whackin' varmints come after us."

Bo was already reloading his revolver. "I'll be ready for them if they do," he said as he snapped the cylinder closed. He holstered the gun and then drew the Winchester from the sheath strapped to his saddle. The rifle was fully loaded. Bo worked the lever to throw a cartridge into the firing chamber.

Bo stood guard while Scratch took a flask of whiskey and a roll of bandages from his saddlebags. After giving Hector a nip from the flask and taking one for himself, Scratch splashed some of the fiery liquor on the wound in Hector's side. Hector's breath hissed between his teeth at the sharp bite of the whiskey on raw flesh. *"Ay, Dios mío!"* he said.

"That'll keep it from festerin'," Scratch said. He wrapped bandages around Hector's torso and pulled the bindings as tight as he could. "You ought to be able to ride now."

"Where are we going? To the rancho?"

Bo shook his head. The bushwhackers hadn't followed them, but he knew it wouldn't be safe to try to make it to the Half Moon again. "I reckon we'll have to forget about those wages we've got coming to us, boys. I don't believe Theresa intends to pay us in anything except lead."

"You think she was behind that ambush?" Scratch asked.

"Cole or Wood may have given the actual order to send some of those gunslingers ahead of us, but she had to know about it. I reckon they figured we might try to join forces with Bodine and Two Wolves, and they wanted to stop us before that could happen."

Scratch nodded in the dimness. "Yeah, varmints

like that usually want the odds as high on their side as they can get 'em. So we're gonna try to make it back to Buffalo Flat?"

"Yeah, I guess. But Cole's liable to have thrown a cordon around the settlement by now. We may have to fight our way through." Bo paused. "The other option is to pick another direction, ride off toward it, and never look back."

"You mean let Cole and Miz Kincaid get away with takin' over the whole damn town? This whole part o' the country, in fact?" Scratch let out a disgusted snort. "Not damned likely. It took me a while to come around to the truth, but I can see now that woman's got to be stopped."

Bo nodded in agreement. "Let's ride, then. That is, if you're up to it, Hector?"

"Try and stop me, Señor Bo," the gritty little ranch hand said. "I, too, have scores to settle."

Night had fallen quickly once the sun set. The three men mounted up and rode grim faced through the darkness toward Buffalo Flat.

Theresa Kincaid sat across the desk from Junius Cole and said, "I don't see any point in waiting."

She had a glass of sherry in one hand and occasionally sipped from it as they discussed their plans. There was an easy elegance about her despite the frontier garb she wore, Cole thought. She was undeniably beautiful, and the ambition and even ruthlessness he sensed in her drew him to her even more strongly than he would have thought possible. For months, he had regarded her as an enemy, an obstacle in the path of his plans, and nothing more. He could see now how wrong he had been about her. They should have been working together all along.

He didn't want to start moving too fast, though. He said, "Maybe we should take our time—"

"Why?" Theresa cut in. "Every day you wait to crush your opposition is another day they can get stronger. I know how Bodine and Two Wolves work. I've had trouble with them before. They'll rally the townspeople around them if you give them a chance. You heard what they did to Braddock and Forrest and Jones. Everybody in town will know about it by morning, if they don't already. That'll give people the courage to stand up to you. You don't want that, Junius."

Cole scowled and shook his head. "Anybody who crosses me will regret it. That's a promise."

"I believe you. The question is, do the citizens of Buffalo Flat?"

"They'd damned well better!"

Theresa took another sip of sherry. "Then you have to do something to *show* them." She paused, then asked, "Can you count on the sheriff to look the other way?"

Cole waved a hand. "Don't worry about Sherman Branch. The only reason he's in office is because of my support, and he knows it. Anyway, he's a small-timer. He's not going to interfere."

"Then as soon as those men get back from disposing of Creel and Morton, our whole bunch should go down and clean out the Silver Belle. You'll never have a better chance to get rid of Bodine and the half-breed. Once they're dead, that redheaded witch and the other whores won't have any choice but to leave town . . . unless, of course, you want to keep them around and put them to work for you."

"You're talking about not even making a show of doing things legally," Cole growled.

"Why worry about that? You already said the sheriff's not going to interfere."

"What about outside authorities?" Cole wanted to know. "What if the governor gets wind of what we're doing?"

Theresa smiled and shook her head. "That's when Sheriff Branch will earn his keep. No matter what happens, he can make it sound like we were in the right, like we were just defending our own interests. If he can't, then it'll be time for another lawman to take over." She laughed. "How does Sheriff Wood sound?"

It sounded pretty good to Cole. He began to nod slowly. She was winning him over.

Theresa leaned forward and set the glass on the desk. "Hit them now, and hit them hard," she said, hatred edging into her voice again. "Once Bodine and Two Wolves are dead, no one can stop us, Junius. We'll run this part of the country like a king and queen."

Cole smiled. He liked the sound of that.

Especially the king and queen part, he thought as he looked at the beautiful and deadly Theresa Kincaid.

"I tell you, I don't trust her," Anna Malone said to Lucas Tate as they sat together at one of the rear tables in the Colorado Palace. "I don't trust her at all."

Tate scowled toward the bar, where Porter Wood and the rest of the gunslingers were gathered, drinking and talking and laughing. They didn't seem bothered by the fact that three of their

number had died earlier this evening in the gunfight with Bodine and Two Wolves. Men like that
knew their lives could end violently at any time,
with little or no warning. That was part of the game.
So they didn't waste much time mourning when
one of their fellow gunslingers was cut down.

Anna looked at the closed door of Cole's office
and went on. "You know she's in there turning him
against us, Lucas. Junius never shut us out like this
before. Not until she came along and offered to
join forces with him."

Tate laughed harshly. "You're just jealous," he
said. "You're afraid the Kincaid woman is going to
take your place."

Anna glared at him. "Don't try to tell me you
don't feel the same way about Porter Wood. You're
not the top man with a gun around here anymore."

"I can take Wood," Tate snapped, but he didn't
sound too convinced of that. "Anyway, we're all on
the same side, ain't we? I got no reason to be jealous of him." He didn't sound convinced of that,
either.

Both of them sat up straighter as the office door
opened and Cole came out, followed a moment
later by Theresa Kincaid. Cole walked across to the
table where Anna and Tate sat.

"I've got a job for you, Lucas," he announced. "I
want you to ride out to the Diamond C and bring
back Barlowe and the crew."

"You want all the hands in town, Boss?" Tate
asked with a frown.

"The gun-handy ones, anyway," Cole decided.
"Barlowe can leave a few men on the ranch, just to
keep an eye on the place. Although I don't think
we have anything to worry about out there."

"Why do you want Barlowe and the others to come to town?"

Cole frowned as if he didn't like having his orders questioned, even slightly. He said, "We're taking over the Silver Belle and getting rid of Bodine and Two Wolves tonight."

"You're gonna send nearly twenty men to get rid of two?"

"How many men have I sent against those two before?" Cole snapped. "I'm through playing with them. They're going to die tonight, and I might just run those whores out of town on a rail." His right hand clenched into a fist and thumped down on the table. "Everybody in Buffalo Flat is going to see that they can't defy Junius Cole, by God!"

Tate nodded and stood up. "Sure, Boss. I'll fetch Barlowe and the boys from the Diamond C. Just don't start the ball until we get back."

Cole nodded curtly. "Don't waste any time."

As Tate left the saloon, Anna glanced toward the bar, where Theresa Kincaid stood talking to Wood. There was a smug, self-satisfied smile on the blonde's face, and as Anna saw it, she knew that it had been Theresa's idea to attack the Silver Belle tonight. She wanted to strike right away, while her partnership with Cole was still fresh. Before Cole had a chance to find out for himself just how treacherous she could be.

Anna drew a deep breath. She knew who her real enemy was now.

The question was, what was she going to do about it?

Chapter 27

The evening was well advanced when the door of the sheriff's office opened and Lucas Tate came in. Sherman Branch looked up from the desk where he had been shuffling through some reward dodgers and trying not to think too much about what was happening in his town. A few minutes earlier, he had heard a lot of horses in the street outside and had stood up to look through the window. He'd seen Tate riding by with Roy Barlowe and half a dozen of the hands from the Diamond C. The gunslinging half of the ranch's crew, Branch had realized. He didn't know why they had come to town, but it couldn't be for anything good.

Now he looked at Tate and growled, "What do you want?"

"Mr. Cole's worried about you, Sheriff," Tate said. "He thinks you've been workin' too hard lately. He sent me to tell you that you ought to go on home and get a good night's sleep. Whatever you hear, just don't worry about it tonight, and everything'll be fine in the morning."

Branch felt something gnawing at his insides. "Cole told you to tell me that, did he?"

"That's right," Tate said. "Because he's worried about you."

The sheriff sighed and reached for his hat, which sat on the corner of the desk. "Well, you can tell him that he doesn't have to worry. I'll take his suggestion and go get some sleep. Reckon it'll be such a sound sleep I won't hear a damned thing."

Tate smiled tightly and nodded. "I'll tell him."

As the gunman started to turn away, Branch couldn't resist saying, "I saw you ride by with Barlowe and the rest of that bunch a little while ago. Looks like Cole's turned you into an errand boy, Tate."

For a second, as Tate's mouth twisted in anger, Branch thought he might go for his gun. But then Tate just spat on the floor and said, "Run home and hide under the covers, tin star."

He stalked out of the office. Branch sat there for a moment longer, looking down at the hat he held in his hands.

Then he put it on and reached for the badge pinned to his vest. He took the star off and tossed it on the desk as he stood up.

As he left the office after blowing out the lamp, he turned not toward his house on the edge of town, but the other way toward the Silver Belle instead.

Only a handful of men were drinking at the bar tonight, and the tables were empty except for the one where Matt and Sam sat with Judge Ashmore. The lawyer looked around the mostly deserted room and said, "It appears that most folks think

Cole won't waste any time taking advantage of the situation, now that he has some new allies."

"Yeah, I reckon most of 'em want to stay out of the line of fire," Matt said as the men at the bar began to finish their drinks and drift out of the place. "Maybe you'd like to mosey back on over to your office, Judge."

Ashmore rejected that suggestion with a shake of his head. "I like it here," he declared. "You understand, courage and valor are not hallmarks of my profession, but hell, even a lawyer's got to stand up and do the right thing every now and then."

Casey McLennan pushed through the batwings and looked around. The newspaperman had a Sharps carbine tucked under his arm. He came over to the table and nodded to Matt, Sam, and Ashmore.

"Thought I'd stop by here for a while, just in case there's a story to cover tonight," he explained.

"Most journalists regard the tools of their trade as pencil, paper, and a printing press," Sam pointed out. "Not a Sharps carbine."

"Well, you never know what'll come in handy," McLennan said.

Matt frowned. "I know you've got a wife, McLennan. What about kids?"

"Three of them," the newspaperman replied with a nod.

"Then you'd better go home to them, my friend," Sam said softly. "That way, if anything happens tonight, you'll be alive to write about it in the morning."

McLennan was pale, and Matt could see the fear in his eyes. But there was something else there, too—sheer mule-headed determination.

"It's because of my family that I'm here," McLennan said. "I like Buffalo Flat. It used to be a good place to live. But it won't be anymore if Junius Cole is running things around here. We all know that."

Matt and Sam exchanged a glance and then shrugged. "Suit yourself," Matt said.

"It's possible that nothing will happen, anyway," Sam added.

But less than five minutes later, the batwings swung back and Sheriff Sherman Branch strode into the saloon. He didn't have his shotgun with him this time. The place was empty now except for the women behind the bar and the four men sitting at the table. Branch walked over to where Matt, Sam, Ashmore, and McLennan waited and gave them a curt nod. Fastening his gaze on Matt, the sheriff said, "I thought you ought to know, Bodine . . . Lucas Tate fetched half-a-dozen gunmen from the Diamond C. They rode into town not long ago, and I reckon they're over at the Colorado Palace now."

Matt nodded. "Added to Wood's bunch, that'll give Cole about twenty men. It figures those are the sort of odds a snake like him would want."

Sam asked, "Are you going to do anything about this, Sheriff?"

"I came and told you about it," Branch said. "That's all I can do."

"You could stay and help us, Sherman," McLennan said.

"I'm not as big a fool as you, Casey. You shouldn't even be here yourself."

"Somebody had to stand up to Cole."

"Somebody has to die, you mean." Branch shook his head. "Well, I warned you, all of you. It's on your heads now. I'm going home."

"None of us are going to forget how you turned your back on the law, Sherman," Ashmore said.

"I might worry about that . . . if any of you were going to be alive in the morning."

Branch turned on his heel and stalked out of the saloon.

It wasn't like a weight had been lifted from his shoulders or anything like that. The weight was still there and probably always would be. But it wasn't like life hadn't already heaped plenty of burdens on Sherman Branch, either. And he thought he felt a little better as he walked away from the Silver Belle. At least he had tried to do something.

Then a dark shape stepped out from an alley mouth in front of him, and a voice he didn't recognize at first said, "I told Cole you'd go running to that bunch in there. I told him it would stick in your craw so bad you'd have to do something about it."

"Wood!" the sheriff exclaimed as his eyes began to make out the short, slender shape of the man confronting him.

"We needed a signal to get things started," Porter Wood said as he lifted his hand. "I reckon this'll do as good as any."

The gun Wood held roared even as Sheriff Branch made a desperate grab for his own weapon. Branch didn't even come close. As the muzzle flash half-blinded him, he felt the slug strike him in the chest like a hammer blow. It knocked him back a step. He sat down on the edge of the boardwalk and tried to draw a breath into his body past the giant surge of pain that seemed to fill him. It was no use. There was nothing left of him except the hurting and a last fleeting thought of his wife. Then he toppled backward into blackness.

Matt and Sam heard the shot outside, not far away, and knew instinctively what was about to happen. "Everybody down!" Matt shouted as he leaped to his feet. "Blow out the lamps!"

A second later, almost before the people in the saloon had started to move, one of the windows exploded in a shower of glass as a volley of gunshots blasted through it.

Matt heard screams of fear and possibly pain as he crouched and drew his guns. He kicked over a table to serve as cover. A few feet away, Sam was on his feet with his revolver in hand. He knelt behind an overturned table, too, as did Judge Ashmore and Casey McLennan. Matt cast a glance toward the bar and saw that Charity and the other women had disappeared. They were down behind the hardwood, which was about the safest place they could be right now. As he watched, Charity stood up long enough to blow out the lamps at each end of the bar. As she puffed at the flame in the second one, she suddenly yelped and fell out of sight.

"Charity!" Matt called. "Are you hit?"

"I'm all right," she replied shakily from behind the bar. "A bullet just came right by my ear and scared me."

"Anybody else hurt over there?" Sam asked.

"We're all fine," Lydia answered.

Matt looked up. The lamps on one of the silver chandeliers were still burning, casting enough light around the room so that the bastards outside could see to aim their shots. He hated to do it, but he tilted up the barrel of his left-hand gun and fired several times, blasting the chandelier to pieces and putting out the lights. Darkness fell over the saloon, relieved intermittently by muzzle flashes from outside as Cole's men continued firing.

"We were lucky no one was hit in that opening volley," Sam said. "But we're in a bad spot anyway. We're pinned down here, Matt."

"I know. Cole's probably got men posted behind the place, just in case anybody tries to get out that way."

Ashmore asked, "Is the door locked back there?"

"Locked and barred," Sam replied. "I took care of that earlier. We couldn't be sure that Cole would make his move this soon, but Matt and I figured we needed to be ready in case he did."

"That's why there are Winchesters and six-guns and plenty of ammunition under the bar," Matt said. "You ladies feel free to help yourselves over there."

"We're already ahead of you," Charity replied, and her words were followed immediately by the sound of a Winchester's lever being worked. "If those bastards get in here, they'll find a hot reception waiting for them."

"Speaking of hot receptions," Casey McLennan said worriedly, "what if they try to burn us out?"

"Not likely to happen," Matt said. "Cole can make use of this building if he gets his hands on it. Bullet holes can be patched and window glass can be replaced, but the place is lost if it's burned down. Besides, in the middle of town like this, if you set a fire you risk it spreading to the rest of the settlement. More than one whole town has gotten burned to the ground like that. Cole won't chance it. He doesn't want to be the boss of a destroyed town."

"So what you're telling us," Ashmore said, "is that they'll sit out there and keep shooting until they've picked us all off."

"That's about the size of it," Matt agreed.

"That's what they plan to do, anyway," Sam said. "What they don't know is that Matt and I have a different idea."

"What's that?" McLennan asked.

Matt grinned savagely in the darkness that now cloaked the saloon. "We're going to take the fight to them," he said.

Bo, Scratch, and Hector weren't very far from the outskirts of town when the shooting started. A single shot rang out first, then seconds later the roar of a veritable fusillade came to their ears through the night air. As they reined in, Scratch said, "Sounds like a war goin' on up yonder."

"Damn it," Bo said. "Cole must be going after Bodine and Two Wolves already. I was hoping we'd get there first so we could give them a hand."

"I reckon we still can. They've probably got those young hellions pinned down somewhere. They won't be expectin' trouble from some other direction."

Bo nodded. "You're probably right about that. Hector, are you sure you're up to this?"

Hector held up his rifle. "Just lead me to the battle, Señor Bo," he declared fiercely.

Scratch grinned and slapped him on the shoulder. "You're a good hombre, Hector!"

"Let's go," Bo said.

They rode on toward Buffalo Flat, halting and dismounting when they reached the edge of the settlement. The shooting continued at the center of town. One good thing about a fracas like this, Bo thought, was that the innocent citizens of the town were probably all lying low, waiting for the shooting to be over. That meant the chances were anybody he and his companions encountered as they made their way toward the Silver Belle would be an enemy.

They tied their horses in a little clump of trees and started forward on foot, clutching their Winchesters. Bo saw orange stabs of muzzle flame up ahead on the right side of the street. A few shots flared in return from the left. That was the side of the street where the Silver Belle was located, he recalled. To a man who had seen more than his share of trouble, the muzzle flashes told the story quite plainly. A smaller force was holed up inside the saloon, while the larger, attacking force had found cover in buildings across the street, and behind parked wagons and water troughs and rain barrels. The air above the surface of the street was filled with a hailstorm of hot lead right now, as shots went back and forth between the attackers and the defenders.

"We can circle around and get behind them," Bo said quietly to Scratch and Hector. "We'll come up that alley next to the building where some of them have taken cover. From the mouth of the alley we'll have a good angle on the ones behind the wagons and watering troughs."

Scratch nodded. "We can cut down some of 'em before they even know what hit 'em."

The three men began working their way alongside one of the buildings. When they reached the rear corner, Bo stepped around it first, only to find himself facing several shadowy figures. Starlight glinted on gun barrels as the men jerked up revolvers and opened fire.

Bo flung himself forward, hitting the dirt as bullets sizzled through the air above his head. His Colt was in his hand and spouting flame before he hit the ground. One of the men grunted in pain and staggered backward. The others lowered their aim and kept firing. Bo rolled desperately to the side as slugs pounded into the ground where he had been lying just a heartbeat earlier.

That distraction gave Scratch and Hector a chance to duck around the corner and open up with their rifles. Like cracks of thunder and lightning, the Winchesters spat death and sent the gunmen tumbling off their feet. Bo scrambled up as the last of the shadowy figures fell.

They were all down and unmoving, he saw. He holstered his gun and fished a match from his pocket. Snapping the lucifer to life on his thumbnail, he held it up and let the wavering glow from the flame wash over the fallen men. He recognized them as four of Porter Wood's gunslingers. None of them was Ike Davis, and Bo was grateful for that, even though he was well aware that they might have to swap lead with Ike before the night was over.

He shook the match out and dropped it at his feet, hissed, "Come on," to Scratch and Hector. They had already whittled the odds down by four, and they were just getting started.

When they reached the alley that was their destination, they started along it toward the street, moving silently through the darkness. Suddenly Bo heard several soft thudding sounds behind them.

Even as he whirled around with his gun in his hand, his brain realized that those sounds had been made by a couple of men dropping to the ground from up above them somewhere. Beside him, Scratch turned, too, but Bo had the sick feeling that both of them were going to be too late to meet this unexpected threat.

The killers had the drop on them. At any second death was going to roar out of the darkness right in their faces, and there wasn't a damned thing they could do about it except try to go down fighting.

Chapter 28

Leaving Judge Ashmore, Casey McLennan, and five of the women downstairs in the Silver Belle to keep firing across the street at Cole's men, Matt and Sam slipped upstairs, accompanied by Charity MacKenzie. They went into one of the darkened rooms and crossed to the window, guided by the faint starlight that came through the glass.

Matt raised the window and threw a leg over the sill. "I'll go first," he whispered. He knew that if Porter Wood, or whoever was directing the actual attack, had posted gunmen behind the saloon, he was taking a big chance by climbing out this way. But there was nothing else he and Sam could do to turn the tide of this battle. He slid over the sill and hung by his hands for a second, poised to drop to the ground below.

In that second a gun suddenly blasted to his left. The slug chewed splinters from the wall next to the window. Matt released his hold and let himself fall. Even as he plummeted toward the ground, a muzzle flash lit up the room where Sam and Charity were. Sam was returning the bushwhacker's fire.

Matt's boots hit the ground in the alley behind the saloon. He let all his muscles go limp and rolled across the dirt to break the force of his fall. As he came to a stop on his belly, he lifted his head and saw another stab of flame as a gun roared. His Colt was already in his hand, and it bucked against his palm as he triggered a round toward that flash.

A man groaned in the darkness, and Matt heard a clatter as something fell. A second later, Sam thudded to the ground beside him. There were no more shots.

"Must've been just two of them," Matt said as he climbed hurriedly to his feet.

"Yeah, and I think we got both of them," Sam replied. "Come on."

They cat-footed off into the darkness as Charity closed the window in the room above them.

Moving quickly, Matt and Sam made their way along the street behind the buildings until they thought it would be safe to cross over and work their way back. No shots rang out as they darted across the street, so Matt hoped that meant they hadn't been spotted. In a matter of minutes, they reached the rear of the building where some of Cole's gunmen had positioned themselves to lay siege to the Silver Belle.

Not wanting to risk any words, Sam touched Matt's arm and then pointed upward toward a second-floor landing that could be reached by a narrow outside stairway. They climbed the stairs, continuing to make as little noise as possible even though it was unlikely anybody would hear them, what with all the hellish racket of gunfire going on.

When they reached the landing, they found that the door was locked. Matt grasped the knob, turned it as hard as he could, and threw his shoulder against the door. It didn't budge. He put his mouth close to Sam's ear and said, "Must be barred on the inside."

Sam nodded understanding and pointed to a window a few feet to the left of the landing. He handed Matt his hat and then swung a leg over the railing around the landing.

Balancing himself carefully, Sam lifted his other leg over the railing and perched at the very edge of the landing. After taking a second to steady himself, he launched out into space, leaping along the wall and reaching out with his right hand for the windowsill. His fingers closed over it and tightened, and he hung there by one hand for a second before he could get the other hand on the sill. The window was raised slightly for ventilation. Once Sam was able to get a good grip, he let go with one hand and pushed the pane up more. Then he hauled himself up and over the sill and through the window, his booted feet disappearing last.

A moment later Matt heard the bar on the inside of the door being lifted. The door swung open and Sam stood there grinning. "Are you half Cheyenne or half monkey?" Matt whispered with a grin of his own. He gave Sam's hat back to him and stepped into the building.

They were in a hallway that led toward the front. As they moved cautiously along it, a door suddenly opened and a man stepped out. The blood brothers' guns leaped into their hands, but before they could fire the man thrust his arms into the air and whispered urgently, "Don't shoot! Don't shoot!"

Even though there was little light in this upstairs corridor, Matt and Sam both had keen eyes and could make out the fact that the man wore a night-shirt. He went on. "I ain't one of Cole's men. This is my building. I run the store downstairs and live up here. Please don't kill me."

"You let Cole's men use your place?" Matt asked in a hard voice.

"I didn't have no choice. I ain't a gunfighter. What would you do, Mr. Bodine, if you was just a normal man and some o' them killers showed up and wanted to be let in?"

Matt shrugged. He supposed the store owner had a point, but there was no time to discuss it now. "Get back inside that room," he said, "and keep on lyin' low."

The storekeeper reached back into the room and lifted a rifle into view. "I want to help you," he said. "I seen you comin' in and recognized you. Folks got to stand up to Cole, or he'll take over the whole town. He damn near has it in the palm o' his hand already."

"Go on back in your room, sir," Sam told the man. "We appreciate the offer, but this is something we're more suited for than you are."

"You sure? I . . . I reckon it's time I took a chance."

"No, Sam's right," Matt said. "We'll handle Cole's gunslingers."

The man nodded and seemed to be relieved. "Good luck to you boys," he said in a heartfelt tone as he faded back into the room where he had been hiding out.

The blood brothers moved on. The shots from downstairs were louder as they reached a set of stairs. Without having to talk about it, Matt and Sam holstered their guns and drew bowie knives instead. If they could deal with the enemies downstairs quietly, they would still have the advantage of surprise on their side.

A slow step at a time, they moved down the stairs. Three men were in the front of the store, crouched by the windows. They had knocked out some of the glass with their rifle barrels and were firing through the broken windows at the Silver Belle across the street. Matt and Sam approached them stealthily from behind.

The men never heard them coming. Matt grabbed one of the gunmen from behind, looping an arm around his neck and jerking him upright. The blade in Matt's other hand swooped across the man's tight-drawn throat, cutting deeply. Matt felt the hot gush of blood over his hand as death spasms shook the gunslinger.

A few feet away, Sam had launched an identical attack and cut the throat of the man he grabbed. But the third man heard the commotion and realized something was wrong. He yelled, "Hey!" and twisted toward them, swinging his rifle around. In a continuation of the same movement with which he had cut the second man's throat, Sam threw his bowie at the third man. With a solid, meaty *thunk!* the blade sunk deep in the hard case's chest. He gasped in pain as the rifle slipped out of his hands and thudded to the floor. For a second he pawed futilely at the handle of the knife before falling to his knees and then pitching forward on his face as death claimed him.

Sam lowered the still-twitching corpse in his hands and went over to the third man to roll him onto his back and pull the knife free. He wiped blood from the bowie's blade on the dead man's vest and then sheathed it.

"That's five of 'em," Matt whispered, counting the two men they had killed in the alley behind the Silver Belle.

"Only fifteen or so to go," Sam responded wryly.

They went back upstairs, where Matt knocked softly on the door of the room where the store owner was hiding out. "We got the ones downstairs," he said when the man opened the door a crack, "but you'd still better keep your head down until all the shooting stops."

"I intend to, don't you worry about that," the man said, bobbing his head in a nod.

The blood brothers went to the door that opened onto the outside landing, exchanging a few whispered words as they formulated a rough plan. They would have to split up now, each of them moving up a different side of the building so they could get behind the gunslingers who had taken cover along the street. But before they could put that plan into action, Sam touched Matt's arm and gestured toward the ground below.

Several shadowy figures were moving stealthily along the wall. More of Cole's men, Matt figured, getting ready to join the fight. He pointed to them and drew his bowie knife again. Sam did likewise. With the agile strength of youth, they vaulted over the railing and dropped to the ground, ready to fling themselves among the enemy with cold steel flickering in their hands.

Two of the three men whirled around with surprising speed, hands dipping toward their guns. Matt was ready to strike first, but Sam abruptly caught his arm and said, "Wait!"

The men froze with their guns drawn but not leveled. One of them said, "Two Wolves? Bodine?"

"Creel!" Matt said in a low-voiced exclamation. "Is that you and Morton?"

"And Hector Ibañez from the Half Moon," Bo answered. "You fellas were right all along about Mrs. Kincaid. Somebody tried to ambush us while we were on our way out to the ranch, and I reckon she was probably behind it."

"So we rode back here to give you a hand if Cole tried to wipe you out tonight," Scratch put in. "From the sounds of all the shootin', that's what's goin' on here."

Sam said, "You're right. We made it out of the Silver Belle, but the others are still pinned down there."

"We're trying to improve the odds some," Matt added.

"We've whittled at 'em a mite ourselves," Scratch said. "There are four of Cole's men back up the alley who won't bother you no more."

Matt let out a low whistle of admiration. "Then between us, we've just about cut their forces in half. That means the odds are only two to one now."

"We can handle that," Bo said confidently. "And when we're done . . ."

Matt nodded, even though they might not be able to see him in the shadows like this. "Then we deal with Cole and Terri," he said.

The Colorado Palace had cleared out. None of the townspeople wanted to sit around drinking or gambling tonight. They all wanted to be home with their heads down, hoping that stray bullets would steer clear of them and their families.

That left Cole, Theresa, Anna Malone, Porter Wood, Lucas Tate, and Ike Davis in the saloon. Wood, Tate, and Ike had stayed to protect Cole and Theresa, on the slim chance that Bodine and Two Wolves might survive the attack on the Silver Belle and come looking for revenge. That possibility was so remote that it was laughable, Cole thought, but at the same time he didn't mind having three tough, fast guns around just in case.

He sat at one of the tables with Theresa while Anna stood at the bar throwing back shots of whiskey. Cole had enjoyed the time he'd spent with Anna, and she had been a dependable partner in his schemes for a long while, but he sensed that in Theresa Kincaid he had finally met a woman worthy of him. Together, there was no telling where they could go, no limit on what they might accomplish—as long as he was careful not to trust her too much.

"Tell me," he said curiously as the shooting continued down the street. "What *really* happened to your husband?"

Theresa smiled thinly. "He was ambushed, shot in the back. Haven't you heard the story? Most of the people in Buffalo Flat seem to think that you ordered him killed."

"They may think that, but it's not true. I didn't have a damned thing to do with his death, although I thought at the time it was a stroke of luck for me." His eyes narrowed as he gazed across the table at her. "It was a stroke of luck for *you*, for sure. You inherited a fine ranch."

"As well as a lot of trouble."

"The Half Moon is worth some trouble. I know you found Kincaid's body. I'm wondering if you found him a little earlier than what you claimed . . . like when he was still alive and never suspected that his loving wife would shoot him in the back."

Theresa just smiled and didn't say anything. Cole knew the truth, though. He could look in her eyes and know who had really pulled the trigger ending William Kincaid's life.

As he poured drinks for both of them, he told himself that he would never make the mistake Kincaid had. He would never give Theresa the chance to get rid of him that way.

"To us," he said as he lifted his drink.

"To us," Theresa repeated as she clinked her glass against his.

And at the bar, Anna Malone threw back another shot of whiskey.

Matt, Sam, Bo, Scratch, and Hector quickly hatched a plan. The five of them would split up and close in on Cole's men from behind. "When we're ready, we'll call out and then take them on," Sam said.

"Why not just shoot 'em *before* we warn 'em?" Scratch suggested.

"We can't do that," Bo said. "It wouldn't be honorable."

"Honor can sometimes get a man killed," Scratch grumbled.

"Yes, but unfortunately, I agree with Mr. Creel," Sam said. "What about you, Matt?"

Matt shrugged. "As long as we ventilate those skunks, I don't much care how we go about it."

"All right, then, it's settled," Sam said with a nod. "Good luck to all of us."

They moved apart from each other in the darkness, slipping around the buildings and through alleys until they were in position behind the gunmen hidden along the street who continued to pour lead into the Silver Belle. Matt hoped no one inside the saloon had been hit, but he knew the odds were against that, considering the volume of fire that had been directed toward it tonight. Soon, though, this fight would be over. He stepped onto the boardwalk, a few yards from a covered wagon parked in front of a building. Two of Cole's gunslingers crouched behind the wagon, one at each end, and they were blazing away at the Silver Belle.

"Hey!" Matt called to them.

His guns were still in their holsters, but he filled his hands as the startled men spun toward him. They were experienced, hardened gunfighters, and their weapons were already drawn. Each man got off a shot, but the bullets whistled past Matt's ears as his Colts began to thunder. The shots rolled out, and the slugs drove the two men into jittering dances of death. They dropped their guns, slumped against the wagon, and then crumpled to the dirt of the street.

At the other corner of the building, Sam Two Wolves stepped out of the darkness and called, "Drop your guns!" at two men stretched out behind a water trough. He knew perfectly well that they wouldn't do it. Instead, just as he expected, they rolled over and lunged upright, crouching as they slammed shots at him from the rifles they held.

Sam flung himself down on the boardwalk, wincing

as slugs tore splinters from the planks and stung his face. He squeezed off two shots that sent one of the gunmen spinning off his feet, then triggered a third time. That slug caught the second man in the middle, folding him over and knocking him backward so that he fell into the water trough with a huge splash. Neither man moved again.

Farther along the street, Bo Creel strode confidently along the boardwalk, and the ringing of his boot heels on the planks made two of Cole's gunslingers jerk around to face him. Bo's hand swept the long black coat back as he palmed out his revolver. Flame geysered from its muzzle as he fired. One of the gunmen was driven off his feet by a slug, but the other triggered two fast shots. A bullet slammed into Bo's left arm, jerking him around. He fought off the wave of shock and pain that went through him and fired again, putting a slug cleanly through the second man's head.

Not too far away, Scratch joined the fight, both hands filled with roaring pistols as he closed in on three of the gun-wolves. Hector Ibañez was beside him. The rifle in the Mexican's hands cracked again and again until Hector went down, his right leg shot out from under him. By then, though, he had blown a hole through one of the gunmen. Scratch accounted for the other two, hammering them with slugs until they went down.

He walked over to the sprawled bodies, kicked them to make sure they were dead, then hurried back to kneel beside Hector. "You all right, compadre?" Scratch asked worriedly.

"My leg, she hurts like el Diablo himself," Hector replied, "but I will be fine, Señor Scratch. What about you and the others?"

Matt, Sam, and Bo came along the street, re-grouping around Scratch and Hector. Scratch said, "We all appear to be fine."

"Speak for yourself," Bo said. "I caught a slug in my left arm."

Scratch came to his feet with a worried frown. "How bad is it?" he asked.

"It's not my gun arm," Bo said, as if that answered everything.

"Sam and I checked the other bodies," Matt put in. "They're all dead. But Cole and Wood and Tate weren't among 'em."

"What about Ike Davis?" Scratch asked.

"That old-timer who wears buckskins?" Sam shook his head. "I didn't see him. Could be he's still down at the Colorado Palace with the others."

"And that's where we're headed now," Matt added. "We still have to deal with Cole and Terri. How about you fellas go over to the Silver Belle and check on the folks over there, let them know this part of the fight is over?"

Scratch looked like he wanted to argue, but after a second he nodded curtly and said, "Bo and Hector need some patchin' up, and Hector can't even walk. Bo, get on one side of him with your good arm, and I'll get the other side."

Working together, the Texans lifted Hector and half-carried him toward the Silver Belle, where Charity, Judge Ashmore, and Casey McLennan had emerged from the saloon, pushing the bullet-riddled batwings aside to step out onto the boardwalk.

Matt and Sam finished reloading their guns, then Sam said, "You ready?"

"Damn straight," Matt said. "Let's finish this."

Chapter 29

Cole began to worry as the fighting down the street grew more intense. The shooting should have been over by now, he told himself. How long could such a motley force hold out?

"You've crossed paths with Bodine and Two Wolves before," he said to Theresa. "Is there any chance they might be able to get out of this?"

Her expression had grown more worried as the minutes went by, too. "I wouldn't put anything past those two," she admitted. "I've seen them fight off long odds before."

Cole nodded. "I think you'd better go upstairs, just to be on the safe side. Take Anna with you."

"I don't like being told to go and hide," Theresa snapped.

Cole reached under his coat and brought out a small pistol. He checked the loads in the cylinder and then placed the gun on the table in front of him. "I don't want to have to worry about either of you if there's any shooting down here," he said. "When Bodine and Two Wolves are dead, I'll let you know."

Theresa still didn't like the idea, but she nodded in agreement. She stood up and went over to the bar to join Anna.

"Junius says we need to go upstairs."

Anna appeared to be drunk. She stared at Theresa for a moment, as if she didn't understand what the blond woman had said, but then she nodded and started toward the staircase, stumbling a little as she did so. Theresa glanced at Cole one more time and then followed her. As they climbed the stairs, the gunfire down the street abruptly fell silent. Theresa's hand tightened tensely on the banister for a second. She didn't know what the silence meant—hopefully, that all of their enemies were dead—but she sensed that one way or another, this would soon be over.

Cole picked up his gun and walked to the bar to join Wood, Tate, and Ike Davis. Wood had a drink in front of him. He threw it back and said, "Reckon it's done. The boys will be along in a minute to tell us that Bodine and Two Wolves are dead."

"They'd damned well better be," Cole grated.

A few edgy moments passed, and then the four men heard footsteps coming along the boardwalk outside the Colorado Palace. The steps reached the corner of the building, where the entrance was located. The batwings were pushed aside. . . .

Matt Bodine and Sam Two Wolves stepped into the saloon.

Porter Wood and Lucas Tate looked to Matt like they wanted to slap leather, but Cole put out a hand to stop them. Cole said hoarsely, "My men?"

"They're all dead," Matt told him.

"That's impossible!" Wood said.

Tate said wearily, "They wouldn't be here if it wasn't true. Son of a bitch. I wouldn't have thought anybody could do that, either."

"You have a choice, Cole," Sam said. "You can keep fighting . . . or you can surrender and wait for some real law to get here from the capital. Either way, you're through in Buffalo Flat."

Cole struggled to get words past the rage and disbelief that clogged his throat, but Ike Davis didn't have a similar problem. The old-timer said, "I'm through, that's for damned sure." He picked up a shot glass of whiskey from the bar and downed it, then wiped the back of his hand across his mouth. "I'm ridin' out, fellas. This ain't my fight anymore."

"The hell it's not," Wood growled. "You take a step toward the door and I'll ventilate you myself, Ike."

"Sorry, Porter. You done bit off more'n you can chew." Ike started toward the door.

He spun after only a step, though, his hand darting toward the butt of his gun. He had to have known that Wood would carry through on his threat, and he was trying to beat him to the draw.

Ike was fast, but not fast enough. Smoke and flame spurted from the barrel of the gun that had appeared as if by magic in Wood's fist. The bullet slammed into Ike's midsection, doubling him over. He had his gun out, though, and he got a shot off as he went down. Wood was rocked back against the bar by the impact of the lead.

"Get them!" Cole roared at Lucas Tate as he jerked his gun up and fired at Matt and Sam.

The blood brothers lunged apart as Cole's bullet whipped through the air between them. Matt's guns leaped from their holsters. Sam filled his hand as well, and the racket inside the saloon was deafening as gunfire filled the air.

Matt went for Lucas Tate, triggering both Colts. A slug ripped through his buckskin shirt, but he barely felt its fiery kiss against his side. Tate staggered, crimson flowers blooming on the breast of his shirt where Matt's slugs had pounded into his body. He slewed sideways, managed to get off one more round that went harmlessly into the floor, and then folded up into a bloody heap.

Even before Tate hit the floor, Matt had turned his attention to Porter Wood. The little gunslinger was wounded, but that didn't mean his fangs had been pulled. The gun in his hand roared and Matt felt his hat go flying off his head as Wood's bullet tore through the crown. Then Matt emptied his left-hand gun into the man, shooting Wood to doll rags and driving him halfway back over the bar.

That left Sam to deal with Cole, who proved that he still had some of the toughness that his hard-scrabble upbringing had ingrained in him by staying on his feet as Sam's bullets smashed into him. He fired twice, the slugs smacking into the floor near Sam's feet. Then Cole stumbled forward, blood welling from his mouth as he said thickly, "Can't . . . can't end . . . this way—"

He collapsed, his face landing on the floor amidst the sawdust and the spilled blood.

"I reckon it *can* end this way," Matt said. "I reckon it has."

And yet, even as he spoke, he knew it hadn't, because Theresa Kincaid—Terri Kelly—was still somewhere here in the saloon. A soft footstep made both Matt and Sam look up sharply. She stood at the top of the stairs, a gun in her hand. Matt fought down the impulse to fire at her, because he saw that even though she held the weapon, her arm was down at her side. She swayed a little. Her face was pale and drawn.

Then she dropped the gun. It thudded at her feet. She fell forward, tumbling head over heels down the stairs. Matt and Sam watched in shocked surprise. When Theresa reached the bottom, she sprawled on her face. The handle of a knife stuck up from the back of her shirt. The blade was buried in her back, in the center of a rapidly spreading bloodstain.

Matt reached her and carefully rolled her onto her side while she still clung to life. "B-Bodine . . ." she gasped. "I . . . I'm sorry. . . ."

"Sorry for all the trouble you caused?" Matt asked with a frown.

"S-sorry I . . . didn't get to kill you . . . before that witch . . . stabbed m—"

She stiffened, and her eyes began to grow glassy. She was gone, but she had been filled with hatred to the end.

Across the saloon, Sam knelt next to Ike Davis, who looked up at him, blinked pain-filled eyes, and struggled to say, "Tell Scratch . . . so long . . . tell him . . . I forgive him for . . . Rosita."

"I will," Sam promised. "I'll tell him that you did the right thing at the end, too."

"M-much . . . obliged . . ." Ike's head fell back, and his last breath came out of him in a long sigh.

As Sam rose to his feet, he looked over at Matt and saw that his blood brother had stood up, too, and was gazing down at Theresa's lifeless body. "What happened to her?" he asked.

"I reckon that gal who was Cole's favorite before

she came along decided to settle the grudge per-
manent-like." Matt drew his gun and started up the
stairs. "I'll have a look around for her."

A few minutes later, though, he returned to
report that there was no sign of Anna Malone. The
woman had fled. With any luck, they would never
see her again.

The batwings were slapped aside. Bo and Scratch
strode in, followed by Judge Ashmore, Casey
McLennan, and several other townsmen. All of
them were bristling with guns. Bo had his coat off
and his wounded arm was bandaged. He glanced
around the now-quiet room and said, "Looks like
it's over for real now."

"Yeah," Matt said with a flick of his eyes toward
Theresa Kincaid's still figure. "It's over and done
with."

Sheriff Branch's body was found on the boardwalk near the Silver Belle. He had been killed by a
single gunshot. Sam's theory was that he had been
shot by Wood or Tate after he had brought the
warning to the saloon. Matt thought that was likely,
but figured they would never know for sure.

There was the question of what would happen
to the Colorado Palace, the Diamond C, and the
Half Moon now that both Junius Cole and Theresa
Kincaid were dead. Judge Ashmore would get the
job of sorting out that legal mess, which was just
fine with Matt. He had no head for such things, nor
any stake in how it turned out. In fact, now that it
looked like Charity and her friends were going to
be running the best and most successful saloon in

Buffalo Flat, there was no real reason for Matt and Sam to hang around.

The same was true for Bo and Scratch. The wound in Bo's arm was a clean one, having missed the bone, and it would probably heal with no problem. The same was true of Hector's injuries. Judge Ashmore suggested that as soon as Hector was on his feet again, he should be installed as temporary foreman of the Half Moon, since he knew the ranch and its operation better than anyone else still alive. The hands who had been left on the Diamond C, who weren't really gunmen, were running that spread for the time being, since Roy Barlowe and the rest of the men had died during the big shoot-out in Buffalo Flat.

The undertaker had been mighty busy for a few days. After attending Ike Davis's funeral, Bo and Scratch went back to the Silver Belle and had a drink with Matt and Sam. Charity and the other women bustled happily around the saloon. A couple of them had been wounded slightly during the fighting, but they were already up and around again.

As the four men sat at a table, Scratch asked Matt and Sam, "Where are you boys headed next?"

"We don't rightly know," Matt replied.

"Generally, we just go where the wind leads us," Sam added.

Bo nodded. "That's a good way to be. Scratch and I have been following that trail for a lot of years now."

Matt grinned. "You mean we're gonna wind up like you two old pelicans?"

"And what in blazes is wrong with that?" Scratch demanded.

"Not a thing, old-timer," Sam said with a chuckle. "Not a blessed thing."

They raised their mugs of beer, clinked them together, and drank.

Despite their friendliness, Matt and Sam sort of sneaked out of Buffalo Flat later that afternoon, heading north toward Wyoming. They worried that Bo and Scratch might want to ride along with them if they gave them a chance to do so.

"I've got a hunch," Matt said as they put their horses into a fast lope away from there, "that trouble follows those danged Texans wherever they go!"